Personal Demons

To Jolene

Tom Stearns

Second Edition 2019

This book was written over a number of years and too many people have been involved in its creation to list here. You all know who you are. You have my eternal gratitude for helping me start this journey.

Chapter One

The splodge on the MRI was larger than Price thought it was going to be. He had expected a small black dot or something suitably abrupt and final; a malignant full stop signifying the end of his life. Instead it was large, shapeless and white. Almost transparent.

He found it difficult to believe that he was looking at a picture of his brain. He couldn't take his eyes off it.

'...any cell in any tissue of the body can suddenly begin to disobey the body's rules regarding its growth and multiplication. There's a mechanism that governs how many cells of a certain type there ought to be...'

What is he talking about? Did you ask him any of this?

'Excuse me.' interrupted Price, suddenly angry at the doctor opposite him. 'If I'm going to die, and I assume from your dull lecture that I am, don't you think it would be more productive to tell me my options instead of providing me with the *fucking history of tumours?* He realised he was crying and switched his attention from the doctor and back to the blob.

When he was younger his mother had entertained him on long trips by pointing out interesting shapes in the clouds. Look; a sheep! A castle! A teddy bear!

The longer he looked at his tumour the more he realised that a cloud was a much better description of the tumour than a blob; yes, a toxic cloud poisoning his brain. He liked it. It had a sense of drama.

Dr. Mason handed Price a paper tissue then looked down at his notes to allow his patient time to gather his composure.

Price dabbed at his eyes. 'I'm sorry.'

The physician raised his palms. *No problem.*

'How long have I got?'

Dr. Mason paused for a moment before speaking in a hushed tone. 'It's difficult to be certain…If I may be permitted to explain?'

Price nodded.

'Intracranial tumours disclose their whereabouts with a combination of interfering with the function of the adjacent part of the brain and by taking up space within the cranium. Over ninety per cent of these space-occupying lesions are neoplasms, and of these, around half are primary tumours which is what you have, Mr Price.'

Inevitably, like the clouds of his youth, the shape on the MRI shifted again. It became a foetus. He could see the head and the arms and imagined it sucking a thumb. He wondered if he should talk to it like a father chattering to a bloated belly. It's a boy! He almost laughed.

The physician continued: 'Most primary tumours are neurological in origin and are called *gliomas.* The gliomas are a mixed group of tumours, but the most common type of primary malignant brain tumour is *Glioblastoma multiforme,* and this is what you are suffering from. It represents approximately fifty-five per cent of all gliomas and is twice as common in males than females between the ages of forty-five and sixty-five years of age. At the present I have no explanation as to why you have developed this particular tumour at such a comparatively young age.'

Then it wasn't a foetus but a clump of worms that writhed and worried and shit in his mind. The worms tunnelled out from the clump to explore their new domain. From their shit grew more worms and they thrived and grew fat off his mind and thoughts. Soon, he knew, his brain would be nothing but a writhing mass of bloated worms.

'So, how long have I got to live?' Never in his worst nightmares would he have imagined asking that at the age of thirty-one.

'Glioblastoma multiforme is a rapidly fatal tumour...the average survival period after the appearance of symptoms being less than twelve months.'

Twelve months. Twelve months. You sit there in your leather chair, in your white coat, and tell me that I have a load of worms shitting in my brain and that I am going to die in less than twelve months and you expect me to take it and

'Oh,' was all he could manage to say.

He had left soon after that. Dr. Mason had tried to explain his condition further, but Price had found it difficult to remain attentive. He watched the physician's mouth open and close but only heard tunnelling worms. Making his excuses, he waved away the physician's protests, telling him that he would make an appointment for the following day.

Dazed, he had staggered past the receptionist and out into the street, consumed by so many thoughts it was as if he wasn't thinking at all, and vomited in the gutter. Next came the tears - restrained and adult at first - swiftly giving way to a heaving, confused bawl.

What was he supposed to do now?

You should have stayed and asked the doctor, wasn't that the reason you went to see him, after all?

But the urge to leave had been overwhelming. He'd stayed as long as he could, but it was as if there was no air in the room. Every time he heard the word tumour it was a struggle to draw a breath. All he could see were black clad mourners stood around his grave as the box containing his worm devoured corpse was lowered into the earth. Running had seemed the only thing to do.

What was he going to tell Julie? Then despite himself he laughed. She had left him nearly eighteen months ago. She wouldn't give a shit about him, cancer or not. He knew he still had feelings for her, the fact that he had thought of her before his current partner, Christine, was evidence of that. At the same time, he knew his refusal to forget the past served only to prolong a pain that had nearly ruined him.

Melodramatic to the last.

Still, Christine was a nice enough girl; pretty, smart, funny. Their relationship was approaching the six-month mark and, so far, none of the usual warning bells had sounded.

She had caught him by surprise, he hadn't been looking for a girlfriend and certainly hadn't wanted a long-term relationship, but things had just happened. He enjoyed her company, they never argued, and she allowed him to be himself. If there *was* a problem, and he had told himself time and time again that he was just picking faults, it was their sex life. It was a disappointing lights off under the duvet missionary type of thing. He supposed that was the real reason he had stayed with Julie for so long. There was nothing she wouldn't have tried at least once. And they had tried everything. Unfortunately for him she hadn't confined her experimentation to their relationship.

He felt the familiar bleakness spread through his chest and wondered how she still maintained such a hold on him after so long. There were millions of people who had gone through similar betrayals and they got over it.

Yes, but you caught her in the act, didn't you? And what had her reaction been to your look of horror, to your eyes brimming with tears? Shock? Did she say it was a mistake?

It was as sharp in his mind as if it had happened only yesterday.

She hadn't even stopped. And what about the time she had called you a couple of days later all apologies, begging for forgiveness and a second chance. You ran to her like a puppy to its master. Now that was something to be truly ashamed of.

He shook his head to clear the memory and began to walk.

He needed a drink.

Chapter Two

Even after Price had thumped the alarm clock into submission the harsh beeping somehow lingered on, aggravating the painful whining in his head.

He lay there, focused on the sluggish throb of his temples and the wasteland that used to be his throat, and slowly began the process of waking up. He was at home and, judging by his reluctance to remove himself from the bed, alive if not well. Determining what day it was proved to be more difficult. The clock told him it was quarter past nine which meant it was too late for work and too early for anything else he normally did. He must have set the alarm for something. It was obvious that he had a hangover which meant that it was Friday, Saturday, Sunday or Thursday. Not a great help.

The fog slowly began to thin.

He remembered drinking. He remembered Dr. Mason.

Tumour.

The realisation poured into him. *For a moment you'd forgotten all about it.*

Would it be like this every time he woke up?

Would he be treated to a few moments where everything was as it should be?

Would he get the full twelve months, or could it end at any time?

Shut up with the questions.

Again, he chastised himself for not asking Dr. Mason to explain everything to him. He would make another appointment.

All of this still didn't tell him why he had set his alarm.

Dismissing the question as a waste of his now finite time he sat up and swung his legs out of the bed. His head came alive with pain.

He needed painkillers and lots of them. As he staggered to the bathroom colours danced before his eyes and the whining in his ears grew louder.

He was not really surprised to find that there were no pain killers in the bathroom cabinet. With a groan he closed the mirrored door and stared at his unhappy reflection. His face seemed to hang untidily from the bone, his eyes were bloodshot, his stubble was dangerously close to becoming a beard, and his hair stood like antlers on his head.

'You're fucking useless,' he informed his reflection. It nodded back at him. He sighed, resigned to the fact that a trip to the chemists was unavoidable.

*

When Price eventually staggered into the chemist, he was relieved to find there was only one other customer: a woman in her fifties with a shopping trolley squinting at bottles of something and coughing. It was the wet gurgle of forty a day.

'Bastard worms,' she said as she spat into a handkerchief. 'Crawling round me night and day shitting all over the place, as if I haven't got enough to do without cleaning up after the likes of them...'

The old woman eyed him with caution and Price tried to gather his composure unsure of what he had just heard. In the most charming voice he could muster, he said: 'I don't mean to be rude, but I couldn't help but notice...Are you all right?'

She showed Price her hankie full of bloodied worms squeaking like children. Price took a step back. The woman's smile didn't quite reach her eyes. 'Yes, yes, I'm fine.' She courteously shooed him away. As Price watched her waddle away from him his headache returned stronger than before. He doubled up, his head clamped between his hands, as white-hot pain rushed through his veins.

Is this what it will feel like when I die? His mind struggled to concentrate on the question. He understood death to be instantaneous and painless; it was the dying that was the hard part. Would he lead a normal life until someone hit his off switch, or would he shrivel away in a bed unable to wipe himself?

Of course, you would know all this if you weren't such a baby and asked Dr. Mason about it. 'Oh, yes Mr Price I did neglect to mention that from this moment on, up until the moment of your unfortunate demise, every waking moment - and a few of your non-waking ones, too - you will be gripped by the most excruciating pain imaginable. I mean really bad. Did I fail to mention that? I'm terribly sorry. You have my deepest sympathies.'

'Can I help you?' Price turned to see a young woman wearing a white pharmacists coat and a displeased expression.

Price struggled to collect his thoughts. 'What?'

The pharmacist repeated her offer.

'Headache tablets: the strongest you have...Please.'

The pharmacist hesitated for a moment while she decided whether this unkempt individual was trouble or not. Price smiled as best he could.

The pharmacist was not impressed. 'What kind of headache is it? Migraine? Hangover?'

Price wasn't very keen on the way she had said *hangover*. It felt like an accusation rather than an inquiry. *Alcoholic are we, sir?*

'I eat the flies off corpses juicy and fat with death. Yum,' she said and licked her lips.

'What?'

'What kind of headache is it? Is it a migraine or a Hangover or?'

That wasn't what she had said. A fly crawled out of her mouth and crawled up her face.

'It's self-inflicted, yes.' But I have a brain tumour too if that's ok with you so ha I win.

The pharmacist placed a small blue packet of pills on the counter. 'These are the strongest you can get without prescription,' she informed him. 'Some re-hydration sachets may help you get back on your feet. They're used primarily for replacing fluids and minerals lost with diarrhoea, but some say they work wonders with hangovers and guilt associated with lies and deceit.'

Price paid and left.

*

All he needed was a day in bed. He was clearly emotionally distressed. Yesterday he had found out he was dying from a fatal brain tumour and now he had a hangover to contend with. Things were bound to go a bit wonky on a person given that amount of stress. A day in bed to get things into perspective would sort him out.

Then he remembered why he had set the alarm clock.

He was supposed to be meeting Christine for a drink at one. His stomach lurched at the thought of alcohol.

Hair of the dog'll do you the world of good.

No, he would have to cancel. *Send her some flowers or something to apologise.*

His mobile was in his coat and he couldn't remember if he had any credit. He was terrible at keeping the bloody thing topped up.

The landline was unplugged as usual. He wondered why he even bothered with it. Every time he plugged the bloody thing in some automated message would ask him if he and his family wanted a cheaper insurance. Well, he didn't have a family so fuck them.

You never will either.

He would have to cancel the date. He shifted himself out of the bed and his guts jabbed at him. 'For fucks sake, I didn't have *that* much to drink.'

He couldn't remember if he had eaten a kebab or any other junk.

It was only eleven o'clock. He decided to go back to sleep for a bit.

*

Price dreamed about the worms.

They were hungry.

While he was awake, they grew fat off his thoughts and daydreams.

When he slept, they starved. Dreams were not real enough for them; it was like trying to fill empty bellies with the aroma of food only and the worms writhed and starved within him. They were desperate to escape, to feed. They crawled down his spine and burrowed into his stomach, into his lungs and he choked and gagged, they slithered through his veins and into his heart and he jerked with pain. Soon they saw a light, a way out, and they crawled out of his eyes and nose and mouth.

Price woke screaming.

He instinctively swiped at his nose expecting to swat away rotten worms. Instead his fingers met only a steady trickle of blood. There was large stain of blood on his pillow.

A nosebleed? Was that a bad sign? It seemed a logical side effect of the tumour. Whenever people got nosebleeds in films it usually meant something was seriously wrong somewhere.

He'd been dreaming too. What was it?

Worms. Jesus!

Worms crawling from under his eyes and out of his nose. He shuddered in disgust. It had seemed quite real. His eyes felt fine, but his nose was sore. Ah, that was it. He'd punched himself in the nose while having a nightmare. The dream had obviously freaked him out and he'd truly believed there were worms coming out of his nose.

Then he noticed something.

The blood on his pillow wasn't just a drip; there were thin trails leading away from it that grew fainter like cracks in a glass.

Don't be daft. You don't have worms in your brain, and they didn't crawl out of you while you were sleeping and wriggle away.

It looked like they had. He lifted the pillow. There were more trails of blood and they seemed to head off under the duvet. He hesitated, then threw open the duvet.

In his bed were hundreds of worms. They were slick with blood and squelched as they writhed.

Price leapt from the bed with a scream and crashed into his bedside table sending a lamp and a pint of water crashing.

The bed was empty. There were no worms. No blood. He wiped at his nose again. There was nothing there.

Something tickled his nose and he instinctively sniffed. The blockage shot up his nose and stuck in his throat and he gagged. With watering eyes, he coughed it out.

A small worm fell onto the bed. At least he thought it was a worm. Fighting the urge to vomit he drew closer. It had tiny slits for eyes and a thin mouth that opened and closed as if trying to speak. Its head turned to face him. He grabbed for it. There was nothing there. The worm was gone.

He rubbed at his eyes like an inexperienced actor trying to convey disbelief. What was happening?

Hallucinations?

You do have a brain tumour.

Was it normal? Why the fuck didn't that Dr. Mason tell him?

Because you ran out of there like a little girl for a cry.

Well, it had seemed like the thing to do.

You're still pissed from the night before son. You had some bad news. The worst news people can get, really. You're bound to be a little messed up.

He couldn't argue with that.

Get some rest and you'll be as right as rain.

He wasn't going to sleep in the bed though.

Idiot, it's like those times you dreamed a spider was on your face and danced round the room like a girl for twenty minutes. You're such a big strong man.

'Fuck it,' he said and slipped back under the covers.

Chapter Three

To his surprise the morning's events slipped from his mind the moment he saw Christine standing outside *The Queens*. She didn't like waiting in pubs alone, she'd told him it made her feel like a loser.

'How long have we got?' Price asked, admiring her curves through her black three-piece suit.

Christine smirked at his attention. 'An hour. Why, what have you got planned for me?'

'Well, it's funny you should mention it because...' He patted his pockets as if he was looking for something, and then sighed. 'Would you believe it? I've forgotten the tickets for Tahiti. I could have sworn I had them.'

She pushed him and laughed, taking his hand. 'Come on, dickhead. You can buy me a drink to make up for it.'

It was strange how he didn't mind her calling him names or teasing him. It always felt good. Right, somehow. Julie had tried it a few times but never managed to keep the chill out of her voice.

I really hope that you are not falling for this girl. Hello, reality check. Tumour. Twelve months to live. Hallucinations. Going gaga.

Oh, and by the way, this raises the issue of who needs to know about your malignant friend.

That was a problem. There was no way of knowing how she would react to the news. After only five months she was perfectly within her rights to walk away. On the other hand, she could become too attached, seeing it as her duty to nurse him to the end.

Either outcome wasn't particularly appealing. If he didn't tell her then things could go on as they were. That suited him but he knew it was selfish. If she liked him, and he was sure that she did, his sudden and unexpected death would - to her, at least - be a devastating blow. The post-mortem would reveal the worms eating his brain and...

And he would be six foot under and unable to explain anything.

He sat down next to her, aware that he was smiling too brightly, and quickly gulped at his pint. She thanked him for the drink and gave him the *'what are you up to?'* look.

Price almost choked on his lager. 'Nothing, nothing at all.'

I'm a big fat liar wriggling like a big fat wormy worm.

'Are you sure?'

'Of course I'm sure. I'm just in a good mood, that's all. Is that a crime?'

She nodded that it was and sipped her vodka. 'I phoned you earlier, you weren't in.'

'I might have been. I unplugged the phone and went back to bed. I had a blinding headache.' Not exactly a lie. Edited truth was a more accurate description.

She reached out and caressed his temple, concerned.

'It's gone now. I took four under the counter industrial strength pain killers which seemed to do the trick.'

'Four! Have you any idea how dangerous that is? Didn't you read the packet? And you shouldn't be drinking.'

'I'm fine. In fact, I'd go as far as say I feel great. That's probably why I'm in such a good mood; high as a kite.'

This did nothing to alleviate her concern. 'Promise me you won't take anymore until this evening.'

Under normal circumstances he would have argued that she was overreacting, but life was now too short. 'I promise. How's work?'

She looked stressed. 'The same as it is every time we have weekend overtime. All the crap that no-one can be arsed to deal with during the week gets dumped on my desk first thing Saturday morning. If I wasn't paid so much, I'd be really angry.'

They both laughed and Price decided that telling her, if that was what he was going to do, could wait until another day. 'Are you doing anything tonight?' he asked.

'Well, I was supposed to be going into town with Janine, but she's just hooked up with a new bloke, *Roland*.' She rolled her eyes when she said his name; she obviously had heard nothing but *Roland* all day. 'And you know what she's like when she gets a new man in her life.'

He did. Janine was the kind of girl who abandoned everything and everyone whenever a man came into the picture. Price had lost count of the number of times she had cancelled nights out with Christine because she had met someone new or left her stranded in the middle of a night-club while she swanned off with someone.

'How does this sound? I'll pick you up tonight; we can go for a meal in that Italian you like then hit the bars in town or wherever you fancy. We'll spend the night in the best hotel I can book this afternoon. My treat.'

She looked as if it sounded pretty good, but: 'That sounds very expensive. Are you sure you can afford it?'

'It won't be that much and besides I'm not going to live forever

That's for sure

'So what better way to spend my money than on a good night out for the both of us?'

Price thought he saw her eyes twinkle. 'Then that's what we shall do. But you must let me pay something towards it.'

He held up his hand. 'Not tonight. Indulge me; this is something I really want to do.' He could see she didn't like the idea which made him even more determined not to concede.

'Okay then, but just this once. I don't want this to become a habit. I like to pay my way, and to prove it I'm getting the next round. And it's a coke for you, this time.'

Price raised his glass. 'Yes, boss.' He felt a few worms drop away from the main clump and he tried to hide his disgust. He knew it was his imagination. It wasn't real. He had felt it happen all the same.

Christine shook her head, mumbling 'fool' under her breath and slid out from under the table. Price watched her make her way through the suits thinking that he was three or four pints from being in love with her. He wondered how much harder it would be to die if she felt the same way. She looked back at him from the bar and winked and he decided that two pints was nearer the truth.

What is wrong with you? It was only a couple of weeks ago that you were thinking of giving her the elbow. You're dying; take this opportunity to spread yourself about a bit. You've always felt as if you missed out on the single's scene. Well, now's your chance.

This was true. His late teens and early twenties were strewn with rejection, ridicule and laughter (there were three clear memories of the latter that still made him wince today).

'Penny for them.'

Price jumped. He hadn't noticed her return. 'A penny?' he replied with mock indignation. 'I'll have you know, my good woman, that the thoughts of David Price are worth considerably more than a penny.'

'It must be a great place, this little private world you live in. I'd like to visit it sometime.'

He tapped his right temple and told her that she didn't have the bus fare. She'd heard the joke before but laughed anyway.

And so it went on until it was time for Christine to return to work. They said their good-byes in the car park, arranging for him to call for her at eight, and they kissed. Price drew her to him; abandoning the perfunctory peck on the lips he had favoured so many times in the past and kissed her deeply. Initially her lips were closed but as they sensed his intention they opened and a small moan of pleasure escaped from her mouth to his. He felt her nails pinch the skin of his back through his shirt and he heard a second moan and felt his heart melt. When the embrace was over, he saw the sparkle in her eyes that must have mirrored his own.

'Wow,' she said, breathless. 'I don't think I've ever been kissed like that before. What brought that about? Can we go to the hotel now?'

'Too much of a good thing can be bad for you. See you at eight.' Price swaggered out of the car park happier than he had ever been before. *Tonight is going to be something else.*

Chapter Four

Christine sank into her sofa and exhaled deeply, glad to have finished the Saturday shift sanity intact. Meeting Dave for lunch had certainly helped, even if it had taken its toll. Three vodkas in an hour and she was exhausted. Four years ago she could have had at least four and been back in the bar straight after work. *And* stayed out all night. Those were the days. Well, some of them weren't much to write home about and most of them she *couldn't* write home about, but she wouldn't change any of it. Not even the bad times. Part of her admitted that she was glad that was all behind her. She still liked to go clubbing but the urge was diminishing almost weekly.

In her twenties if she couldn't go out at the weekend (and in those days Thursday to Monday was her weekend) for whatever reason she would go absolutely nuts. These days if she had to stay in she hardly noticed; especially if Dave came around. He was the best thing that had happened to her in years.

Instead of promoting himself like most men did he had done the opposite. She had always had a soft spot for self-depreciation providing it wasn't all consuming.

Recently she had thought he was losing interest...but today. Warmth spread between her thighs at the thought of it. Maybe he was realising that all women were not soul-destroying bitches like that last one he had gone out with.

He was so vulnerable when they met. The very fact that he was dating her seemed to bring a lot of the bad things to the fore, and she had to be sure that he wasn't with her to heal the pain. She was nobody's rebound girl. When she had eventually managed to get him to talk about Julie, she found it difficult to believe that anyone - other than a man - could be that cruel.

There was a knock at the door, confident, loud. Not that of a friend. Curious she padded to the door cursing her aching feet.

The man standing on her steps struggled to be seen behind an enormous bunch of roses. 'Miss MacNeil?'

'Yes?'

'Could you sign for these, please?'

She scrawled her name, hardly able to drag her eyes away from the flowers, then handed the pad back to the man who dumped his delivery into her arms. Thanking him she closed the door and wondered who they were from. This was the first time in her entire life that anyone had sent her flowers. The address on the envelope wasn't in a handwriting she recognised. The handwriting inside, however, was and she almost dropped the gift. Although in her heart she had always known they were from him the message inside was not what she expected.

You bring the colour to my world David

He had said some nice things to her in the past, but this took her breath away. Maybe this was his way of saying he was ready for a serious commitment, that he wanted to move the relationship to the next stage. She hoped so. Janine told her that she was daft to act like this after only five months but, as far as she was concerned, when you were in love you were in love and that was that. Reading the words over and over again she took the flowers into the kitchen.

Chapter Five

The smell hit him as soon as he descended the stairs to the restaurant: a pungent aroma of garlic and cheese. On any other occasion it would have caused his stomach to grumble in anticipation. Tonight it was overpowering, catching in the back of his throat.

Like a worm trying to escape?

This was beginning to look like a bad idea.

For a start he knew he was going to have to spend the whole evening watching what he said. Hiding things from women was not something he was good at and he had to keep a lid on his 'news'.

Also, her insistences on thanking him for the flowers at every opportunity were beginning to irritate him. If he had known she was going to go on about it so much he wouldn't have bothered.

If he hadn't made such a fuss about it he would have called Christine and cancelled. All he wanted to do was crawl under the duvet and sleep.

Th waitress handed them both menus

Christine smiled at this. 'You know, I think I've had everything on this menu at one time or another. Except for anything with prawns in, we don't get along.' She patted her stomach.

Dave felt irritation crawl through him.

'This is nice,' she remarked, her smile faltering when she noticed her date was elsewhere. 'Dave?'

'What? Oh, I'm sorry what were you saying?'

'Are you okay?'

I'm dying, what do you think? 'Yes, I'm fine. I think I'm coming down with something...a cold maybe. I don't feel too good.'

She reached over and touched his forehead, then his cheeks. 'You do feel a bit hot. Do you want to leave? I don't mind.'

He took her hand in his, the knuckles of his free hand whitened under the table as he tried to keep an inexplicable anger in check. 'Don't be daft. I said this was going to be a good night out and that is what it will be. Don't worry, I'm fine. Really.'

What is the matter with you? Why was that so hard for you to say?

'Are you sure? I really don't mind leaving.'

Are you fucking deaf or something? I said that I was fine!

'No, don't worry about it. Please?' His lip curled into a sneer and he quickly disguised it by kissing her hand. 'I'm just going to the toilet. I'll be back in a minute.'

Lowering the toilet seat, he dumped himself down, his head between his knees, and ran his fingers through his hair. He was uncomfortably hot. It reminded him of the stiff and itchy church clothes he'd endured every Sunday until he stood up for himself. He loosened his tie and undid his collar wishing he had chosen less constricting attire.

It was difficult to breathe. He should have accepted her offer to go home. A fantasy formed in his mind of him lying naked on his bed under the cool breeze of a fan. His temperature lowered from a cantankerous boil to a churlish simmer.

Pull yourself together. She wouldn't accept his assurances that he was fine for much longer. Despondent, he buried his head in his hands. His nose began to tickle and he sat upright just as the sneeze tore itself from him with a roar. He caught the flying mucus in the palms of his hands. As reached for toilet paper he saw the mucus was crawling with tiny worms. The longer he stared the fatter they grew. He tried to blink them away, but they persisted. With a yelp of horror, he threw them in the bowl and flushed.

The toilet gagged on the worms and vomited the water back out, showering him with a noxious mixture of shit and wriggling bodies. He squealed and tried to brush them off him.

The worms fell to the floor with a wet slap and started to crawl up his shoes. The speed of them astonished him and he began to kick his legs wildly, gibbering as he did.

The toilet belched out more water and the worms flooded over the bowl. Price stomped on them, his feet sliding on their guts.

Then he was just stamping in a puddle of water like a child with new Wellingtons.

He ran his fingers through his hair and stifled a sob. What the fuck was happening to him?

Stop your whining. You had better get back out there.

When he returned to the table Christine was heavy with concern. 'Are you okay? You were gone for ages.'

'I'm feeling much better now that I've took this tie off,' he gestured to the open collar. 'Plus, I've just had the biggest sneeze in my life. Best orgasm ever. Much messier, though.'

He watched as the concern lifted and her nose wrinkled. 'That's foul,' she laughed.

Price poured himself a glass of wine, drained it in one, and then poured another. He nodded in approval: 'Impudent little number.'

Christine leaned forward, her left eyebrow raised slightly. 'Slow down or you'll be too drunk for later.' She gave his knee a squeeze under the table. 'Now, what do you fancy? I've gone for the tortellini alforno.'

As he scanned the menu and found he wasn't hungry. 'I think I'll just have the small lasagne. I'm not as hungry as I thought I was,' he explained, thankful that she didn't ask him if he wanted to go home again. 'So, Janine's out with Roland tonight, then?' he enquired, hoping to shift the attention away from him.

'She's quite taken by him.'

'That must mean he's loaded.'

'Yes, he's got a bit of money, but she seems to like him for him, if you get what I mean? She says he's funny and treats her like she's someone special.'

'I know that she's your friend and I apologise if I'm out of line, but she wouldn't have given him the time of day if he was broke. He might make her laugh, treat her well, and all the rest of it, but it was his bank balance that afforded him the opportunity to show her that side of him.'

Christine did not comment so Price continued. 'Take Craig, as an example. Both you and I agreed that he was perfect for her. You said he was gorgeous, although I couldn't see it myself, but he was intelligent, well spoken, and had a great sense of humour. They hit it off instantly. She was all sweetness and smiles for months. Then his contract ran out at work and he was let go. She dropped him quicker than a hot coal, and you can't deny it.'

'Security is very important to her. She has every right to make sure she's well looked after.'

Angela returned and took their order, Price asked for a second bottle of wine.

Christine continued the conversation when she left. 'All women think like Janine to a certain degree.'

'You don't.'

'Not where money is concerned, I can provide that for myself, and anyway that's not what I mean. I want emotional security. To be able to live my life without having to answer suspicious questions, or not worry my bloke cheating on me. Or spend every waking moment wondering if he's happy with me.'

Her voice trembled as a distant recollection became painfully clear. This time it was Price who leaned forward and squeezed a knee. 'And I am. Very.'

Christine's hand found his and returned the pressure. 'I am, too. I know it was difficult for you at the beginning, but I need you to know that I care for you a great deal.'

'I know you do, and I feel the same way. It's just that I find it hard to express myself properly.'

'The message with the flowers said it beautifully. You bring the colour to my world, too, Dave.'

Had he really written that? It was so unlike him. The message was his in the sense that he remembered scratching it onto the card, but that was all. The process of constructing the words wasn't there. It was almost as if the words had been put in his head for him to find.

He raised his glass. 'To us.'

'To us and may this night never end.'
I'll definitely drink to that.

*

As Price picked at his lasagne, he began to feel hungry again, the food waking his sleeping stomach and it growled for more. He regretted not ordering some garlic bread to go with it.

'You *are* feeling better, aren't you?' Christine had stopped eating to watch Price shovel the food into his mouth.

He nodded and smiled, before washing the food down with a swig of wine. 'I'm absolutely starving,' he said. 'I must have been too hot before.'

'Or maybe you're hungry because you're pissed.' There was no reproach present in her voice, only amusement.

Price adopted an exaggerated expression of contemplation. 'You know,' he concluded, 'I think you might have something there.'

'I know I have because I'm pretty much in the same state as you are. You're a bad influence, David Price.'

He smirked. 'And you love me for it.'

'I do.'

Price ignored that last comment. They had that conversation quite often. Not about the drink, specifically, usually it occurred when Price displayed an unattractive characteristic, such as belching or breaking wind. He would do the deed and Christine would push him or prod him in the ribs and say he was disgusting or something similar, to which he always replied, *'and you love me for it.'* This remark would receive the sarcastic reply of '*oh, I do*' or '*how could I not?*' Only on this occasion she had sounded as if she meant it.

He busied himself with the pasta, knowing that she was watching him carefully. The tips of her fingers touched his wrist and he raised his head. 'I love you, David.'

Just say it. Four tiny, insignificant words. I love you, too. Only four, you've already exchanged hundreds this evening. What is your problem? Four. What time is it? Four. Where are the toilets? Four. What is your name? Four. I Love you, too.

Somehow, they were too heavy to be only four words. If only he hadn't sent her those bloody flowers. Yet it wasn't the flowers that were responsible for this. It was the message. Had he written *See you tonight* or *Thinking of you* or anything like that would he be in this mess, now?

Then it came to him.

It was the tumour! He thought and, to his horror, almost said aloud. He remembered thinking to himself earlier today while she was getting drinks, that he was three or four pints away from being in love with her. He eventually decided that it was closer to two. He was never sentimental like that, even when he *was* in love, it wasn't his style. *So what you are saying is that there is a tumour inside you that has made you fall in love. You're insane.* He was inclined to agree with himself on that one. It was possible that it wasn't as straight forward as that.

'Say something.' Her silent pleading had given way to a thinly veiled fear of rejection.

Just say it.

'I love you, too.'

'I'm so happy.' She leaned over the table to kiss him. 'For a second there I thought that you were going to leave.'

'I'll never leave you,' he said and regretted it. In less than a year he wouldn't have any choice in the matter. His days were numbered.

'And I'll never hurt you, never.'

'The same goes for me,' he said, wondering if he had just made a promise he couldn't keep.

Chapter Six

After several drunken attempts to swipe the hotel key through the reader, and Christine's remark that it happens to all men sometimes, they spilled into the room. Price fell flat on his face and Christine collapsed on top of him. They laughed hysterically until they cried, and Christine closed the door. Through the alcoholic blur, she located her bag and disappeared into the bathroom.

'Get into bed,' she whispered before she left.

Crawling along the floor and onto the bed he sprawled himself out on his back and he sank into the mattress. He allowed himself to descend further as the room drained into him like the waves of an unfathomable dark ocean.

The door opened and the light from the bathroom streaked across his eyes.

Christine was standing in the doorway, striking a pose in a very short nightdress.

Price sobered himself almost immediately and, judging by her seductive walk to the bed, she had done the same.

She straddled him and lowered her head to kiss him. Price reached out and cupped her breast with an eager hand, but she removed it, pinning it to the bed by the wrist above his head. Sensing that he would try to touch her again she secured his second curious hand with the other and kissed him. She drew herself from him slowly, teasing out his bottom lip with hers before gently biting it. Keeping his hands in place with her left hand she delved between her thighs with her right. Price strained his neck to see what she was doing and when she removed a red silk scarf, she pushed him back down again.

The drink had, up until now, delayed his arousal but when he felt the silk tighten against the flesh of his wrists, he knew that was an obstacle he no longer had to concern himself with. She reached down towards her thighs again and Price felt her undoing his belt. Next came the buttons followed by his zip. Her hand wandered inside his trousers caressing him through the thin material beneath and he arched his back to encourage her to sneak her fingers further. She immediately removed them and began to unbutton his shirt. He exhaled, the disappointment only adding to the excitement.

She kissed at his bare chest, rubbing her crotch against his hardness, lightly at first but gradually increasing the pressure until she sat upright and began to gyrate as if he were already inside her. Her breath began to quicken, as did her movements. Then suddenly she stopped, smiling at his pained expression. Christine shuffled down his legs and moved into a kneeling position, his legs between hers, and pulled down his trousers. His boxers released his erection and she seized it in her hands and took it into her mouth. The suddenness of her action after the teasing stole a gasp from Price which evolved into a moan as her tongue worked on him.

His back arched again, his climax building, he knew it was too soon, but he was helpless. Feeling the tension in his loins she stopped, not wanting the game to end without him inside her.

Price felt the warmth as she lowered herself onto him and his pleasure increased as he caught sight of her expression; eyes closed, biting her lower lip, her features contorted in what looked like a grimace of pain. She began ease herself up and down, gently urging him deeper and deeper. She knew he was almost there, his body becoming more rigid, but could contain herself no longer and she increased her speed. He stiffened and she felt his release, pushing herself down to meet his final thrust.

In the panting silence Christine untied his wrists and snuggled in beside him, the need to be close to him overwhelming her. He held her tightly, his long-satisfied exhalation saying more than his words ever could.

'I'm glad you enjoyed it,' she whispered, kissing his chest.

'Give me a minute and we can do it again,' said Price.

Christine said that would be fine by her.

They were both asleep less than a minute later.

Chapter Seven

Christine was at home sleeping it off and Price was bored.

Sundays were just another day of the week nowadays, thought Price, as he sat on his front steps. Childhood Sundays were tainted with Church and closed shops. It was unmistakeable, in much the same way the clip round his ear for fidgeting too much during the service was. Whenever Price heard the peeling of church bells he would suffer the same tightness in his chest beget by hard benches, damp air and the monotonous regurgitation of the scriptures. His mother had despaired at his lack of enthusiasm for her faith. He had tried to accommodate her, but it was, he had explained, unfair of her to expect him to be interested when the priests evidently lacked enthusiasm themselves.

The small shopping parade opposite his house was as busy as any other day of the week. The newsagents-cum-grocers had opened at 6 a.m. as it did every day. The off-licence, card shop and betting shop were also ready for business.

Price heard a child crying and turned to see a red-faced boy pulling against his father's arm. The boy was about seven and the dad looked annoyed.

'I've told you already. No more sweets.'

'But dad I need them.'

'You don't need them, you want them. That's two different things.'

'But I will need them to get the taste out of my mouth.'

'No sweets until after dinner.'

'But Nan tastes funny. I don't like it.'

'There's nothing wrong with your Nan's cooking. Now, stop being silly.'

'Not her dinner! She puts her boobs in my mouth an' makes me suck them like a dummy till stuff comes out.'

'You will enjoy it and tell her it's lovely'

'The stuff has lumps in it, and they get stuck in my throat and they move inside me.'

Price felt the worms inside him lurch. It was as if they wanted to see for themselves.

He needed to clear his head. Walking was as good a way as any. The urge to drink away the day in the pub was strong. What the hell. It wasn't as if he was going to go into work tomorrow. A nice leave of absence until they sacked him was in order. So a day getting sloshed in the pub it was.

As he crossed the road a number 15 pulled up and a passenger stepped off. Normally he wouldn't have paid her any attention but something about her caught his interest. He couldn't shake a sense of familiarity, although he was sure he didn't know her.

She was in her thirties he guessed with dark brown hair and was pretty enough to make an impression without turning heads.

'Price!' she shouted and gave him a wave. She knew him, then. Where from? As he started walking towards her, she set off down the road.

He stopped and looked behind to see if she had waved at somebody else. The road was empty.

She was talking to you.

Then why did she walk off?

I think she wants you to follow her.

The woman was stood at the entrance to an alley between a row of terraced houses. She beckoned him again with smile and a curling finger then slipped past a pile of rubbish and into the alley.

Price followed.

She was waiting.

'I think you should grab me by the cunt and drag me behind these wheelie bins.'

'What?'

'You heard me; I need you to clean me out.' She rubbed at her crotch.

'I don't know what you mean?'

'Get the worms out of me before it's too late.'

She began stripping off her clothes. 'Do I have to do everything myself?'

Price held up his hands in what he hoped was a halting gesture. 'Stop please. What are you doing?'

She kicked her knickers off and Price saw there was blood and worms in the crotch. She lay down and opened her legs.

'Slice me up, doctor. A nice deep cut from me tits to me fanny. Make sure it's not the other way around though. I'm a lady: tits first.'

Price stared at the worms wriggling out from her vagina.

'Come on,' she urged. 'I haven't got all day and its freezing out here in me nip!'

The worms crawled on the floor towards him. Tiny mouths whined and moaned. The sound grew until he was forced to clamp his hands against his ears.

Price vomited a twisting mess of worms onto the ground. He vomited again bringing up blood. The worms squeaked with delight.

The woman patted his back. 'Good lad,' she said. 'Get them all out. Set them free. '

Price blacked out.

Chapter Eight

Christine was in bed reading a magazine when the phone began to ring. It was 11:20 p.m.

'Hello,' she said into the mouthpiece.

Silence.

'Hello?'

The line crackled. Silence.

She was about to put the phone down when something occurred to her. 'Gary? Is that you?' she asked, timidly.

The line went dead.

Oh, my God.

She threw the phone away as if it were crawling with insects, covering her mouth with a trembling hand. *How did he find me?*

Christine MacNeil slept very little that night.

Chapter Nine

The bones crumbled beneath him as he scrambled towards the summit, clouds of decay rushing into him as his lungs gasped for air.

Sharp edges clawed at his flesh, drawing blood. He stopped, watching as the bones absorbed the viscous fluid. The mountain grew higher, extending silently upwards. The movement lacerated his skin, tearing thin rents deep into his flesh, spraying hot blood in a thousand painless directions.

The bones absorbed the life he had brought to them. Veins appeared, entwining, welcoming his blood as if it were their own. Muscles formed, glistening in the dead sun before hardening under its glare to form a brittle covering. Limbs developed, twitching with new life. He saw new-born fingers drumming impatiently on the crest of a skull while its features took shape.

A bleached pelvis transformed into a pouting bald vagina in an instant. The pubis sprouted black hairs that grew to an impossible length, falling either side of the opening which moistened with desire. The lips parted with a squelch, inviting entry and Price fumbled for his penis but touched only blank flesh. He wailed in frustration.

The mouth of the vagina opened and closed, drooling like a hungry infant searching for its mother's nipple. Price felt its hot fetid breath against his face and he stretched his fingers towards it, hoping they could satisfy its lusting.

With an angry burbling of fluid the vagina snapped its maw at the offered digits before scurrying deep into a pile of quivering limbs.

The hill shifted as the limbs crawled in search of their kin; calf seeking knee, arms creeping towards shoulders. Each *locked together with a sickening crunch and he fell to the ground, unable to maintain his balance on the writhing mass.*

His eyes stared up at the golden shimmer of his goal, obscured by the mountain of corpses, then turned to the eyes of the dead as they bore into him.

Mouths stretched wide, emitting feeble moans of rebirth that rose to a mournful screeching. As one, the dead stretched their fingers down to him and their screeches became a roar of rage.

*

It was a quarter to nine when Christine arrived at the smoking room at work for her morning coffee. It was a small stinking box, with white walls stained brown from years of cigarette smoke. Christine had given up the dreaded weed a year ago and only came here because Janine smoked like a chimney.

When Janine entered at five to, it was with an air of contentment. *Somebody got laid*, Christine thought and bit her lip to stop the laugh springing forth.

'Good morning,' chirped Janine on her way to the vending machine.

'It's Monday,' corrected Christine.

'Sorry. Hello, Chris.'

'That's better. You sound cheerful this morning,' she remarked, wincing as her coffee burned the tip of her tongue.

'It's a wonder I can even walk.'

'I take it you had a good weekend, then?'

Janine dumped her handbag on the table in front of Christine then sat opposite. 'The best,' she said, her hand emerged from her handbag with a packet of cigarettes.

'So?' prompted Christine, bursting with her own news but knowing Janine wouldn't be able to focus until hers was exhausted.

'I slept with Ronald last night,' she explained as she lit a cigarette.

'I guessed that.'

'You should have seen the size of him.'

Christine raised her eyebrows. 'Really?'

'I mean, I thought I'd seen big, but this...' her words trailed off as the memory floated before her eyes. 'It was the biggest one I've ever seen. Ever.'

'How big?'

She dragged on the cigarette, 'It was about ten inches, I swear to God.' The words left her mouth in long grey clouds. Ignoring her friend's whistle of approval, she continued. 'We'd started getting a bit frisky in the cab on the way to his place, just a few kisses and a few playful gropes...and it didn't *feel* like he had much to offer...'

'You felt his balls in a taxi?'

'I was drunk, and I was horny, what'd you expect?'

'Slut,' said Christine benignly.

'Anyway,' a slurp of tea, 'we got to his flat, and by then we were both pretty much gagging for it, so we went straight to bed. He took of his trousers and...' She paused, more for effect than to flick ash, 'and this monster appeared. I took one look at it and said 'Oh, my God.''

'You didn't?'

'I knew it was a mistake. I could feel his ego swelling even as the words left my mouth, but I couldn't help it. I thought to myself, there's no way I can take all *that*. It sort of killed the mood, if you know what I mean. But he seemed to know what he was doing. He didn't rush into it; he was really gentle, considerate. He made sure I was ready before things went further.'

She stabbed out the cigarette and reached for another. 'And when he did...' She paused to light it.

'Go on.'

'I tell you something...I've never come like that before in my entire life.' Both women erupted in fits of laughter, leaning close, their eyes alight with mischievous glee. When the laughter diminished Janine said, 'I'll never say that size isn't important again.' Fresh laughter.

'I have some news of my own,' whispered Christine.

'What?' asked Janine; curious, but also slightly annoyed that the attention had moved away from her so soon.

Through beaming white teeth, she said, 'I told him.'

Janine's eyes widened. 'That you loved him?'

A nod.

'What did he say?'

'Well, what do you think?' she said, pointing to her grin.

'He feels the same way?'

Christine nodded emphatically.

'Wow. I'd take that over a ten-inch dick any day.'

'No, you wouldn't.'

She thought about it. 'You're probably right. So, tell me about the night of passion at the Palace.'

'Well, you know how I've been holding myself back in that department.'

Janine nodded. 'Waiting for a commitment, right?'

'Not just that. Waiting for a sign that he was happy with me and not just what I could do for him. Not like Mark.'

Janine nodded. Christine had dated Mark for about four months, enjoying a frequent and adventurous sex life, before his absence during her periods became apparent. Christine had suggested that they abstain from sex for a couple of weeks to see if they could get along without it: a simple request and an effective measure of where they stood with each other. He had left her after three days.

Christine drained the last of her coffee, the grains of sugar rough on her tongue. 'So, I tied him up and gave him a blow job. You should have seen his face.'

'Dirty bitch. I take it he was pleased, then?'

'Delirious, I think is the word you're looking for.

'Keep your eyes open, though. He's still a man.'

'Talk about killing the mood.'

'I'm sorry. But I'm your friend and it's my job to make sure that you're okay. I really do think that Dave is a nice guy, but as I said he's a man and they're all bastards when they want to be. Just don't let him give you the run around, that's all.'

'I know what you're saying, but Dave would never do anything to hurt me.'

Janine nodded, and glanced up at the clock. 'Shit,' she said, stabbing out her cigarette. 'Time to go.'

Chapter Ten

Price's eyes opened at the insistence of the telephone. It took a while for the shapes of his bedroom to fall into a recognisable order; when they did, he turned to his alarm clock. 6.29. The red dot at the top right-hand corner of the nine told him it was evening. He rubbed his neck to ease the stiffness.

He didn't remember going to bed. His head was heavy, indicating that he had slept for a considerable time. He was fully clothed and hadn't even taken off his shoes. He must have hit the sauce pretty hard.

'Hello?' he croaked into the receiver; his throat dry.

'Dave, are you all right? I've been so worried about you.'

'Chris? I thought you weren't calling until Monday?' He rolled off the bed and stood up.

'It *is* Monday, and I've been trying to get through to you all day...'

Monday? It can't be Monday. Today was Sunday. You dropped Christine off at midday, and then ...?

'...and your work said that you hadn't come in. I explained to them that you had a cold, so I assumed that you were in bed...'

A baby crying...then he followed it, no, that wasn't right...the pub?

'...phoning you all day. I was so worried.'

Must have made my way back here at some point? Why can't I remember? Why didn't I hear the phone?

'Chris I'm fine, honestly. I went straight to bed when I got home yesterday and unplugged the phone so I could get some peace. I was going to plug it back in tonight so you could call me, but I must have slept right through.'

'Dave, there must be something more to it than a cold if you can sleep for thirty hours without waking.'

'I feel fine, my throat's a bit dry, but that's probably because I haven't had anything to drink-'

'What did you go to the doctor for on Friday?'

The question took him by surprise. 'How did you know about that?'

'Your mate Mike from work told me when I phoned.'

Bloody Mike, how the hell did he find out? His grip tightened on the receiver. 'It was nothing.'

She wasn't convinced. 'David, I know you; it must have been more than nothing for you to go to the doctor. Is it something to do with how you're feeling now?'

'No. I've been getting headaches and the doctor sent me for a scan-'

'A scan! Is it serious?' She managed to express both shock and concern at the same time.

'No, no,' he said, wishing he hadn't mentioned it. 'It turned out to be a false alarm. It was just a precaution. Please don't worry.'

Silence. *Here it comes.* 'Why didn't you talk to me about it?'

'Because there was no need. It turned out to be nothing and I didn't want you to worry unnecessarily.'

'You should have told me'.

'I know, I'm sorry, I should have told you, it was stupid of me not to. It just didn't seem worth worrying you about. Am I forgiven?'

Christine said that he was, but the way she said it suggested otherwise.

For crying out loud!

'Do you want to come round tonight?' he asked, hoping to lighten the mood. 'We could re-run the Palace Affair.'

'I'm a bit tired tonight, actually,' her voice was distant, as if the line was failing. 'To be honest, all I want to do is-'

Stay home and sulk?

'-have a bath and an early night. You don't mind, do you?'

'Of course not. I'll give you a bell tomorrow.'

'Okay, bye.'

'Love you.'

'I know you do,' she said and hung up.

Price removed the receiver from his ear and glared at it. His hand tightened on the plastic and it creaked under the pressure, fuelling his anger. He slammed it down, panting. *'For fuck's sake, woman, what do you want from me!'* he shouted at the phone and kicked the bedside table. *I'm not a fucking baby, you don't have to check I'm still breathing every five minutes. It's not my fucking fault if I slept through your bastard phone calls, is it?*

But did you? Can you remember what time you came home on Sunday? He couldn't.

He lay back on the bed, groping in the dark for the remote control, and clicked on the Television without thinking.

The room came alive, the walls dancing with the images on the screen. Absently he flicked through the channels and when nothing grabbed his interest, he pressed PLAY on the remote.

Cum sluts 17 filled the screen.

He stared at the images; his eyes unfocused, aware only of the rhythmic movement; his ears numbed to the contrived, dry squealing of the woman. He felt nothing, the unbuttoning of his jeans a reflex action. His organ was unimpressed. The tired routine played before him: meeting, strip, cunnilingus, fellatio followed by penetration, change of position, withdrawal, and ejaculation; always the same.

It wasn't enough.

Price watched as a thin, blonde woman wearing black stiletto heels was roughly twisted from a supine position onto all fours. Her eyes darted briefly to the left of camera and she obeyed the instruction to moan raucously. Price rubbed his still unresponsive penis. She had been in every film he had ever seen. Not her exactly but women identical to her in every way, down to the noises they made when they allegedly reached climax. Blonde, fake breasted, size ten. Where were the real women; the individuals who resisted the stereotypes? The fat women, the old women, the thin women, the ugly women, the women who had sex because they enjoyed it not because they were being paid.

Or even the women who didn't enjoy it and weren't getting paid and were lucky if they escaped with their lives.

He stiffened at the thought of weeping, submissive women beneath strong hands, the tearing of delicate unprepared flesh as entry was forced upon them, a chorus of pitiful sobs and pleas. His strokes quickened.

The screen blurred, then edged slowly back into focus. The woman had changed. Although only the rear of her shoulders and head were visible as the man thumped into her, he knew it was true. The build was similar but the hair, which had previously been a shoulder length blonde, was now a short black bob. He knew it was Julie before the camera focused on her libidinous grin. Her tongue slicked her lips in exaggerated lasciviousness, and she winked as his eyes met hers. 'Hello, Davie. Care to join us; two cocks are better than one.'

He jumped up and punched the off button.

Zipping up his jeans, he stopped the video recorder and removed the cassette. The label read *Cum sluts 17*; it was his. It was also an original copy, so nobody could have recorded over it.

Inserting the tape, he switched on the television. *The Antiques Roadshow* filled the screen before the video took its place. It was a close up of a man's face. His brow was furrowed as he rocked back and forth, eyes down.

The camera cut to the object of his attentions.

'You didn't expect me to have gone away, did you?' hissed Julie.

Too horrified to move, he watched as Julie tipped him another wink, pushing harder onto her lover. 'He's so much better than you, Davie boy. OOOh, yes, I'm going to *come*. Yes. You never made me come, Davie boy. Although I expect your pathetic little droop already knew that-'

The rewind button silenced her. He allowed the tape to reverse a full minute before pressing play. The blonde was back, writhing in her unconvincing way. He watched as the scenario reached its inevitable outcome before a change of scene introduced two blonde women who explored each other's bodies without conviction.

No Julie. He rewound the tape again to make sure.

The room was plunged into darkness; his breathing and the dying whine of the video recorder the only sounds. It was probably the fuse in the video plug again. He knew he should get rid of the ancient thing, but he was too attached to some of his VHS films.

At first he mistook the sound for his own. Then it became louder. He held his breath. The sound of the breathing continued. It was low, throaty. It sounded like someone was ill.

'Who's there?' he called feeling foolish.

The breathing continued, rattling with phlegm.

'David,' the whisper seemed to come from right by his ear and he spun around blindly in the dark.

'Who the fuck is there?' he ran to the door and yanked on door. It wouldn't open.

The breathing grew louder, more strained. It sounded as the owner was getting exited.

'David, will you be my friend?' the voice asked with mocking tones. 'Let us play together. Just me and you.' Price shuddered as he felt something caress his neck. He spun around and lashed out with his hands. His eyes were becoming accustomed to the darkness and he could make out some of his furniture. He made out enough to know he was the only person in the room.

He was almost gibbering with fear. 'Where the fuck are you?'

'I love you David. David. Stick it in me, David; pound your frustrations into me. I can take it. Make me bleed.'

The lights blinked on.

The woman was naked and standing before him, her eyes sewn shut with clumsy stitches, her face was alive with cuts and bruises. She hugged her stomach as if she were freezing cold. 'Love me Dave, the way only you can. Make me alive with your pain.'

She opened her arms to embrace him.

Her stomach was a criss-cross of slashes. Without her hands to keep them closed the flaps burst open and her stomach spilled onto the floor. It was a heaving pile of steaming viscera and worms.

'God damn it,' she said. 'Can't a woman hug her man without her guts falling on the floor?'

He watched as more worms fell from her vagina. She bent down and scooped up and handful and thrust them back inside.

'I love it when they wriggle around in my cunt. It makes me come big lumps of death, David.' She lay on the bed and spread her legs showing him the worms. 'Lick them out of me, please baby.'

He found himself moving towards her. He could see her gaping holes and wondered what it would be like to fuck her inside out. Stick it in her stomach and out her vagina.

'Why don't you try it and see? It sounds fun,' she said pulling out worms from her stomach to make room for him.

As he stripped off his clothes he began to choke. He gasped for breath, but his windpipe was blocked. He thumped at his back, trying to dislodge the blockage, feeling the pressure in his head as he struggled for oxygen.

He fell to his hands and knees and retched great huge heaves like a cat trying to bring up a fur ball. Consciousness was fading.

With a roar of relief he spat out a worm. The worm flopped about on the floor and Price slumped on to his side, exhausted. The worm was bigger than he had expected, it was as thick as his index finger.

They grow fat off your mind, David. Tasty nomies for them. Nom.

The worm began to pulsate and grow. Price could hear the cells of its skin stretching to accommodate the new bulk. Flesh split and eyes peeked through the slits. A mouth cracked open and it began to moan and whine. The sounds grew in volume until Price was forced to protect his ears with his hands. The whining grew louder and higher and he felt the pressure on his eardrums increase. His teeth rattled. He felt that they might shatter under the pressure.

Mercifully, Price blacked out.

Chapter Eleven

After this drink she was going home. Margaret Henderson came to the single's night at the *Montrose* every Monday; the ale was cheap (okay, the lager was watered down, but it was a double's bar) and the majority of people were her own age. Her friends, who lessened the sting of desperation these evenings held for her, weren't here tonight and she felt exposed. Clare had pulled out because she couldn't find a baby-sitter and Allison had given this week a miss because her husband was convinced she was having an affair. It wasn't true; Allison came to the *Monty* to support Margaret that was all. Unfortunately for Allison single's night was the only time Margaret felt confident enough to venture out. In her opinion, she possessed neither the youth nor courage to hit the town at weekends, which had become a lurid and baffling experience. Margaret was forty-three and, although she would never accept the compliment, was often told didn't look a day over thirty-five. Her features, which had known little make-up in their time, were naturally attractive, and her tight frame of black hair had yet to capitulate to the grey life had tried to give her.

Her husband left her ten years ago for a younger woman, and her self-respect had gone with him. Margaret, who had grown from a bridal size twelve to, in her husband's vociferous opinion, a shameful sixteen blamed herself for his departure; slipping into a depression that haunted her even now. It was, she told Allison, like suddenly watching the world through an old black and white television; everything was foggy and slow. Things were improving though; she was down from sixty milligrams to twenty.

What was she doing here? She had hoped that someone would talk to her. Monday nights had figured on her agenda for nearly two years and she recognised a few faces, but no one had glanced at her, let alone approached her.

Margaret threw back the last of her brandy and coke.

'Not leaving us so soon, are you?'

She turned towards the voice and into the brownest eyes she had ever seen. 'Yes,' she replied, as she slung her handbag over her shoulder.

'It's easy to forget how much they make our evenings, isn't it?

She peered intently at him. 'Who?'

'Our friends. It's never the same without them. I always feel conspicuous when they're not here for me to hide behind. They've all got girlfriends now, the people I used to come with, and this place is too sad for them. So they say.'

He smiled and Margaret found herself smiling, too.

'At least stay for one more drink.'

'I don't know...'

It's only a drink. You've sat here wanting someone to come over and when they do, you don't know!

'Okay, sure. But just the one,' she warned.

'Great. I'm Tony by the way. What can I get you?'

'My name is Laura.'

Better to be safe than sorry. 'A brandy and coke, please?'

'Coming right up,' he said before he left.

Margaret couldn't believe her luck. He was gorgeous; and those eyes. All the same, she was aware of the age difference, she estimated him to be about ten years her junior and she knew what men his age thought of women her age: they were all desperate, lonely, and an easy lay. She wasn't going to make the same mistake she had made with that bastard Ed.

It had been the week the doctor upped her from forty to sixty milligrams and things were looking as if the colour was never going to come back. Allison had dragged her here to try and perk her up. She had gone along without thinking. Allison had started a conversation with two men at the bar and brought it back to Margaret with the drinks.

'You've got to get laid,' Allison explained to her later in the toilets.

'You want me to shag him?'

'You've done it before.'

'I know I have, but that was when I was too drunk to know any better.'

'So, get drunk, then.' She watched as Allison raised her eyebrows: *It's that simple.*

And simple it had been. Ed needed little encouragement and they had returned to her house after the club closed, Ed far more eager than she. Margaret had been in no mood for sex and had taken him home to prove to Allison that the old Margaret Henderson was alive and well. What harm would it do to let this man pound away at her and then sneak away in the middle of the night? After all, it wasn't like she hadn't done it before. It was, however, the first time she hadn't been drunk enough to forget about her hysterectomy scar. Her attempts to conceal it had roused Ed's suspicion and when he saw it he had tried to disguise his revulsion. His suddenly limp penis had betrayed him. She hadn't bothered with anyone since. That was a year ago. She came, she drank, she wondered, she went home.

'Here we go.' Tony handed over the beverage and Margaret thanked him. He settled himself on the stool in front of her, taking a swig from his bottle of lager. 'So where are your friends tonight?'

'What friends?'

'You're usually with two others.'

Caution returned. 'Usually?'

'I'm not a stalker,' he blustered. *Was he blushing?* 'It's just that I've seen you in here a few times and you were with the same two women, that's all. I didn't mean anything by it.' He *was* blushing.

'So, you decided to take advantage of their absence and make your move.'

'No,' he protested. 'Well, yes...women, when they're in a group, can be a bit catty. Not that you're like that...oh, dear, I'm not very good at this.'

Margaret couldn't help but grin at his awkwardness. It had been a long time since she had affected a man in that way. It was customary for her to be the one stuttering and blushing and saying the wrong things. The reversal was refreshing. Her guard lowered a little. 'I know what you mean,' she assured him and was pleased to see some of his anxiety lift.

'Thanks. I thought you would. The first time I saw you I knew you were someone who was different.'

'Really?' This wasn't a new one on her. They usually told her she was beautiful, or didn't look her age, or some such nonsense brought on by alcohol or throbbing genitals. This one seemed to mean it. It was still a line, cast out in the hope that she would bite, but it seemed sincere. Her guard lowered further.

'I could see that you were tired of the meat market and were looking for something more. I wanted to talk to you the first time I saw you, but I didn't want you to think I was only after one thing...and I have a real problem talking to attractive women.' He blushed again and averted his eyes as he gulped from the bottle. 'I'm sorry.'

'For what?'

'For blurting all that out. I didn't mean to, but seeing as I had plucked up the courage to finally come over I thought I should say what I'd wanted to say for weeks.' He drew in a much needed breath and asked her if she wanted another drink. When she replied that she would like the same again he disappeared to the bar once more.

Margaret was still undecided. Either he was a very slick operator, or he meant every word. Her mind favoured the former, but her heart opted for the latter. Seeing as both had let her down on numerous occasions, she remained cautious.

As the night went on her caution gradually slipped away. Tony proved to be a warm hearted, funny man and Margaret found that she enjoyed his company a great deal. He was thirty-nine-year-old postal worker, divorced with no children. She disclosed a few minor pieces of information; that she too was divorced, with no children and told him that she worked in a bank. *A little white lie never hurt anybody.*

The music softened and the lights on the dance-floor ceased their manic blinking. Margaret watched as Tony voraciously swallowed the dregs of his lager, and she considered his question before it was asked.

'Would you like to dance?'

'Yes.'

He offered her his arm and she took it; her initial misgivings long forgotten. They pushed through the usual uneasy shufflers to the dancefloor. After finding a space they stood facing each other for a few moments. Tony placed his hands on her waist and began to sway with the music. Margaret, who had expected to initiate the move, did the same, glad he felt comfortable enough to take the lead. Tony said something she didn't hear and pressed his body closer. She braced herself for the inevitable drunken thrust of his groin and was relieved when it didn't come. She rested her head on his shoulder and felt his hands shift to encircle her back. He held her firmly. The embrace, she surmised, of one who needed someone to hold. She returned the gesture and realised how much she had missed the feel of a man in her arms. Her friends had convinced her that she didn't need a man, and she had agreed. She had her own place and a career that ensured that she could keep it with change to spare. But to be desired; that was better than those things. If she could hold onto this feeling she wouldn't need even ten milligrams.

Sure, lots of men wanted to fuck her, but they were two a penny. A woman only had to approach a man for sex and nine times out of ten he would oblige. This one was different. He wanted her. He saw her as another human being, and not simply another notch on his headboard. If things continued as they had done so far, tonight was going to be his lucky night.

The thought of sex raised the issue of her scar and her mood darkened. *Tell him. If he leaves now, so be it.*

It'll hurt, but not as much as watching his penis droop before your eyes will. Margaret, reluctant to share such a personal piece of information, wasn't sure that things would get that far. She was ready, but what Tony wanted was a different matter. The impression he had given her was that of a man who was looking for something more than a one-night stand. Did that mean he wouldn't sleep with her tonight, or did it mean that he would, but only on the understanding it progressed further?

Margaret reached up and kissed him. He responded stiffly, mouth closed. Sensing his hesitation, she gently urged his head closer with her hand and kissed him again. Margaret gripped his hair as his lips parted and his tongue sought out hers. The ardour of his embrace was unexpected and she succumbed to it, returning his probing, urging it deeper. For all his conversational fumbling, he certainly could kiss, and Margaret sensed her own pleasure begin to rise.

The music stopped and the DJ said his goodbyes. The house lights blinked on and the doormen began ushering people towards the exits: *'Come on, boys and girls, can you drink up now, please!'* and *'Let's take the talking outside!'*

'Would you like to come home with me?' she inquired softly.

'I would,' he whispered, then added, 'But I'm not into one-night stands.'

That answered one question. 'There's something I have to tell you,' she said before she had a chance to talk herself out of it.

He pulled away. 'You're not married, are you?'

'No, nothing like that,' she assured him. 'I... I have a scar on my stomach.' It was like releasing a great burden into the smoky air.

Tony looked confused. 'So?'

'A big one.'

'So?'

'*Lads and lasses, let's have your glasses!*'

It was her turn to blush, and she stared at her feet. 'The last person...man to see it-'

'Am I him?' His voice had become hard. Not quite angry but clearly displeased at her unspoken accusation. When she didn't answer he asked again, 'Am I him?'

'*Do your talking while you're walking!*'

'No,' she said.

His hand beneath her chin, he raised her head so that she was looking at him. 'Then there's nothing to worry about, is there?' He pecked her cheek.

'I'm sorry,' she said, feeling foolish.

'If there's anyone who should apologise, it's me. I'm sorry I raised my voice, I just don't like to see people put themselves down like that, it makes me angry. You could be covered in scars from head to toe but that wouldn't change what's inside. Anyway, you haven't seen me naked yet. Now there's something for you to worry about.'

She laughed and they kissed, and the cries of the doormen fell on deaf ears.

*

Margaret carried the cups of coffee into the living room. Tony sat on the edge of the sofa, hands on lap, striving to look relaxed and failing miserably. 'I'm sorry I haven't got anything stronger,' she apologised as she handed him the drink.

'Coffee's fine.'

Margaret sat in the armchair opposite, emulating his rigid posture, and resisted the temptation to put her feet on the coffee table as she often did. This was the part of the evening she disliked intensely. They both knew the reason they were here, and conversation became strained as it was difficult to focus on anything else. Tony dragged his eyes away from the cup. 'Nice place,' he said.

'Thank you,' she replied, also finding her steaming mug unusually enthralling. The quicker she drank it, the sooner she could put this part of the night behind her.

'What bank do you work at?'

The lie that had flowed so easily earlier fazed her. At the time it was a sensible precaution, but if they continued to see each other it would become a problem. She briefly wondered how he would react. 'The one on the corner of the High Street.'

He nodded slowly. 'I know it, yes. Worked there long?'

'Not long. How about you?'

'All my working life. Started off as a postman, did that for seven years. I drive the vans now. You know, collecting the post from the pillar boxes that sort of thing. Why don't you sit here, Laura?' He nodded his head to the empty space beside him. When she did, Tony put his cup down on the table and reached for hers. Anticipation quickening her pulse, she allowed him to take it from her.

He shuffled closer and touched her cheek with the backs of his fingers, smiling. She also smiled, conscious that she was holding her breath, then pounced on him. Their lips connected hungrily, eager fingers scrabbling at clothes. He unbuttoned her blouse deftly while she struggled with his shirt. 'Rip it,' he hissed, and she felt herself gush at his words. Buttons flew as she tore it open, licking at the flesh she revealed. Tony pushed her on her back, lifting her bra over her breasts, sucking roughly at her nipples. She groaned, her hands searching for his zip to release his hardness.

She felt his attentions move from her breasts to her stomach and she stiffened as her inhibitions returned. His tongue dispelled them as it ran the length of the scar culminating in a gentle kiss. Her sigh of relief stopped in her throat as he hoisted her skirt and descended between her thighs, then rushed from her in a gasp as he pulled aside her panties and his tongue stabbed at her moistness. She spread her legs to accommodate him and he plunged his tongue deeper.

'Put it in me,' she breathed.

He pulled open his fly, released his penis, and thrust into her in one swift motion. Margaret was dimly aware that they had omitted to take precautions, but it felt too good to stop.

'Pull out before you come,' she gasped in his ear, not caring whether he heard her or not.

Price grunted and she mistook this for agreement. His movements began to slow as the initial pleasure of entry diminished, the sensation slowly fading until it was as if he were fucking thin air.

It's always the same. The need. The hunger. No man can resist the lure of their moist flesh, the desire to sink his phallus deep within is irresistible. Long has this been the cause of his

61

ruin. Those stretched and slimy slits that control it all, that contaminate it all. With each release they steal another piece of his soul, draining it into their bodies until nothing remains of him but a shadow of a shadow. The reward for his sacrifice? A split second of dribbling relief. It's not enough.

'It's not enough,' Price snarled.

'What?' she said, her concentration broken.

His climax was drawing near and it had never felt so dull. 'It's not *enough!*' He withdrew, jetting sperm over her body, smirking as it spattered her face.

She wiped it away, her disgust clear. 'What are you doing?'

'It's not enough!' The words tore themselves from Price in a roar and Margaret recoiled. 'Don't you understand?' He was almost pleading with her.

Margaret collected herself. 'Get the fuck out of my house!'

Price climbed off her, rubbing his now flaccid organ, as he paced up and down the length of the sofa. 'It's like having an itch you can never scratch, do you see? Pathetic couplings like these don't even come close.'

'Get out! Get out!'

Price stopped and jerked his head towards her violently. Margaret took one look at his clenched teeth and braced herself for a blow. Instead, he eyed her coolly. 'It's not your fault. You're controlled by that *thing*,' he indicated between her legs. 'That's all you are, Laura, nothing more.'

Margaret closed her legs as fear chilled her. His eyes were dead; they looked in her direction, but they seemed to be blind to her at the same time. She watched his expression change from confusion to revulsion to anger and back to confusion in the space of seconds. He was clearly deranged. *Please don't kill me. Please don't kill me.*

Price zipped himself up and sat in the chair opposite, visibly calmer. 'Don't worry; I have no intention of hurting you. I *like* you. Really, I do.' He took a swig of her coffee. 'That's good stuff, what is it?'

'Gold blend...de-caf.' She was weeping softly.

'De-caf...no shit? I think I've just found my brand.' He tasted it again, then stood up, smacking his lips. Margaret flinched. 'Well,' he said, stretching tiredly. 'I'm going to go now. I'm sorry things didn't work out better, I think my problem is I'm too picky, so try not to take it to heart.'

He paused at the door. 'One more thing, Margaret.'

She jumped at the sound of her name. He wagged his finger in admonishment, adopting the tone of a scolding parent. 'If you must persist in bringing people home under a pseudonym, you really should hide you mail beforehand, don't you think?' He frowned as confusion returned. 'I also know, and please don't ask me how,' he countered with a raised hand, 'that you are an English teacher at St. Joseph's High School. Funny that.' He dismissed it with an impatient exhalation. 'Anyway, as I was saying, don't think of calling the police. I know where you live,' he pulled a dopey face, sweeping his arm in explanation, 'obviously. And your friends; Allison lives at 34 Green Close, correct me if I'm incorrect; and Clare lives at 22a Fulham Heights. Rosie's such a lovely child, wouldn't you say? Ripe.'

He laughed at Margaret's stunned and teary expression.

'That is amazing! I have absolutely no idea how I know that. None at all. Do you? No, of course you don't. How could you? Anyway, consider yourself cautioned. If the boys in blue come knocking at my door I'll gut all four of you like pigs, okay.' This was said as casually as if he were arranging to meet again. 'Just put it to the back of your mind like you did that business with Ed. Besides which, I haven't really done anything wrong. Not really. You consented, even enjoyed it-'

'Just go,' she sobbed. *Please just leave me alone.*

'Fair enough. I know when I'm not wanted,' he waved his farewell; a childish opening and closing of his hand. 'Bye-bye.'

Margaret ran and bolted the door behind him, slipping the security chain in place as an added precaution. She put her eye up to the spy-hole to make sure he was really gone. She watched as he reached the bottom of the path, opened the gate, and closed it behind him. He looked up straight at her and waved again, blowing a kiss.

She collapsed to the floor and tried to scream a scream that wouldn't come.

*

(I am lost)

He is at the top of something older than time. Not a mountain or a building but something in between. It is not truly alive although it shifts and groans in pain. He looks down and his head spins with the height.

It is the city: a ruin without life and without hope of rain; a timeless colossus with no end or meaning.

Then he sees them.

*Distracted from death they shuffle silently, eyes down,
through the dusty ruins. He calls to them, but they do not hear.
Not a flicker of anything on the drawn blank faces.*

Except one.

*It raises an empty brow to the heavens and speaks to him
in a voice like jagged fingernails on silk:*

*'I can feel myself going wrong. Through the flesh that clings
to my frangible bones, through the stretched paper, blank and
bloodless. Through all this I can feel it...'*

He watches and listens and understands.

To end their death, he must bring them life.

Life through suffering.

Chapter Twelve

The bus to work was packed with the same old faces, thought Price. From his position at the rear of the single-decker he watched as his regular travelling companions filed on at their regular stops, their faces weighed with sleep and the burden of the day ahead. There were no conversations, no smiles of recognition; only a silent shuffling on and off, eyes down.

The crackle of sulphur to his left and he knew without looking that it was the plump, bottle-blonde twenty-something partaking in her 8.20 nicotine fix. Smoking was banned on all buses, but no one complained or coughed in disapproval. Price wondered if anyone noticed apart from him. The smoker was quite attractive, her features retaining their shape despite the weight; strong, high cheekbones, autumnal sky-blue eyes. Her figure – somewhere between sixteen and eighteen, he guessed - was strangely alluring; the rounded curve of her stomach and her hips seeming more than just fat. He pictured her naked lying on his bed, her soft flesh trembling as he touched it. His hands grabbed at her hips as he entered her, his fingers sinking deep into the folds. He turned her onto all fours, reaching underneath her to squeeze her stomach as it sagged. She moaned as he penetrated her again, digging his nails into her hips to aid his thrusts. Her skin broke under the pressure and blood oozed between his fingers. 'Harder,' she begged, but she was too big for him now. She bucked wildly, her fat hole dribbling copiously as he tore fistfuls of flesh from her hips. 'More,' she demanded. He smacked her buttocks, sending waves of blubber up and along her back, bile scorched his throat.

He threw her on her back, gagging as her stomach wobbled in a grotesque parody of a waterbed. And then his hands were around her neck. Her eyes bulged and her face began to redden but she did not struggle, the only movement the frantic urging of her hips for more; more penetration, more pain. 'Kill me,' she spluttered, and Price began to shake her, retching as the scent of her poison filled the air.

Then he was back on the bus. He adjusted his trousers to conceal his erection and looked at the girl out of the corner of his eye. She was grinding the cigarette into the floor with her shoe, staring with disinterest out of the window.

Price shuddered. The feel of her throat in his hands had seemed so real. His palms sported four thin crescents where he had dug his nails into the flesh. He massaged them away and he rested his head against the window.

A woman stepped onto the bus and paid her fare. She took her usual seat; four rows down on the left. Today there was something different about her. It wasn't her clothes, or hairstyle. Price sniffed. There was a scent of something. He moved to the seat behind her aware he was ignoring an unwritten protocol of bus etiquette.

The woman's long brown hair draped over the back of her seat, shining in spite the grey sun. Unable to resist the temptation, Price reached out and stroked it. He returned his hands quickly to his lap fearing that the contact would be noticed. She didn't move. Invigorated by this clandestine connection he touched the smooth locks again. He closed his eyes enjoying the coolness against his skin.

He sniffed his fingers. The odour was present; hidden beneath shampoo and smells of femininity. She had made love that morning; and during the thrash of naked limbs her lover's scent had bled into her. It was as distinctive as her cheap perfume. Eager to taste more he bowed his head, tilting it as close to the woman as discretion would permit. He feigned a pose of contemplation to try and disguise his intrusion. He breathed deeply, drawing her into his lungs.

His nose caught the real scent beneath the deception. It was a rich, cloying fragrance unlike anything he had encountered previously. The worms squirmed in his guts, appalled by the stench. He could feel them crawling up his gullet trying to escape.

Price staggered down the walkway covering his mouth to keep the worms inside. The bus eventually crawled to a stop and he pushed through the doors before they were fully open, knocking shoulders with those as keen to board as he was to alight.

He supported himself against the bus shelter and swallowed huge gulps of crisp October air.

The hiss of the doors closing signified that the bus was about to depart, and he turned to look at the woman. All the passengers faced him; instead of amused expressions or concerned frowns, he saw only eyeless agonies of brittle flesh pressed against the glass. He saw thin mewling mouths moaning his name, decayed fingers jabbed at him.

The bus pulled away and the passengers now hammered at the windows screaming. Only when the bus turned the corner did the screaming stop. The hallucinations were worsening. He could accept worms - a natural enough offshoot from the pink elephant - but a busload of eyeless corpses shrieking at him and accusing him of killing them? That was much harder to swallow.

Deep within himself he knew they were as real as the tumour eating away at his brain.

Tumour. He blanched. How on earth could something as terrible as that slip his mind so effectively? He only knew that it had. *If you've got a brain tumour then why are you going to work?*

'I don't know,' he muttered, and truly didn't. He'd woken with the alarm seven thirty, showered and dressed and left the house at eight o'clock to catch the eight-o-five to work just like he always did. He had performed these tasks automatically, without thinking. Strange.

Somewhat stranger was the fact he couldn't recall what he had done the previous night. Arguing with Christine was the last definite recollection. There was, however, a strong essence of Julie about the evening. Had he spoken to her? It was unlikely. Even so he couldn't shake the notion that she had been there?

As if to answer this question Julie stepped into view across the street. The shift from the internal to external took a second to register. He glanced at his watch. It was twenty to nine. She was wearing black jeans and a navy blue fleeced jumper that meant she wasn't going to work. She normally wore a suit.

He followed her brisk determined strides. The denim hugged the thighs he had laid between so many times. *You and all the others. How many others were there? More than you could even bear to think about.*

(He danced up the stairs to their bedroom. It was his lunch hour and he was hoping to catch her still in bed. She was taking a day's leave from work and he was after a little lunch-time loving. He heard her moan and his penis indicated its impatience by pressing uncomfortably against his trousers. She had started without him, just how he liked. He pictured her hand working frantically between her thighs, aching for him.)

Price crossed the street, keeping what he hoped was a sensible distance between them. The jumper didn't quite cover her buttocks, and he noticed she had put on some weight. It annoyed him that she looked better for it.

(He paused at the door, holding the knob, then swung it open. The words of greeting choking in his throat.)

Seeing Julie in the flesh made the memory somehow more; her presence adding something tangible to it. The rage he had hidden for so long surged to engulf him. His legs buckled under the weight of it.

(The scene failed to register. She was bouncing up and down on the bed, a glistening penis sliding in and out of her body. Everything was as it should be, except he wondered why he could see his own penis like that. Then he realised he was standing at the door.

Julie turned to face him, laughing. 'Hello, David,' she said, not interrupting her movements. Upon hearing a name other than his own, the man raised his head. He saw Price at the doorway and a look of absolute horror seized him; the antitheses to Julie's unrepentant smirk.

'Julie?' he whimpered.

The man threw her off him and scrabbled for his clothes. 'Look, mate, I didn't know she was living with someone, in fact I didn't know she even had a bloke, I wouldn't have done anything-'

All Price could see were Julie's eyes. He'd never seen them so cold. They stared at him with defiance, regarding him without fear of reprisal or indication of culpability.

'What are you doing?' He sounded amazed, confused.

She shook her head. 'I'm having a shag, what does it look like?' She said as if he had walked in and found her reading a book.

'I don't understand?' he gasped.

'For God's sake, David, get a backbone, will you. You're pathetic.'

Anger finally began to rise. 'How could you-'

'Fucking get out!' she screamed.)

When Julie turned into the High Street he didn't follow. He knew where she was going; the place they had first met. He dumped himself in the bus shelter opposite and watched her enter the cafe. He smiled at her predictability. A big English breakfast was a daily requirement for Julie, and it was because of a mix up with his order and her own that they became friendly.

He smiled at the impression he still held of her then: charming and funny and so demurely sexy. Compared to the Julie he knew now it was like they were two different people.

He kicked at the shelter. He should have killed her when he had the chance; he might even have got off with the murder charge. Crime of Passion wasn't it? If he had the opportunity to do things differently, he'd have gutted her.

He ground his teeth together. *You should have tied her up and worked on her. A few strategic cuts, here and there. A few subtle slices of guilty flesh, filling the wounds with salt. Better still, you could have scrubbed her cunt out with a brillo-pad and bleach. Her agony would have lasted for days. The delights you missed, Davie boy. The inexpressible joy of correction.*

In his mind's eye she struggled against the restraints. She was tied to a gynaecologist's bench, her legs bound tightly to the stirrups, and leather straps secured her head and wrists. Her naked body glistened with fear. He stroked her; amused by the way her skin crawled away from his fingers. At first, she mocked him; called him spineless, impotent, everything her feeble mind thought would wound him. The taunts faded a little when he produced the knife, but soon her misplaced courage returned. It was only when he used the knife to explore her softest flesh that she began to beg.

There's still time to reacquaint yourselves, who would suspect you? It's been nearly two years since you last saw her, what is your motive? And besides, you are in love with a new girlfriend now and are very happy.

He coughed up the first worm of the morning onto the pavement. The creature raised its head to him as if in recognition. Price managed a nervous smile. Its features began to form, and it was already ten times the size it had been.

They grow up so fast.

It whipped away down the street with a whine. Price released the breath he was holding, noting that his fear of these things was decreasing. It was only three days ago that he was running away terrified at the sight of them.

('Fucking get out!'

'I thought you loved me, you bitch!' He moved to the foot of the bed, fists clenched in anger.

She began throwing cushions at him. 'Love you?' She gave him the laugh again; terse and humourless. 'How could any

*woman love a man without a backbone? Any other man would
have killed the pair of us, but you just stood there looking like
a wounded puppy, whimpering! Now get OUT!')*

*That was when you should have killed her. You could have
snapped her neck, or strangled her, or simply stamped on her
face until it was nothing more than an unrecognisable splat.
Imagine the feel of her skull crunching beneath the heel of your
boot. There would have been none of this pain for you after
that. No self-castigation, or nights blubbering lost in a haze of
alcoholic self-indulgence. You should have answered your destiny
that day. Became the man you always dreamed you would be.*

A smile flickered briefly on his lips.

The man she wanted you to be.

It wasn't often you got a second chance.

*

At one p.m. Janine entered the smoking room. By
the time she had taken the six steps to the vending
machine, she managed to inhale a deeply satisfying
lungful of secondary smoke and light one of her own.
She stabbed at the buttons for her tea, her right eye
watering as a wisp of white from her cigarette
aggravated it. She stole a quick glance over her
shoulder to see if Christine was eating her lunch at the
usual table. She was, but she looked miserable.
Collecting her drink, depositing a small clump of ash
to the floor in the process, she rushed to the table.
She asked her if everything was all right.

'I think Gary's found me,' she said flatly.

Janine's heart sank. 'What? He knows you're in
Liverpool?'

'He phoned me at home, Jan.'

'Oh my God,' said Janine, reaching out to touch Christine's arm. She gave it a squeeze and asked 'When?'

'Sunday night and today; about twenty minutes ago.'

'He phoned you on Sunday and you didn't tell me until now?'

'I wasn't a hundred percent sure it was him, then.'

'But you are now?'

Christine nodded.

'What did he say?'

'He didn't say anything.'

'Then how do you know it was him?'

'Because he hung up when I mentioned his name.'

'But he didn't *say* his name.'

'I'm not making this up.'

'I know you're not, Chris,' she said sincerely. 'But you've no reason to assume it's him that called you, either. It could have been a wrong number, or kids messing about. Anything.'

A frown. 'I know all that, don't you think I've thought this through. I was willing to put it down to my imagination but when it happened again this morning, I knew.'

Janine squeezed her friend's arm once more. 'You've got to call the police,' she said.

'I don't think so,' dismissed Christine, moving to the vending machine.

Janine waited for her to return, not wishing to continue the conversation at a distance. She took the opportunity to light another fag 'Why not?' she asked on Christine's return.

'Because I know what they'll say. How do you know it's him? Call us when you've something more to go on than woman's intuition.'

'You've got to do something.'

'I know, I know.'

'Why don't you get Dave to move in with you for a few days.'

She considered this. 'What would I tell him?'

'You could tell him the truth.' At the look of horror that washed over Christine she quickly added, 'Or just the fact that you've been getting funny phone calls and you're frightened. Come on like a frightened rabbit, men like that. It brings out their protective instincts.'

Christine smiled. 'Dave the Protector, I've never thought of him like that before.'

Attempting to keep the smile on her face, Janine clasped her hands to her chest, fluttering her eyelids wildly. 'Oh, Dave, I just don't feel safe without a man to protect me. And you're such a man.'

Christine giggled. 'Fool.'

'If he doesn't go for it then he's not the man you thought he was,' she jiggled her eyebrows. 'If you know what I mean?'

Christine's smile widened and Janine, now that a temporary solution had been reached, changed the subject. 'I was talking to Roland last night-'

'Seeing him on a Monday, that's not your style,' remarked Christine with an intrigued expression.

'Well anyway,' she dismissed the jibe, glad that her friend was back to her old self again. 'I thought it would be a good idea for the four of us to go out together.'

'What, me and Dave? On a double date?'

'You don't have to make it sound so unpleasant, Chris. Roland was pretty keen.'

'Oh, I'm sorry,' she assured her. 'It just sounds so U.S of A.'

'You mentioned double date, not me.'

'I know I did but I'm not sure whether it would be a good idea. I mean none of us have met him-'

'Well how else are you going to meet?'

'I suppose you're right,' she conceded, hoping Dave would be willing to come along after her little tantrum on Monday. She hadn't meant to act like that, after all it was his business. She had no idea why she had let things go that far. Trust her to mess things up. 'How about Friday?'

'The very day we had in mind.'

Christine hesitated. 'You *would* warn me if he was a wanker, wouldn't you?'

*

Price had followed Julie to the hairdressers.

When the woman with the blonde streaks exited ninety minutes later he almost let her go. He had been so focused on Julie's familiar black bob.

Yet another indication of your innocence. Blonde, officer? No, no, Julie had black hair. She dyed it? Well, as I said, I haven't seen her in nearly two years...

Her screams would certainly warm his cold heart; her blood would bring spring to his dry skin.

(The scene failed to register. She was bouncing up and down on the bed with a glistening penis sliding in and out of her body. Everything was as it should be, except he wondered why he could see his own penis like that. Then he realised he was standing at the door. He freed his hardness from its constraints,

stroking it, his eyes drawn to the copulation on the bed. His bed. Their bed. Watching her moist flesh being penetrated by another was strangely intoxicating. He worked on himself frantically, her infidelity proving to be the ultimate aphrodisiac. It wasn't enough.

He moved to the bed.

The yelp of pain when he stuck it in her ass soon gave way to an inhalation of surprise, then a groan of pleasure. 'Oh, Davie, I never knew you had it in you,' she exclaimed in staccato gasps.

He turned to face the man she was riding and gazed without surprise into his own. They exchanged a wink.)

Price let Julie go. *Now is not the time. You must be patient. Acquiring the skill with which to equal the pain she has inflicted onto you is a lengthy process. It requires practice.*

Price considered where such practice could be found.

Chapter Thirteen

The bus jerked to yet another sudden stop. Christine mumbled curses under her breath. In the last ten minutes the bus had moved less than twenty feet. The grim acceptance of being trapped in rush hour traffic had deserted her today.

Work had been shitty, first the call from Gary then Mrs. Moore moaning about her using the phone too much. What did she care? She didn't pay the bloody bill, and none of the other supervisors worried about it so why should she?

But the real source of her frustration was Dave. He hadn't gone to work again today, and he wasn't at home. Or if he was, he wasn't answering the phone.

She really needed to apologise for her behaviour on the phone yesterday. She shouldn't have acted like that. He had said that it wasn't worth worrying her about and he was right. The sooner she told him this then the sooner things could get back to normal.

But when she eventually rapped her knuckles on the door of 57 Winterburn road, there was nobody home.

Chapter Fourteen

Susan Lally jabbed two fingers at the driver of the cab as it passed. That was the second bastard to ignore her. *Weren't they supposed to give priority to women after midnight?* She snorted indignantly. *Too busy pissing off to town for the big fares to worry about that sort of thing.*

She tugged her skirt down an inch to try and keep the wind at bay, the sweaty heat of the club long blown cold. *They all told you he was no good; your mother, friends. You had insisted that you could change him, told them that they didn't know him like you did, fooled by the times alone together without his mates to egg him on. They were a bunch of useless bastards as well, looking up to him like he was Buddha or something. They'd get a shock if you told them it had taken him three months to get into your knickers, even though he told everyone he'd 'done you in' on the first night. That would dent his star status. Tosser.*

When he had called to cancel their night at the cinema, she had thought nothing of it. Andy frequently did that sort of thing; usually ending up in the club, bragging about how he had kept his woman in line. Tonight she had intended to rumble his little display. And rumble it she did. However, instead of finding him pissed and showing off to his mates she had spotted him off in the corner snogging the face off some trollop. *You should have gone over and said something, slapped him, and her. Slag!*

But she hadn't. She had backed away unnoticed as the crowd enveloped her, numbed by the discovery. Only when the biting wind outside whipped at her face did the tears eventually fall. At first she had chided herself for going to the club, her muddled mind reasoning that what she didn't know wouldn't hurt her. Then came a bewildered rage that focused inwards, scrabbling for explanations and concluding that she was at fault. If she had been a better girlfriend, if she had done the dirty things he had wanted then there would have been no need for him to stray. That was soon dismissed; Andy Baker was a pervert and a bastard and that was all there was to it.

She stood on the corner of Cotton Road, the din of the club now a distant thumping. It was far too cold to hang around waiting for cabs that wouldn't stop. She began to walk.

It wasn't far - about a fifteen-minute hobble in heels. It meant cutting through the estate but her familiarity with the area kept the trepidation a stranger would have felt at bay.

It was more like a maze of narrow roofless corridors than a housing estate; the architect living in a world where shadowed corners weren't home to rapists and thieves or didn't consider such things.

She stopped. The lamp ahead was smashed and the passageway was engulfed in darkness. Her mind quickly calculated it was the only way forward if she didn't want to retrace her steps back to the club and walk around the estate. Her confidence faltered. Walking here was ok as long as she could see where she was going.

It's not that far, the path follows an L-shape, once you turn the corner you'll see the light from the other side. Fifty yards max.

A noise from behind her and she spun around. As far as she could tell there was nobody there. A gust of wind ruffled her hair and she pulled her leather jacket tight around her neck. Footsteps, she could just make out the sound. Heavy. Male.

She walked into the darkness, shifting her weight on the tips of her toes to stop the clicking of her heels, thinking it was Andy mucking about. The shoe slipped from her heel and scraped the concrete, the sound amplified by the confined space. She heard the footsteps break into a run, becoming louder. Removing her shoes she pushed herself up against the wall confident that the night would conceal her. *If it was that bastard, he was going to be sorry.*

The footsteps slowed, shuffling, unsure of the direction the sound had come.

'Su-sie?' called the voice, playfully singing the words. She froze in terror at the sound of her name. It wasn't Andy. *Oh, my god it was a mugger or a rapist or a murderer and he knows my name and*

'Su-sie. Come-and-play-with-me.' Then in a hushed, sinister tone: 'I promise I won't hurt you...' A cold, humourless laugh. '...much.'

She clamped her thighs together in case she wet herself. She had needed to go before, now she was desperate. From her position in the darkness she searched the illuminated street beyond. She was certain the voice had come from there, but the wind could have carried it. *You should have run the moment you heard it.*

A figure stepped into view and she pushed herself against the wall, the noise of her jacket brushing against the brickwork deafening to her adrenaline fuelled ears. Thankfully the man hadn't heard it; he was facing to the left, then to the right; uncertain.

Then his head turned slowly towards her.

Her breath caught in her throat as her whole being tensed. She remained there unable to move as he strolled towards her hiding place, his face obscured by the poor lighting, and then by darkness as he stopped at the entrance. His voice no more than a whisper, he said, 'I think you're in there.'

He stretched his arms, resting his palms against both sides of the narrow walkway, his silhouetted frame filling it entirely. '*Are* you in there?' The man leaned forward, close enough for Susan to hear his breathing, it was calm like his voice. 'You *must* be in there...I tell you what; I'll go around the corner, close my eyes, and count to ten, I promise I won't peek, and then I'll come in and get you. Won't that be fun?' He disappeared.

You've got to move.

With this thought she padded silently into the dark, ignoring the pain as pieces of stone imbedded themselves in the soles of her feet. She broke into a sprint when she turned the corner and saw the light ahead.

She wasn't to know he was waiting for her.

*

Price could hardly contain himself. The anticipation, he discovered, was everything. She had no idea he was there, the potency of that information exhilarating him like nothing else. The patter of stockinged feet drew closer and he hoped the tension would last. He raised his fist.

When he was sure she was almost out of the walkway he swung his arm. His fist smashed into her nose and his heart danced at the feel of her beneath his knuckles. Susan immediately collapsed to the floor and her left leg folded awkwardly under her body. Price was disappointed when he didn't hear it break.

Price stepped out of the shadows, regarding the prone body. She looked no more than eighteen years old, but these days' appearances were deceptive. His nose wrinkled. The smell of her soiled flesh reached him even at this distance. Her youthful looks no distraction to his finely tuned senses. She was out cold, her face covered in blood. In the darkness her blood looked almost black. He opened and closed his fist, massaging the wrist. He licked her blood from his glove, smacking his lips then returned his attention to the girl.

He bent down, grabbed a handful hair and dragged her back into the darkness. Susan began to stir, so he slammed her head against the concrete, feeling the excitement return at the dull sound it made.

Trembling fingers traced the outline of her lips, moving down to her chin. How he wanted to hurt her, show her his suffering through her own. It burned him.

He resisted the temptation. The area was not secure, and he would need time if he were to do it correctly. It was enough to know she was his. The delight of showing her the error of her ways could wait for another day.

Another face.

*

Mrs. Lally initially woke at her husband's furious departure from the bed. Then she heard the hammering.

'What is it?' she asked, alarmed. Only bad news came knocking at your door at a quarter to five in the morning.

'If she's forgotten her bloody keys again...' His words trailed off to an irate mumbling as he descended the stairs.

Mrs. Lally followed her husband's progress from the warmth of the duvet, ears straining as he unlocked the door.

'What's happened?'

Upon hearing his startled exclamation Mrs. Lally bolted from the bed.

She screamed when she saw the blood, rushing to Susan and throwing her arms around her. Her husband, however, was shouting; he wanted blood of his own and he knew where to find it.

'For God's sake George call the police!'

He stopped as if he had been slapped in the face and dialled 999.

Three quarters of an hour later an area patrol car pulled up outside.

'About bloody time too,' muttered Mr. Lally from the window.

'George!' Again, he fell silent.

Susan was sitting on the sofa in the front room, her face had been washed and she held a bloodied tissue up to her still bleeding nose. The skin around her eyes was already bruising. Her mother, sitting beside her, stroked her head, cooing. 'Everything's going to be all right, darling, you'll see. We're here now, okay, sweetheart? Sweetheart?'

It was as if she hadn't uttered a word, Susan continued to stare blankly ahead, shivering. The blanket draped across her shoulders failed to warm her.

When the two officers entered the room, male and female, the situation suddenly became more ominous. The WPC crouched before Susan while her colleague hovered by the door.

'Hello, Susan, can you hear me? My name's WPC Parr, and I would like to ask you a few questions, if you feel you're up to it?' Her voice expressed a well-rehearsed compassion.

The male PC asked Mr. Lally if he'd called an ambulance.

He could have kicked himself. 'No, it didn't occur to us. Our first reaction was to call you.'

The PC nodded and called for one on his radio.

'Can you tell me what happened, Susan?' asked WPC Parr.

Mr. Lally exploded. 'Isn't it bloody obvious? She's been attacked by that yob she's been knocking around with. Just wait 'till I get my hands on the little bleeder!'

'George!'

'It wasn't Andy,' said Susan.

Parr shifted her eyes to the mother who sighed. 'Andy Baker, her boyfriend,' she explained.

A snort from Mr. Lally.

'George, stop it!'

The female officer ignored the parent's squabbling. 'Can you tell me what happened, Susan?'

'There was a man,' she sobbed. 'In...in the estate...he...he...'

'Which estate was this?'

'The Mandern estate...I couldn't get a taxi.'

'And what time was this about?'

'I'm not sure...around midnight, I think. I'd just been to the club on Cotton Road.' She began to cry silently, 'I'm sorry.' Her mother held her tightly.

'It's okay, Susan, you're doing just fine.'

'There was...a man following me...he...he knew my name.'

'And it was this man that attacked you?'

Susan nodded.

'What time did this happen, Susan?'

'About ten past twelve...

'Can you remember what the man looked like?'

'It...it was too dark.'

'Can you remember how tall he was?' When Susan didn't answer she said: 'Was he as tall as your Dad?'

Susan glanced at her father. 'Taller, about six foot four.'

The male PC's radio burbled into life and he excused himself and stepped into the hall.

'Can you remember anything else about him, what he might have been wearing, anything he might have said-'

Susan stiffened.

'Did he say anything to you, Susan?'

'He said...he wanted me to come and play with him and that he wasn't going to hurt me much...but the way he said it I knew he was lying.'

'Did he have an accent?'

'No.'

It was at this point that the paramedics arrived. WPC Parr let them examine Susan and asked her mother to gather some of Susan's things in case the hospital detained her overnight.

Mrs. Lally jumped at the chance to do something useful. Parr gave her a reassuring smile as she left before asking Mr. Lally if she could have a word with him in the kitchen.

It was there that she asked him for the address of Andy Baker.

*

Here the night devoured everything; the moon, the stars, the life from all things. All that remained was the blackness.

And the sounds of the dead.

The pitiful wailing drifted through the dusty land like the wind. It was everywhere. It was everything.

Price was moving. He had been lying at the foot of the hill of corpses when the sun had finally died. For an eternity he remained there, deprived of sight, breathing in dust and listening to the moaning accusations from above.

Then there was light. Myriad yellow eyes blinked into existence at once. He brought up his arms to shield himself from the glare and found himself moving, carried along on the backs of his brethren.

He did not resist. They knew him; every thought, every festering desire.

There was nothing to fear.

Price's bed was covered in worms, his sleeping form oblivious to the creatures as they crawled over him.

They warmed themselves on his body heat, curling up beside him, rubbing their heads in appreciation against his nakedness.

A smile stretched his lips as a worm caressed his cheek. It grew wider as another rubbed itself against his groin making him hard, the resulting climax destined to be explained away as an erotic dream.

*

The two police officers who had responded to Mr. Lally's call drove away from Andrew Baker's house.

'What do you think, Geoff?' WPC Parr asked her colleague.

He indicated left and moved into second gear, lazily turning the corner. 'I don't think he knows anything about it.'

'I'm not so sure, there was something iffy about him?'

'You just don't like him because he was shacked up with another bird when she was attacked, that's all.'

She shook her head. 'Susan said he knew her name.'

'I expect lots of people know her name, and the girl swore blind she was with him from about eight o'clock and listed three bouncers who could confirm the time they left.'

They headed to St Anne's Hospital, resigned to the fact that if Susan Lally couldn't remember anything else and Baker's alibi checked out, they would have next to nothing to go on.

Chapter Fifteen

The worms carried him into waking. The afternoon sun burned his face through the window. His stirring brought hisses from all around him. He opened his eyes and the bleary shape of a worm's head began to form. They were growing bigger all the time.

'Hello,' he said, and yawned. The worm rubbed its muzzle against him affectionately.

Price reached out and tickled the creature under what he hoped was its chin. It acknowledged his gesture with a delicate whining sound. The sound rose to a crescendo as others took up the call, nudging Price for similar attention.

He sat up, spilling the creatures from his body. 'I *am* popular this morning,' he commented as he took in the countless intertwining bodies that covered his bed.

'And what have I done to deserve such attention?' The worms slicked themselves around his limbs and tightened. He found the sensation oddly pleasing as their body heat penetrated his skin, spreading warmth to his cold bones; their blood slick skin working him liked a masseuse's oily fingers.

He sighed, reclining gently back on to the bed. The worms wriggled under his weight, and Price smiled as they massaged the tension from his shoulders.

His penis twitched into life and he took it in his hand. It felt good; not because of the rhythmic movements he employed but because of the epiphany.

Women devoted their lives to perfecting the art of deception. It was taught to them from birth; how to daub their masks, how to contort and shape their figures, how to disguise the stench of their poison with perfumes and toxins.

All this effort and it was of no consequence. He was immune. There was nothing they could offer that his mind and the worms couldn't emulate.

He closed his eyes and saw a woman. Her features were a blur, as if she were a smudged charcoal sketch. The shape of her body was more clearly defined; small white jagged stretch marks on the hips, two moles beneath the navel. The smell of her moistness permeated the image as it came into focus. His hand mimicked her softest flesh perfectly. He ran his tongue across a scar on her stomach, tasting her sweat. The scar split, releasing a thick clear liquid. He drank from the wound and his tongue probed for more. Blood turned the liquid red. Price continued to feed.

His semen dropped without sound onto his stomach and legs. The worms crawled over one another to feast on his seed. He waited while they diligently cleaned him up then rose to make a cup of tea. The worms followed loyally behind.

The local paper was waiting for him in the hall. He picked it up, flicking through the pages. He stopped when he came across the *What's On* section. 'Now,' he said to the wriggling creatures congregating at his feet. 'Let's see where all those sly little sluts are at tonight, shall we?'

They moaned their approval.

The *Inferno* was offering a mid-week promotion: two drinks for the price of one. The ad boldly claimed that it was the *only* place to be. He seriously doubted that. However; he did believe there were a significant amount of people who would believe the claim to warrant a visit. *An opportunity may even arise for you to punish their gullibility.*

That sealed the matter. 'The *Inferno* it is, then,' he said, throwing the newspaper over his shoulder.

The worms were gone. The house suddenly seemed very empty without them.

The sound of knuckles rapping against his front door startled him. And he glared at the person he knew to be on the other side. Every normal person who came to his house used the doorbell. He saw no reason why she should be the exception. Perhaps she believed herself to be above such things, that she was something special. Well, he knew otherwise.

*

Christine was about to knock again when the door opened far enough to permit an eye but no more. She watched as it looked her up and down.

'What do you want?'

Christine, although expecting the cold shoulder, was surprised by his hostility. 'Erm, can I come in?'

'What for?'

'To talk.'

Let her in. The door swung open, Price concealing himself behind it. She stepped inside and wiped her feet on the mat. Price remained behind the door and directed her towards the living room with a curt nod of his head. As she entered the living room, she heard the front door close and his footsteps move in the opposite direction. She turned to see what he was doing. He was naked, his body glistening with sweat. He seemed different. Not only in the way he had spoken to her but in the way he moved. It was slow and deliberate; but with an agility that she hadn't noticed before. He ran up the stairs two at a time.

Christine sat on the sofa, taking in the emptiness of the room. The walls were stripped and bare, a few scrapings of wallpaper piled here and there on the bare floorboards. Apart from the sofa she was sitting on, and a wooden coffee table, there were no other pieces of furniture. He had mentioned last month that he was in the process of decorating the entire house. This was to be the living room. It looked to her like very little progress had been made.

The sound of footsteps bounding down the stairs signified his return and she shifted her eyes to the door. He entered, wearing a pair of blue shorts and a white v-neck T-shirt. 'I suppose you want a cup of coffee or something?' There was something missing from his voice, it was cold.

'A coffee would be great.' She smiled, hoping it would show him that she hadn't come here to prolong the argument. His expression remained blank and the smile died on her lips.

He said something as he left but she couldn't quite hear it. It sounded like: If you say so.

'How's the decorating coming on?' she shouted. The pronounced movement of cutlery was her only reply. She slumped back in the sofa. He wasn't going to make this easy for her.

The kettle roared to the boil and she heard it click off. It was followed by the sound of him stirring the coffee; brisk and impatient.

He handed her the brown mug without a word. 'You not having one?'

He shook his head and remained standing, his eyes darting about the room.

Christine cleared her throat. 'I'm sorry about the other night.' She looked up at him, but he was facing away from her. 'David?'

He turned at his name. *Make her sweat.* 'Other night?' *Good.*

Christine groaned inwardly. 'When I was abrupt with you on the phone on Monday. I had no right to interrogate you like that.'

'You're right. You didn't.'

She watched as a look of thunder clouded his features. This was a bit harsh, wasn't it? She'd apologised. What more did he want? 'There's no need to be like that about it.'

The thunder boomed. 'Isn't there?'

She countered the volume as best as she could. 'No there isn't. Whatever I said was out of concern for you. Imagine how you would feel if I went for a scan without telling you about it. You wouldn't be too pleased.'

'It's your body. It's up to you who you divulge its problems to.'

She snorted. 'Don't lie, David, I know you better than that. You'd be furious, and don't try to deny it.'

Tell her about the tumour. Enjoy the sight of that stupid face shattering with shock. That'll shut the bitch up. Go on.

That would be so funny.

She caught his grin. 'I don't think this is funny, David.'

'I know it isn't, Chrissy,' he sat beside her and put his arm around her. He saw a wriggle of baby worms on the settee. 'I love you, Chrissy and I don't ever want to fight with you. I'm the one who should apologise. I should have seen that you were worried.'

He opened his arms and she fell into them, holding him tightly. 'I love you, Dave,' she breathed into his neck.

The heat of her words against his skin made his worms churn.

She kissed him, open-mouthed, tongue lolling like a juicy worm. *Yum yum.*

He matched her passion with difficulty. His mouth was drenched with saliva. It reminded him of how his body would lubricate his alimentary canal whenever he needed to vomit. He brushed away the notion of emptying his stomach down her throat; another time, perhaps.

Tell her to undress.

'Get undressed.'

She pulled away from him, smiling in seductive shyness. Slowly, she unbuttoned her blouse. Price lifted off his T-shirt and tossed it to the floor. Christine made a grab for his shorts and he knocked her away. 'No,' he said softly. 'I want to watch you undress. Take of everything.'

His eyes roamed over her pale unblemished flesh, noticing its frailty for the first time. He searched for areas that would benefit most from his attention, dismissing the obvious. The flesh of the armpit looked sensitive

(A scream tore from her lips as he pushed the burning needle into her stubbled, sweaty armpit. He heard the hiss as the flesh burned. Worms rushed into the wound.)

It could be a perfect opportunity for him to experiment with little amateur piercing of the genitals. It astounded him that such fun could be had with just a heated pin.

She was fully naked now, supine and spread kneed. He traced his fingers along her inner thighs, searching for possibilities, working his way lazily up towards the area she most wanted him to touch. Instead of obliging he brushed his fingertips against her pubic hair, smiling as she trembled beneath the slight contact, and moved on to her other thigh. He repeated the performance, again enjoying the way he teased her into life then ignored her.

'Turn over,' he barked, and she did. He smiled again, but it lacked warmth, quickly contorting into a sneer once her back was turned. She was helpless. There was no need for courtesies here. The woman before him was no longer Christine but something else. The poison that flowed throughout the veins of all women was now in control. He could smell the change.

'Don't move,' he said and jumped off the sofa.

Christine shifted onto her side. 'Where are you going?'

'I'll be back in a minute, hold that position for me. Don't move,' he said without turning.

She heard the kitchen door open, then, a few seconds later, heard him bound up the stairs. Almost immediately he rushed down again. The door opened and he marched into the room, panting slightly, his hands concealed behind his back.

She tried to see what he was hiding as he sat back next to her, darting her head left and right. 'What have you got there?' she laughed.

'It's a surprise. Lie back down on your stomach and I'll give it to you.'

She tried to read his expression then gave up.

'Do you trust me?' he asked, smiling wickedly.

'Of course I trust you,' she said, misinterpreting the smile, and rolled over on to her stomach. 'This had better not tickle.'

'I promise it won't tickle.' He began wrapping a grey and blue diagonally striped tie around her head. Christine began to laugh, her head shaking, hindering his work.

'Keep still.' He wasn't smiling anymore.

The tie slipped over her eyes, Price tightened it, then tied a knot.

'David Price you're such a kinky bugger,' she squealed with obvious admiration.

'Now,' he said evenly. 'Whatever happens, don't remove the blindfold. Do you understand?'

'Ooh yes, Master,' she laughed, trying to sound as submissive as her giggles would allow.

'Good.'

The steak knife gleamed as it caught the light.

The stupid bitch had no idea how close she was. All it took was one swift slice. That was all.

The tip of the steel dragged along the soft flesh of her buttocks and they responded by clenching. 'What's that?'

'No more talking,' he said, not quite managing to conceal his irritation. He was sweating now, beads collecting in his eyebrows. Power rushed through him. His muscles felt stronger and his mind utterly focused. It was a good way to feel. It was the *only* way to feel.

He could hear the scratching of the blade as it scraped through the fine, almost invisible hairs on her buttocks

(before ramming the blade between them. The body thrashed silently; there were no screams, only the thudding of his heartbeat in his ears. He put all his weight behind the knife forcing it deeper. Blood jetted up the blade and onto his face, he opened his mouth to drink)

bringing goose bumps to the flesh.

'Is that a knife?' She sounded worried.

Did she ever sound anything else? 'You weren't in when I phoned, are you all right? Why didn't you tell me about the appointment?' Someone should shut her up.

He stopped, the knife weighing heavy in his palm. He tucked it away under a cushion. The smell had gone. There was no poison to be found here. It was Christine.

'No,' he said to both himself and her question, then buried his head between her thighs.

*

Christine was fully dressed when he returned with a fresh mug of coffee. She was pleased to see he had decided to join her. She held his gaze.

'What?' he asked, squirming beneath the attention.

'All this time and I never realised what a rude little boy I was dating.'

He flushed. 'Well, you started it.'

'Don't get me wrong. I'm certainly not complaining. Far from it.' She shrugged. 'I'm surprised that's all.'

'I like to keep my women on their toes,' he claimed, hinting that there were more.

'Oh really?' She leaned forward, holding the mug above his head. 'This is very hot, Dave.'

'Didn't you know? You're my Wednesday girl. I have one for each day of the week.'

'My hand is slipping,' she warned.

'Come on,' he said with a wink. 'You know you're my one and only true love.'

'That's better,' she said gulping a mouthful of coffee. 'Are you going into work tomorrow?'

His head began to ache. His mind was suddenly a jumble of images; half caught words, blurred faces. There was something. A name? A name he couldn't possibly have known but was certain it was correct. Susan. Susan Lally. It blinked into his mind as if someone had pressed a button. The headache faded. He recalled the thrill of the chase. His nostrils full of her terror, his penis pulsing with the blood of his power. The joy of her nose exploding under his knuckles-

'Dave?'

'Sorry,' he said, rubbing his temples to lend credibility to the lie he was about to tell. 'I'm still a bit under the weather. It comes and goes.'

'Why don't you come and stay with me tonight. I can pamper you back to health.'

'I have to admit that sounds pretty good.'

The worms chewed at his stomach. They were angry.

'We could pick up a few films on the way.'

He could feel strips of flesh peeling away from his insides.

'What's the matter, Dave?'

Price scrambled off the sofa, his mug falling to the floor and smashing. He ran out into the kitchen.

She followed him.

Price was humped over the sink with her back to him, vomiting.

He stopped when he heard her footsteps. 'I don't think I should come round tonight,' he said.

'My poor baby,' she said. She couldn't see the manic grin stretching across his lips as he cooed at his worms in the sink.

'Could you get me my T-shirt. I'm freezing,' he explained. He shivered for effect.

When she had gone, he quickly gathered up his children and placed them in a Tupperware dish. 'Have a sleepy bo-bo's, daddy will be back soon." he whispered as he put the dish under the sink

'Here we go.'

He groped for the garment, his head still in the sink, and slipped it on without turning, tucking it into his shorts. Christine placed a hand on his shoulder. He ran the taps to wash away the imaginary vomit, slurping a handful and swilling it around his mouth. He spat it out with a sigh. *This performance is worthy of an Oscar.* He dug his nails into his palms to keep his smile hidden.

'You should go straight to bed.'

The sooner this stupid wench is out of your house, the sooner you can go to work. 'I think you're right.'

'I know I am. Come on,' she said taking his hand and leading him up the stairs.

He fell onto the bed, eyes closed. If he had looked into her eyes he would have burst out laughing. Her concern was too much to bear; the way her eyebrows steepled comically in the middle of her crumpled forehead, her bottom lip protruding slightly. It was a ludicrous sight. 'Do you want me to stay with you?' she inquired, taking his temperature by pressing the palm of her hand against his brow.

'No,' he said. 'I'm really tired. I'll be asleep in a minute.'

'Are you sure?'

Do you think me a fucking moron woman? Of course I'm sure! 'Really, there's nothing to worry about.' He forced a yawn.

She was reluctant to leave. 'Will you promise me something?'

'What?' He said sleepily.

'Will you promise to go and see the doctor tomorrow?'

Anything, just get the fuck out of my house! 'I promise.'

He opened his eyes and was relieved to see her pained expression had lifted. 'Is there anything I can get you before I go?'

'Could you unplug the phone for me? I want to try and get a full night's kip.'

'Have you had it unplugged all this time? Only I've been trying to get in touch with you for the past two days. I called round yesterday and you weren't in.' He knew she wanted an explanation.

The lie slipped easily from his lips. 'I was at the chemists picking up some lemon drink stuff.'

The merest hint of doubt flickered across her face. 'What time was that?' She asked, smiling too innocently.

He could have kicked himself. There was no timetable for this sort of thing with Christine. She came when the urge took her. He hadn't been home all day. Damn.

Then he knew. It blinked in his mind as clearly as the name had.

She called at 6:07 p.m. and waited for fifteen minutes.

'I left at about six, then walked around for a bit; the fresh air cleared my head. I got back at about half-past.'

She seemed to sigh with relief. *Do you see her suspicion? It is the nature of all her kind. They are consumed by deceit and lies. Trust is something they cannot comprehend.*

'Well look, I'll call round after work and check you're okay,' she said. She leaned over and kissed his cheek. 'Sleep well, sweetheart.'

Price waited for the sound of the front door closing behind her before getting out of bed.

He rubbed his hands busily together. 'Right,' he said with a clap. 'Time to get your pulling gear on, Davie boy. There's work to be done.'

Chapter Sixteen

The nightclub was heaving. Price stood on the balcony looking down. Below him was a tumultuous sea of dancing, heads bobbing on the surface like dead fish. He wondered why the gulls hadn't yet pecked out their eyes.

He gripped the brass rail and forced himself to look closer. He sneered at the writhing, sweating bodies jerking to the latest choon from DJ Piggy Wiggy. How he pitied them.

His eyes fastened on a plump woman wearing a long black dress. She feigned a yawn and released a thick cloud of poison from her mouth. It hung like a pregnant raincloud before her then thinned into tendrils that probed the sweaty air like fingers, flowing over shoulders and between legs, searching.

The fingers headed gracefully to the centre of the dancefloor, a victim located and rushed into a man through his nostrils. The man delayed sipping from his pint and turned to the woman in the black dress. He smiled when she beckoned him closer with a smirk and a curling finger. He made his way eagerly towards her, his mind lost to the poison.

Price turned away from them, sickened by the sight of the man's impending demise, and scanned the bodies at the bar. They squealed and fidgeted like swine at the trough. Sweaty snouts snuffled, trotters gestured crudely, and they grunted to each other suggestively.

The bar staff were busy filling metal buckets with lager, watched by the pigs who squealed as the brimming pails were brought up to the bar. Sticky tongues lolled. A scuffle erupted as the larger animals pushed the runts and piglets to the rear. The bar staff took hold of the buckets, glanced at each other to check they would be pouring at the same time, then emptied the buckets over the bar. The screeching drowned out the flatulent oinking of DJ Piggy Wiggy as the swine slurped and sucked noisily at the liquid gushing over the bar.

Except one. A sow with short brown hair was leaning against the wall. She snorted sadly, obviously too weak to fight her way to the front.

Perfect.

He swaggered over, blinking away her snout and the parallel lines of brown nipples that ran down her front.

'Hello,' he shouted over the din.

She nodded with a disinterested smile and looked away.

'My name's Mark. It's a pleasure to meet you.' He offered his hand.

The girl looked at it, then at him, then returned to whatever she had been watching. Her poison sweated from her in thin willowy strands. It drifted towards him then recoiled suddenly as it touched his body retreating swiftly back into her. She turned to face him.

She knows.

'Hi,' she smirked with lifeless eyes.

Leave her. He jammed his hand up to her face, thumb and forefinger held a centimetre apart. 'You were *this* close,' he roared.

The sow tried to appear shocked. 'What?'

He spat at her feet then walked away.

The swine at the bar were still feeding; some were licking the drink from each other's mouths, others rubbed their corpulent bodies together, slavering profusely. His stomach rolled over when a bloated sow regurgitated a thick brown substance over an auburn-haired piglet wearing a white blouse and a black mini skirt. It dropped on all fours to feast on the vomit, its curly pink tail trembling while it lapped up the liquid. It shrieked when a muscular boar with narrow ebon eyes penetrated her from behind, grunting angrily. The bloated sow watched, rubbing between her sweaty legs with a trotter.

Calm yourself. You mustn't show that you can see things as they really are. Price relaxed. The voice soothed him and gave him strength. *Now listen carefully,* it purred. *Look to the far end of the dancefloor.* He did. *Can you see the blonde whore in the red dress?* He nodded. *She is the one. Approach her.*

'What shall I say?' he murmured. *Ask her if she would like to buy you a drink.* 'Then what?' *Just do it.*

His legs seemed to move under their own volition. The girl was dancing languidly, her arms swaying at her sides. Occasionally she would gyrate her hips and bend her knees, lowering her body, knees slightly parted to offer a taste of smooth inner thigh. A lesser man would have been impressed. Price remained unmoved.

He stood before her, exhibiting his most disarming smile, but she was focused somewhere behind him. He craned his neck to catch her attention, broadening the smile as their eyes met. 'Would you like to buy me a drink?'

'Why would I want to do that?' she asked apathetically.

The line slipped from his lips effortlessly. 'Because it's the least you can do in return for a night of hot and un-complicated sex with no strings attached.'

Her eyes narrowed suspiciously.

Price waited to be given the words to reassure her; none were forthcoming. 'Er...my name's-'

She silenced him with a finger. 'No names,' she said. 'What would you like?'

Again, the voice was silent. 'A bottle of Budweiser, please.'

'Wait here.' And then she was gone.

She returned five minutes later with his drinks and a small glass containing a brown liquid for herself. Price thanked her and drank from one of the bottles, placing the second on a table to her left. She sipped from her glass, watching him carefully.

Feeling uncomfortable under such obvious scrutiny, he swigged again. *Should I say anything?* Silence.

The girl consulted her watch then drained her glass. 'I'm going to freshen up. Meet me outside.'

He nodded without smiling and watched her go. There was something about her that worried him. She made him nervous and he didn't know why. Could she be a prostitute?

He finished his bottle, dribbling some down his chin. Belching, he wiped his chin and made his way to the exit.

He concealed himself in the crowds until a group of drunken males shambled towards him. He allowed them to pass then shuffled in close behind them, laughing along with the joke he hadn't heard.

Once outside, and far enough from the snarling doormen, he removed himself from the group, ambling casually, hands in pockets, back towards the club.

The girl in the red dress stepped out on to the street. Snarls became leers as the thickset men drooled. Price hung back to avoid any association being made. He was fortunate. A group of near naked fifteen-year olds stepped into the chill air. The men, aroused by the scent of fresher meat and the sight of wind-stiffened nipples, lost interest in his prey.

He waved. She smiled thinly in return and walked towards him. 'I need to ask you one thing,' she said. 'You are perfectly clear that this is only a one-night thing and can't ever progress further?' Her eyes tried to read him.

'I am,' he replied evenly.

She paused. 'Good. We can use my place.' She began to walk.

Price followed her without a word.

*

Before he had time to engage in any small talk, she had ushered him in the front door and into her downstairs bedroom.

The girl closed the door behind him but did not turn on the lights. Price remained stationary, unsure of how to move in the unfamiliar darkness. Cold hands brushed his neck and he felt them pull him down. He complied, feeling her tongue force itself through his lips.

No words were exchanged, no verbal justification for their actions. No connection established. He had anticipated an offer of a drink at least. At any other time he would have admired her forthrightness; now it simply sickened him.

She dragged him by the front of his shirt. He bumped into something and instinctively reached out. He caught hold of the lamp before it toppled to the floor. He clicked it on.

The darkness crept back a little, the bulb replacing black with a murky brown. She shook her head and made to turn it off.

He grabbed her wrist. 'Leave it on.'

She shrugged, falling back onto the bed, pulling him on top of her. She hoisted her dress over her hips then guided his hand between her legs.

She wasn't wearing any underwear, and he shivered as he touched clammy, eager flesh. Her warmth oddly chilled him.

'Put this on.'

The voice startled him. 'What?' He felt her push something in his hands. He tore the wrapper and removed the condom. He slipped it on quickly, not out of urgency to be inside her but because he wanted to protect himself from her poison.

When he entered her he felt nothing at all. A moan escaped from her and she licked her lips, yet he was unaware of anything he had done to provoke such a reaction. It was flesh in flesh, a compulsion to do what they were created to do and no more. He wondered why he was even bothering. She lay there, eyes closed as he thrust into her with indifference, making no effort to kiss him or acknowledge that he was there. Her tongue snaked from her mouth. Only this time Price realised that the gesture was entirely for his benefit. It did not signify her pleasure, instead it was a well-rehearsed action to show she was enjoying his attention even though the stink of her told him she obviously wasn't. *Only to you, Davie boy. You're the only one smart enough to see through it. Imagine how many soulless wretches she has deceived before tonight, how many men she has drained of their seed.* She scratched at his back then gathered up her hair, bunching it over her had in another well practised pose.

What does the whore think she is doing? Look at her. Is that supposed to make you desire her?

He felt something tickling at his pelvis and his eyes dropped to see her stimulating herself. *Are you even here?* Disgusted he felt his erection soften and he ceased his pumping.

'Don't stop, don't stop.' she gasped to whoever she thought she was with, masturbating frantically. Bile scorched his throat. Without thinking he grabbed a fistful of hair. She moaned again and motioned with her hips for him to continue. He did, tightening his grip on her hair, and she pulled at his wrist urging him to do it harder.

He obliged and she winced. 'Not so hard.' *Harder.* 'Not so hard.' More urgent. *Harder! Please, harder!*

Her eyes opened wide for the first time since he had penetrated her in time to see his fist smash into her face. There was a dull crunch as her nose broke and Price felt himself stiffen inside her. She started to scream but a second blow silenced her with such force that his penis slipped out of her. He smashed her three more times, each as satisfying as the last.

Her head lolled to the left. He straightened it, pulling open her lids to gaze into sightless eyes, then removed himself from between her legs and padded to the kitchen.

He returned with a steak knife, straddled her and sliced her throat. To his surprise she regained consciousness and even began to struggle as her life's blood jetted warmly into his face. He laughed as she gurgled and flapped her arms then wrapped her hands around her neck in a futile attempt to stem the bleeding. Price put his index finger to his lips and shushed her.

Gradually the jet diminished to a dribble and her eyes rolled back into their sockets. He took her chin in his hands and shook her. No response. He slapped her. Still nothing. *The bloody cheek of her.*

He entered her again, enjoying the way his testicles splashed in the puddle of her urine. With an exasperated sigh he cut off her eyelids and threw them across the room.

She would look at him now.

*

He was running through a corridor; blank, grey walls that disappeared far into the distance.

He felt the pleasure as his manhood grew, felt the throbbing power of it. The woman he was chasing was tiring. She stole a quick glance behind her. He almost came when he saw the terror twisting her features. She stumbled, hitting the ground with the hard slap of bare flesh against cold stone. She turned on to her back, panting.

The arms of the dead broke through the ground around her. They pinned her arms and ankles. Lifeless hands pulled her legs wide apart, cracking her pelvis, allowing other monstrosities to probe her most intimate regions. Her skin stretched and bled as they prepared her for him.

Price towered over her, his penis hissing wickedly. He glared at the hands between her thighs. 'I am ready,' he breathed. The hands removed themselves from her genitalia returning once more beneath the earth.

He paused to look at her bloody orifice.

His worm leaped deep inside her.

*

Sleep deserted him in an instant and he sat upright, shivering as the icy fingers of the nightmare clawed at the nape of his neck. Sweat dripped from his brow and he could feel that his clothes

I slept in my clothes?

were soaked through. He mopped his brow with a shirt sleeve, dragging the material from left to right, and shivered. It was cold.

He dived back under the covers and pulled them over his head.

He slept; unaware that his clothes were not drenched in sweat but soaked with blood.

Chapter Seventeen

Detective Inspector Brian Darrow's head had just touched the cool softness of his pillow when the phone rang.

He nodded silently as the duty sergeant relayed the details to him. He replaced the receiver and threw back the duvet. After dressing, he opened his bedside drawer and swallowed three paracetamol for the headache he knew would be his reward for missing the second night of sleep in a row. He removed his car keys, his warrant card, penknife and a packet of spearmints, placing each item in a different pocket, reversing the process of only ten minutes ago.

He heard the banging of the cat flap followed by a delicate purring as Sapphire, his Burmese blue, jumped on the bed. She rubbed herself again his hip and he gathered her up in his arms, tickling behind her ears. 'I'm sorry, Beautiful. You'll have to find someone else to curl up against.'

The cat meowed its displeasure.

'I'm sure it won't be that much of a problem for a good-looking girl like you.'

Sapphire leapt from his arms and put on an elegant show of stretching before haughtily leaving the room.

It was 9:02 a.m. when he pulled out of his driveway. The roads were busy; the commuters of rush hour replaced by keen shoppers making their way to the city centre. He knuckled away an itch from the corner of his eye, wondering when he was ever going to get some sleep. Last night had been spent wrestling with crime statistics, the night before interviewing a suspected armed robber.

He turned into Hall road, spotting the area car and the coroner's van at the far end, and pulled up beside them.

Sitting on the wall was a blanched PC Rawlins, his helmet upturned on his lap as though he was about to vomit into it. Darrow heeded the omen and steeled his stomach.

When he stepped into the hallway, he heard crying. He nodded to a few familiar Scene of Crime officers who pointed him in the direction of the body. Before he entered the bedroom he saw WPC Parr in the kitchen trying to placate the source of the wailing. She wasn't having much luck.

His eyes moved instinctively to the bed. He saw the body and reached for his spearmints. He quickly crunched and swallowed one then popped in another to replace it.

He didn't know where to start. It was a girl; the killer hadn't sliced her breasts off entirely. He had, however removed her eyelids and, unless there was a new fashion craze he was unaware of, he had shaved her head and eyebrows. Her throat had been cut; the murder weapon imbedded vertically in her stomach. Darrow counted twelve stab wounds to the torso before he decided he had counted enough.

'Sir?'

Darrow dragged his eyes from the body. Detective Constable Jay approached, notes in hand. He was only twenty-one, a boy in Darrow's forty-five-year-old opinion, barely six months out of uniform. Jay bid him good morning with a genuine smile. Darrow admired his ability to remain unaffected by death. Sometimes he pitied it, but mostly he admired it.

'Pamela Bell. Twenty-six. A student nurse. Her flat mate Catherine Smith found her at 8:30 this morning. No sign of forced entry.'

'Cause of death?'

'The coroner says she died as the result of an incised knife wound to the throat. The height of the blood stains indicates that she was alive when it happened.'

'Time of death?'

'Coroner said roughly, and not officially, between three and four this morning.'

Darrow scanned the room for the coroner but only found the photographer dancing round the bed and a bald man in a white paper suit dusting for fingerprints. 'Who was it?'

'The coroner?'

Darrow nodded.

'Reifert, but he's off on another call.' To his superior's raised eyebrows, he added: 'Pensioner found dead by her daughter this morning.'

Darrow's mouth formed a silent O. It locked when he noticed the bloody mess where her pelvis should have been.

'Where is it?' he asked.

There was no need to point. 'Oh, you're going to love this,' said Jay without humour, and beckoned Darrow with his finger to follow him; a little too informally for his liking. He led him to what he assumed was the dining room. There was a large table dominating the room, covered with a white sheet which rose to a peak about fourteen inches high in the middle. Darrow noticed the white cloth was spotted red in places.

'We had to cover it up. Smith wouldn't talk to us until we did. SOCO said it was okay.' Jay gently lifted the sheet to reveal the object.

At first Darrow only saw the medical encyclopaedias. Then he saw the dried flowers. Slowly his mind accepted what his eyes were showing him. The encyclopaedias had been employed to keep the pelvis upright, one either side, vagina facing upwards which, in turn, had been utilised to hold the dried flowers. It too had been shaven.

Another spearmint.

'Like the joke,' mumbled Jay.

'What joke?'

'The one where the woman runs home to her friend and tells her that she's just saw her friend's husband buying a big bunch of flowers,' he began tonelessly, returning the blanket over the abomination on the table. 'So, the friend goes to the woman: 'Shit, that means I'll have to spend the entire night lying on my back with my legs open.' Then the friend says: 'Why don't you use a vase?''

Neither man laughed. 'Could be our killer thinks he's a comedian?' suggested Jay.

Darrow shook his head. 'I don't think he's got much of a sense of humour. It's a statement; the woman is an object. The shaving of the head probably to validate the statement, robbing her of her femininity. Did you notice the eyelids?'

Jay told him that he had.

'He cut them off so she could see him. He needs her to know his power. Either that or he's one of those dickheads that likes to stare into his victims' eyes when he kills them.' He sighed. 'Any boyfriends?'

'Too many by all accounts. She liked to play the field-'

'I hope you're not suggesting that justifies this, Constable?'

DC Jay shrank beneath his superior's icy stare. 'Not at all, Sir.' He hadn't but Darrow made him believe that he had.

Darrow held the gaze a little longer. 'Go on.'

'Erm, Wednesday was her day for the house...' He chose his phrasing carefully, 'Smith would go and stay with a friend, returning in the morning. Sometimes her partners were still here when she got back but not always. And not today.'

'Were there any regular 'partners'?'

Jay heard the quotation marks around his words. 'None that she was aware of, no, Sir. But she's in a terrible state.'

Darrow indicated his understanding with a raised hand. 'Anything else I should know?'

He flipped through his notebook. 'Knife handle's clean. No semen, and the killer scrubbed her clean with bleach, even under the fingernails. Either a part of some cleansing ritual or to cover his tracks, I reckon. We dusted the bottles. Clean.' He cleared his throat. 'Erm, Smith said that she picked...met her partners at the Inferno Club on Kenworth Avenue. It was a regular thing, every Wednesday.'

'On her own?'

'Yes, Sir.'

He shook his head and sighed, feeling like that was all he ever did. 'Come on, let's have a word with Miss Smith.'

'There is one other thing, Sir.'

Darrow delayed his departure, gesturing impatiently for the constable to divulge the information.

'The coroner said the removal of the pelvic area was a clumsy job, but indicated an individual with above average strength, as he would have had to hack through bone. The knife would have been difficult to manoeuvre through the flesh. He said the flesh sometimes acts like a suction, holding blades-'

'Spare me the details, Jay. Is there a point to all this?'

'He said it could have taken anything up to an hour for him to remove it, Sir.'

This meant to him that he was either a cocky bastard or too involved in his work to care. Neither conclusion was any comfort.

WPC Parr stood to attention when Darrow and Jay entered the kitchen, her chair scraping harshly against the tiled floor. Catherine, who was also seated at the small table, flinched at the sudden noise, raising her head from her hands. Her eyes were red with tears and she dabbed at them with a scrunched piece of kitchen roll. Darrow committed her features to memory, a habit he found impossible to kick, then asked the constable softly: 'Is there anyone she can stay with?'

'She called a friend about ten minutes ago. They should be here any minute.'

He nodded her out of the room, sitting himself in the chair she had just vacated and folded his hands neatly on the table. 'Hello, Catherine. My name is Inspector Darrow, and this is DC Jay. I know this is a difficult time for you, but I would like to ask you a few questions.' He smiled, just enough to indicate warmth, nothing more.

'Cathy.'

'Sorry,' he apologised. 'Did Pamela mention anybody special to you, Cathy? Perhaps someone she had started to see.'

She shook her head.

'Or someone she had stopped seeing. Someone who would have held a grievance towards her.'

'Pam was very selective about who she brought home. She made it clear to them from the start that it was only a one-night thing, and if it looked like that was going to be a problem then she wouldn't take things further.' Her voice was calm, the words spoken carefully. The lull before the storm, he mused. It wouldn't be long before she lost it completely.

'And did she mention anyone who looked as if they were going to be a problem?'

'No.'

'Was there anyone she saw more than once? Maybe even months apart?'

She appeared to think carefully for a few moments. 'No.'

Darrow nodded. 'You told my colleague that Pamela went to the Inferno Club on Wednesdays, is that right, Cathy?'

'Yes. It was two bottles for the price of one.'

'This was every Wednesday?'

'Every Wednesday,' she confirmed, her lower lip beginning to tremble.

'Did she go there on any other nights?'

Catherine told him that she didn't.

'Did you ever go with her?'

'I'm not really into clubs and all that. I went once or twice when we first moved here, just to check it out.'

'I understand. How long have you lived here?'

'About Fourteen months.'

'Pamela also?'

'Yes.'

'Do you know who her next of kin is?'

'There's nobody. She was an only child, and her mother died when she was fifteen. She didn't know who her father was...She could have been lying there for hours before...I don't usually disturb her if she's not up, but we had to study for an exam...Oh, God. Who could do such a thing..?' She buried her head in her hands and began to sob. Darrow turned to WPC Parr who was already making her way towards Catherine.

He waited, resisting the urge to drum his fingers on the table. Cathy had his sympathies. The sights in the bedroom and on the table were something nobody should have to try and come to terms with. At the same time, however, he needed answers to his questions and her grief was preventing him from asking them. He must have faced a hundred Catherine's in his time and always left the comforting to someone else. He found it far easier to empathise with the dead. There was probably a reason for that. He chose not to dwell on it.

'Do you have a recent photograph of Pamela, Cathy?' he asked, when she had collected herself.

She nodded slowly. 'I think so.' The nodding became more emphatic. 'Yes.'

'Could you get it for me?'

'Now?'

'If you wouldn't mind. It *is* important.'

After Catherine had left the kitchen to get the photograph WPC Parr explained to Darrow that she would have to go to hand over the shift. Darrow waved her away, tilting back in his chair. Damn, he'd forgotten to leave Sapphire some fresh water.

'Where's Kate?' asked Catherine upon her return.

'I told her to go back to the station. Is that the photograph?'

She looked down at her hands as though she had expected to find them empty. 'Oh, yes,' she mumbled and handed it to him.

Darrow cast his eyes over the image before him. It was taken indoors, possibly a pub or club. Pamela herself was exceptionally attractive, standing hands on hips, wearing a huge smile and a short, tight, red dress. The photograph had been taken lengthways, stopping just above her knees.

'It was taken three weeks ago at the Inferno. It was her friend's birthday...Helen Jarvis I think is her name. She's wearing the same dress as she wore last night. Funny, isn't it?' She sounded as if that was the last thing it was.

Pamela's face was striking; blue eyes and full red lips. Darrow also noticed lines of disillusionment creeping onto her brow and around her mouth, suggesting an individual who frowned a lot. She was blonde, naturally so as far as he could ascertain, and it was gathered on the top of her head in an elaborate fashion even he struggled to describe.

As if she had read his thoughts Catherine said, 'She loved her hair. It was her pride and joy.'

'And she had every right to,' he said, trying to keep his mind from comparing the photograph to the bald, bloodied corpse on the bed. 'What kind of person was Pamela?'

She considered the question for a while. 'She was quiet, reserved.' She noticed Darrow glance back at the photograph. 'Not when she was out, Inspector. She was a completely different person then.'

'In what way?'

'During the day she was...not exactly unhappy. More...weary. She told me once that going out on the pull was the only time in her life that she felt completely in control. It was her choice, you see. She liked the idea that she could sleep with anyone she chose to. I couldn't see it myself, but I suppose that was why we got on so well. Opposites.' She paused. 'Pam was good at her studies but that wasn't enough. They were someone else's guidelines to success. She liked to be in control.'

'Cat!'

Darrow turned to the door and saw a black woman in her mid-twenties, wearing a white flannel dressing gown and matching slippers, rush towards Catherine with open arms. The Friend.

Upon seeing her Catherine burst into tears, diving headfirst into the approaching woman's chest. Darrow watched as Catherine's body sagged under the weight of her sorrow and resigned himself to the fact that he wouldn't be able to ask any more questions. 'Could you leave a contact number with my colleague?'

Catherine, who was by now inconsolable, did not hear the request. The friend blurted the details to DC Jay before dragging Catherine to the car.

Darrow walked into the hallway, and to the small table upon which sat the telephone. Snapping on a pair of latex gloves, he picked up the small notebook beside the phone. He turned to J and found no entries. Then he flicked back to H. There he found what he was searching for.

There were two Helens, both with local numbers, one of which he assumed was Helen Jarvis. He removed his notebook from his inside jacket pocket and began copying the numbers into it. When he finished, he picked up the phonebook and flung it at DC Jay, who dropped his own notebook to catch it.

'A little job for you. Copy all the male numbers down.'

'Now, Sir?'

'Can you think of a better time?' he as he dialled the first number on his mobile. He let it ring for a full minute before terminating the connection and dialling the second number.

It was answered after six rings. 'Hello?'

'Can I speak to Helen Jarvis, please?'

'Speaking.'

'My name's Detective Inspector Darrow and I was wondering if I could speak with you this morning?'

A pause. 'What about?'

'I'd rather discuss it with you in person, if I may?'

Again, a pause. 'Okay, what time?'

'Now, if it's convenient?' He walked back into the kitchen and began flapping his arms at DC Jay, who responded with a puzzled frown.

'I suppose I could wait in for you-'

'Could you give me your address, please?' He shot a withering expression at Jay.

She gave it to him, then, 'Look, what's this all about?'

'I'll explain when I arrive. I shouldn't be longer than ten minutes.' He snapped the mobile shut. 'For God's sake leave that will you.'

Jay regarded his superior with a blank expression.

Darrow turned on his heels. 'Come on, come on,' he shouted behind him.

Jay rolled his eyes heavenward and trotted after him.

Chapter Eighteen

Christine had no idea how long she had sat at the foot of her stairs. She was vaguely aware that she should have left for work some time ago, but that was all. Her time was no longer determined by hours, minutes, and seconds but by periods of crying and not crying.

She had noticed the small brown envelope by the front door from the top of the stairs. There was no address or postmark, so it was obviously hand delivered. She twisted it in her fingers; it was thin, not rigid enough to contain a card. She tore a small strip off at the corner, then inserted her finger and ripped across the fold.

Inside was a small piece of white lined paper folded once in the middle. She unfolded it. The words blurred as tears filled her eyes and she staggered back collapsing on the stairs. She wanted to tear the obscenity into a thousand pieces, crumple it up, burn it. But she held on to it, her mind numbed by the words.

I'm coming tO Rip Out YOUR cUNT.

It was from Gary, of that she had no doubt. She could hear his voice snarling the words as clearly as if he had spoken them to her. She pictured his face, taut with rage, as the threat hissed through gritted teeth, his eyes burning maliciously. She knew things were going to be bad for her when his eyes blazed like that. She froze like a rabbit caught in the headlights of an oncoming truck, knowing what was coming, but praying it wouldn't.

Sometimes it worked. It was as if there was a valve inside his head that would release the pressure before he blew. When that happened, his face would fade from red to pink, then to white as the rage diminished into profuse apologies. Only sometimes he would forget to turn the valve and his face wouldn't stop burning. He would choke on the pressure building within him until the veins in his neck jutted out. Once that happened there was nothing you could do to calm him. Except wait until he was finished.

Her hip still gave her trouble during the winter.

She untied her dressing-gown and strained to see the scar. The sight of the six-inch line of white allayed her fear, despite the memories it evoked. Everything heals, she told herself. He hurt you, but you tended your wounds. The flesh first, then the soul. You are stronger now. He can't hurt you anymore. If he thinks that you are still the timid punch-bag he once knew...well he's in for a shock.

With that thought in mind she dialled the number for Price's house, consulting the clock as she did: 9:12. No answer. Of course, she had unplugged the phone, and the chances of him having his mobile near him where nil.

She flipped through her address book to the letter P. There she located the number of the local police station her mother had insisted she kept.

Without hesitation she dialled the number.

Chapter Nineteen

The smell woke Price up. What *was* that? It was a rich, almost metallic scent. And bleach. He sat up, feeling his shirt cling damp and heavy to his chest. Without looking he tugged it free. The garment separated itself from his skin reluctantly as if it were held with paste.

But it was blood.

And he knew who it belonged to.

Pamela Bell, aged twenty-six. Her favourite colour was red, and her favourite film was *The Wizard of Oz*. He knew this with a conviction and clarity of mind that astounded him. But, how could he? He had no memory of meeting this woman and hadn't even heard of her until now.

(He removed his shirt and used it to mop his brow. The knife was stuck fast. Gripping the handle firmly, he pushed down on her freshly shaven pubic mound with the heel of his hand and strained to remove the blade from her groin. It came free with a gruesome sucking sound and he fell off the bed. This was proving to be a problem. It was a nice idea, but he hadn't realised it would require so much effort. But in the words of Magnus Magnusson: I've started so I'll finish. He thumped the blade into her pelvis once more.)

'No!' He dug his fingers into the sides of his head, as though he were trying to claw the thoughts from his mind.

(His frustration peaked, and he vented it by stabbing her stomach and chest repeatedly. He must have punctured a lung, the hissing sound of her last breath escaping made him giggle.)

Diving from the bed he tore off his clothes in a frenzy and threw them into the corner of the room. The blood was everywhere. In his hair, underneath his fingernails, even his penis was a dirty rust colour. Tears blurred his vision as he ran to the bathroom.

He twisted the shower knob to full heat and stepped under it. The water stung his skin, but he hardly noticed. He emptied an entire bottle of shower gel over his head, shifting the bottle to pour the dark blue liquid over his shoulders as well. He worked his hair up to a thick lather, scooping handfuls of the scented foam and rubbing them about his person. The white turned pink then red with blood.

But it was still all over him. He scrubbed himself with the flannel, wrapping it around his index finger to apply more pressure. He threw it away, frustrated with its ineffectiveness, and opened the shower door and groped for his toothbrush. After rubbing it roughly in a bar of soap, he rigorously attacked his palms. Still the blood wouldn't come off. His skin began to peel; yet still it remained. He stopped, watching his own blood mingle with the girl's. He began to cry, sliding his back down the shower wall. Hugging his knees, he rocked back and forth.

It was all there. Names, faces, unspeakable acts. He saw his stalking of Susan Lally and the assault, the names and addresses of Margaret Henderson's two friends, his semen jetting on her frightened face.

Oh, God. What have I done? He saw bloody hands diligently hacking away at Pamela Bell's pelvis and felt his tongue kissing her vagina before he put the dried flowers in. He retched up a worm.

He must have left his fingerprints all over Pamela's bedroom. *You should have worn the gloves.* What if Margaret had phoned the police? They would have a description of him by now. He was certain Susan hadn't seen him, but what if somebody else had? The police were sure to ask around. He beat the side of his head with a clenched fist.

Why? Why? They had done nothing to him.

And Pamela. No-one deserved to die like that. No-one.

Well, except Julie. The tears stopped. And a smile curled the corner of his mouth. *That would be a real pleasure.*

No! No! No! What are you thinking? You're a murderer for fuck's sake. You have to turn yourself in.

Murderer? You're an artist! You worry too much. Margaret didn't phone the police. Think about it. What could she tell them? 'I brought a complete stranger called Tony to my house to have sex with him, he come on my face, shouted for a bit, and then left.' If you are that worried about it, we could always sneak back and slice her throat for her.

'What is happening to me?'

Calm yourself. There is nothing for you to be concerned with.

His head jerked. 'Who's there?' he called, his heart thudding in his throat. He opened the shower door an inch, holding his breath. Through the gap and the open bathroom door he could see a small area of the landing. He searched for shadows that would indicate a presence. There were none. 'Hello!'

There's no-one there, David.

He jumped, spluttering for fresh air. He was close, whoever it was. And the voice was eerily familiar. 'Who's there? Show yourself!'

If only I could.

Price jumped again, his hands pushing against the walls of the shower in preparation for a swift exit. Then he realised the voice was his own. Not his spoken voice but the voice of his mental processes. The voice he used to mull over decisions; only it was louder, more distinct. Separate.

'Hello,' he said feebly.

Good morning.

The voice drowned out the steady roar of the shower. It was in his head.

'Who are you? What are you doing in my head?'

What kind of question is that, David? I'm you.

'No!'

Who else can I be, David? I am you and you are me. I've always been here. Up until now you have chosen to ignore me, something which you were perfectly within your rights to do I might add. But it's hardly my fault if you have decided suddenly to start taking my advice, is it?

Price scrambled to his feet and burst out of the shower, running into his bedroom. Damp, red footprints marked his progress.

Where are you going?

Panting, whining, clawing at his matted hair, he paced up and down the length of the room.

I really can't see what all the fuss is about.

'Can't see what all the fuss is about! Are you fucking serious?'

I'm always serious. It's one of my great failings.

He pulled at his hair and collapsed to the floor, weeping pitifully. 'I didn't mean it. I didn't mean it.'

For God's sake pull yourself together. You're acting like a fool.

'It wasn't me. It was the worms.'

The worms?

'Fucking right the worms. Jesus, they are fucking everywhere, bastard things.' He tried to retch up a few but nothing happened.

I see, so you are blaming your actions on hallucinations now. I think you had better spend some time perfecting your performance if you are to convince a jury of that. Personally, I feel claiming that God told you to do it would be much easier for them to swallow.

'It has to be them,' he repeated, his conviction fading.

There is a much simpler solution.

'Like what?' he said, mournfully.

You're off your rocker.

'Get to fuck!'

Have it your own way, but I assure you I cannot simply 'get to fuck' as you so pithily put it. All you have to do is ignore me. I merely suggest courses of action. The decision to follow my suggestions is entirely your own.

'Yeah, right.'

You overruled me with Christine, didn't you?

That was the last thing he wanted to hear. The truth of it chilled his bones. He sunk to his knees, mouthing a silent denial.

I suggested a course of action and you ignored it.

'It was the worms,' he whimpered.

Worms! Laughter rung in his ears like tinnitus. I thought you were better than that. I really did. Sometimes I think Julie was right. To watch you work on Pamela I believed all that was behind you. It was such a pleasure to be a part of such a work of art. I mean, the flowers...that was all your idea. Genius. I could never have come up with something like that.

'Just one more word out of you and I'll...'

You'll what? Kill me? Now that would be clever. I'd like to see you try.

Chapter Twenty

Christine stood in the kitchen waiting for the kettle to boil. She stirred the coffee and sugar at the bottom of her mug with disinterest. The kettle clicked off and the sound of bubbling water faded. Her eyes dragged themselves from the cup to the steaming kettle. The kettle's colour changed from cream to blue. And the dimensions of the kitchen contracted, the spotless fitted units now peeling and stained, the wallpaper stripped from the walls. The sunlight outside her window had died to a mournful black. It was night. Nine years ago.

She had also been making a drink then.

She was a student; working her way steadily towards a two/one in Economics without any clear idea of what she was going to do when she achieved it. The house was a two bed-roomed terraced which she shared with a fellow Economics student, Barbara Mallow. Barbara had gone home to Manchester to spend time with her father who was recovering from a stroke. And although Christine was sad for her friend, she was glad of the opportunity to spend the weekend alone with Gary.

Gary was a joiner and she had been seeing him for four months, mostly at weekends. He was the antithesis of the shiftless, stoned morons she had dated during her first two years at Leeds University. He was tall with short, neat hair and, although not exactly fashionable, took great pride in his appearance. She first saw him in the student union;

his toned body standing out a mile next to the bony, baggy clothed intellectuals.

Looking back at it now she realised that, apart from his looks, he had very little to offer her emotionally. Gary was not concerned with current affairs and the only thing he ever read was the *Daily Star*. But he was a man in a world where she saw only boys.

She heard the front door open and Gary announce his presence. From the kitchen she listened for the sound the spare set of keys landing onto the table and the heavy clump of his work-bag hitting the floor, the same as it did every Friday at five.

'I'm in the kitchen,' she called.

'Anything for tea?' he asked tiredly.

'You know my grant doesn't come until next week.'

He nodded. 'I'll get a take-away. Chinese, sound okay?'

She put her arms around his waist. 'That sounds yummy.' She breathed in his sweat and dirt. 'Hard day?'

'The worst.' He tipped his head towards the kettle. 'Make us a cup, princess. I've got a throat like a nun's crotch.'

'Gary!' she chided.

He smacked his own hand. 'Sorry.'

'I fancy staying in tonight,' she said as she poured the boiling water into a mug and stirred. 'There's a good film on the telly.'

'I thought we were going out. If money's a problem, then I'll pay. Or I could lend you it, if you want.'

She squeezed the tea bag against the spoon with her thumb. 'But we've got the place all to ourselves for once. It would be a shame to waste it.'

'But we always go out on a Friday.' He leaned against the fridge.

She offered him the brew. He ignored it, staring. 'Don't you want to spend a night in with me?' she asked, pouting slightly.

He averted his eyes. 'I suppose I could pick up a few cans from the offy...'

She smiled and offered him the tea again. 'See, that's not hard, is it.'

'Are you trying to be funny?' The sudden aggression in his voice hit her like a punch in the face.

'No,' she responded immediately.

'Then why are you speaking to me like a three-year-old?' His eyes were burning, and he was panting slightly.

'I'm not. I just thought it would be nice to spend an evening in together.'

He acted as if she hadn't spoken. 'Just because I'm not clever enough to go to university like you and all your posh friends-'

'Gary-'

'Are you interrupting me?' She lowered her head. 'I said, are you interrupting me?'

'Gary-'

'Don't you ever interrupt me when I'm speaking. Do you understand? *Do you understand?*'

She nodded slowly.

'I can't hear you.' He cupped a hand to his ear.

'Yes,' she mumbled.

'I don't get you sometimes,' he snatched the mug from her hand. 'I come home from work and offer to buy you a meal and take you out and all you can do is bitch about staying in.' He snorted. 'There are loads of women who would love to be treated as well as I treat you. Loads. But if you really want to stay in that badly we'll stay in.' He gulped down a mouthful of tea. 'Are you happy now?'

'Yes,' she said softly; the memory of a slapped face from two weeks ago preventing her from arguing further.

The turning of some invisible valve released the pressure within him, he kissed her head. 'I'm sorry for shouting. I had a rough time at work.' The end. Forget it.

And she did.

Later.

The foil cartons were strewn across the floor and Christine, who was lying on the couch in her nightie, dipped a prawn cracker in the remains of a chicken curry. Gary was sitting in the armchair, pulling the tab on his sixth can of Export. He belched and Christine giggled. His head snapped sharply in her direction and he glared at her. But she continued to laugh, and his eyes softened and he belched again. 'Better out than in,' he chuckled.

Christine nearly choked on the cracker, sitting up.

'Serves you right,' he sneered at her crimson face. He held out his can. 'Here. Drink some of this.' Coughing, she took the can and slurped from it. 'Are you sure you don't want any? I bought plenty.' He patted the carrier bags that contained ten more cans.

She shook her head, coughing, then drank some more. 'No, I'm fine. I was just going to make a cup of coffee anyway.'

He took his can back and shrugged.

When she returned from the kitchen, steaming mug in hand, he said: 'I thought you said there was a film on?'

She cleared her throat. 'There is. It's not on until half-nine.'

He checked his watch. 'It's only just gone seven. What's on now?'

She shrugged. '*The Bill's* on at eight. You like that.'

'Don't tell me what I do or do not like. Chuck us the remote.'

He caught the requested item in his left hand and spent the next five minutes flicking through the channels, lingering no longer than a few seconds each time. He threw the remote back in disgust. 'Some night in this is,' he muttered just loud enough for her to hear.

She flicked the channel to three and *Family Fortunes*. An elderly member of the Armstrong family had given an answer that wasn't on the board. A large cross appeared on the screen and a double rasping sound indicated her error.

Gary mimicked the rasping, 'Wah-wah!'

Christine giggled again. *God*, she thought in the present, *she was such a stupid cow*.

Pleased with this response, he took it upon himself to declare the wrong answers personally. 'Wah-wah! Daft cunt!'

The host, she couldn't recall whether it was Bob Monkhouse or Les Dennis, led two opposing family members, both men, to the podium for a starter question. 'We asked a hundred people for something you would wear in bed...' Both contestants slammed their hands down violently. The host turned to the man on the left. 'Shoes!' he answered proudly.

Gary spluttered lager. 'Shoes!' he exclaimed. 'Fucking shoes, the daft twat! Wah-wah!'

When the answer was revealed to be incorrect, he turned triumphantly to Christine. 'See! I told you.'

She smiled silently, knowing that anything she said was apt to be misinterpreted, and turned on to her stomach. Her nightie crept up over her hips, revealing smooth rounded buttocks. She tugged it down again. But it was too late.

His eyes crawled over her bare flesh like hot breath and he squeezed his testicles through his dirty jeans. 'I know what we can do while we wait for the film.'

'Mmm?' She was too engrossed in the television; answer number three had yet to be revealed and she felt sure that *nothing* was the answer.

'Why don't you suck me off?'

She turned her head, peeling her eyes away from the screen at the last moment. 'What?' Then she saw his penis drooping out of his zipper.

He smiled, rubbing his flaccid organ. 'Get your gums around that.'

It wasn't even hard. There was nothing to indicate that he was in any way aroused. Her eyes bulged. 'No,' she said.

'Come on,' he urged.

'No.'

'Come on, princess. You know I like the way you do it. You're the best.'

She shook her head.

'Come on, please. It won't take long.' She regarded the floppy thing lolling on his lap coolly. It amazed her how all men, even the drips at university, were all alike once they got an itch in their pants. It was pathetic. The way they begged and moaned like a baby for their dummy.

'Please, princess. I want you bad.'

She sighed and moved over to him on her knees. Scooping it up in her hands, she heard him shudder with delight, and felt the throbbing in her palm as the blood rushed to it. Semi-erect, she lowered her mouth. Then pulled away.

'Have a bath first,' she said. 'You're all sweaty.'

'So?'

'What do you mean 'so'? You wouldn't go down on me if I was all sweaty like that.'

'Yes I would.'

'No, you wouldn't. I'm not saying I won't do it. I'm saying have a bath first and I will be glad to do it.'

'Wah-wah!' he rasped and grabbed her head and yanked it down. 'Suck it!'

Christine pushed her hands against his knees to extricate herself, grunting under the effort, but his grip was like a vice.

'Suck it! Suck it, now!'

'Gary!'

'If you don't suck my cock now, I'll fucking kill you!'

Before she had a chance to answer he punched her in the side of the head. She fell back under the force of the blow and sprawled to the floor, dazed.

Gary rose to his full height. 'Why are you so mean to me?'

She burbled something unintelligible in response.

'I don't ask for much do I? I take you out, I feed you, I pay your bills and all I ask in return is a blow job. Five minutes of cock sucking for a meal in your belly and a night out whenever you want, is that too much to ask?'

'Gary.'

'We asked a hundred people for one good reason why you shouldn't suck your boyfriend's cock...' He raised his right knee until it was level with his waist.

'Please.'

'Wah-wah,' he said and stomped on her stomach.

The breath whooshed from her in a blinding white flash of agony. She convulsed, desperately trying to force fresh air back into her body.

Gary raised his knee again.

Christine flapped her arms, gasping, choking. The foot crashed into her stomach; vomit sprayed from her mouth. She rolled over, retching.

He began undoing his belt. 'You think you're something special, don't you princess?' He pulled his jeans off over his steel-toed work-boots. 'But I've got news for you.' Next his underpants. 'You're just the same as every other bitch on this fucking planet: nothing more than a cunt on legs.'

'Please...don't,' she wheezed. 'I'm...sorry.'

'Wah-wah,' he roared and kicked her in the hip with a steel toe.

Christine's scream of agony became a despairing gurgle as fresh vomit blocked her throat.

He kicked her again. 'Now, what else doesn't my poor ickle poncy posh princess like to do?' His hands stroked his now fully erect penis. A theatrical smiting of palm against forehead. 'Oh, yes! You don't like it up the arse, do you?' Another vicious kick. 'Well, my little princess,' he said, turning her on her stomach and positioning himself between her legs. 'You've got no fucking choice in the matter. And when I'm finished, I'm going to rip out your cunt!'

Christine jerked herself back to the present, the memory of the rest of that evening too painful to think about, even after all this time. She pressed the back of her hand to the side of the kettle. Cold. She switched it back on again and went back to idly churning the contents of the mug with the spoon.

*

DI Darrow and DC Jay travelled in silence. Helen Jarvis had given almost identical answers to Catherine Smith. No, she didn't go out with Pamela Bell often. No, she didn't know of any regular partners and, no, she couldn't think of anyone who would have wanted to kill her. Darrow shifted down a gear and gently applied the brakes, hoping the lights ahead would change from red to green before he had to stop. They were on their way to another call; a nuisance caller that had upgraded to sending poison pen letters. Normally, he would have left it to uniform but he was glad of the excuse to leave Jarvis to her tears. The lights refused to change, and the car crawled to a stop.

'Any ideas, Simon?' asked Darrow without taking his eyes of the road ahead.

DC Jay looked up from his notebook, taken aback by the use of his Christian name. 'I think it was random. But I do think that she was selected.'

'For her lifestyle,' agreed Darrow with a nod. 'Which would mean that he's been a regular at the *Inferno* himself.' The car began to move again.

'Seems reasonable.'

'Or a nosy neighbour that's witnessed the comings and goings at the house. Have you checked out the neighbours?'

'Uniform's on it now.'

'Good.' Darrow pressed his foot on the accelerator to beat an amber light. 'Do you think that Bell saw anyone more than once and Smith knew nothing about it?'

'It's a possibility, but I think that Bell was too careful about that sort of complication.'

'I agree. Was there a diary?'

'Not that I saw. I looked briefly in the drawers, but I couldn't do a more thorough search until SOCO had finished.'

Darrow turned the car sharply to the left. 'I'll drop you back off at the house. See what uniform have come up with, if anything. And try and find a diary, love letters anything at all. I'll be with you as soon as I've finished with Miss MacNeil.'

'Right, Sir.'

*

Christine was sitting in silence on the sofa when the doorbell rang. She jumped, spilling a few drops of untouched coffee on to the floor. She walked to the front window, pulled back the net curtains and saw a man in a neat grey suit. He was tall, fit and with short efficiently cut grey hair. He looked about forty years of age. Everything about him screamed Police.

'Who is it?' she called, tapping on the window to attract the man's attention.

He stepped towards the window and pressed his warrant card to the glass. 'Detective Inspector Darrow, Eastern Road CID. You called the station?'

She nodded.

Darrow stared at her. 'May I come in?'

Letting the curtain fall back in to position she padded into the hall and opened the door.

Darrow thanked her, resisting the urge to sneak a look at her exposed cleavage.

'Would you like a cup of tea? Coffee?' she offered, thinking, for some reason, that it was expected of her.

'No, thank you, Miss MacNeil. Could you show me the note?'

She plodded lifelessly through a door and Darrow followed. Catherine pointed to the table displayed upon which were a dying bunch of red roses in a vase, a brown rectangular envelope and a small lined piece of paper. He leaned over and read the note. He winced. Not much left to the imagination there.

'Have there been any other notes?'

'No, this was the first.'

'Mm.' It was hand-written at least. Black ball-point. The author had tried to disguise his handwriting with various styles of lettering, and by applying different levels of pressure. She must know him. It looked to Darrow like a right hander; no smudging. 'Have you any idea who sent this?'

'Gary Jennings; date of birth twentieth of the first sixty-nine. He assaulted and sodomised me on the twenty-first of the eleventh nineteen-ninety.' She reeled of the facts without emotion, staring coldly into Darrow's eyes.

He scribbled the details in his notebook, keen to avoid her dead expression.

Christine continued. 'He was sentenced to three years. He was my boyfriend, I was wearing a short nightie and he was fully clothed, and his defence convinced the jury that my previous *promiscuity-*' Darrow detected the first inflection of emotion '- somehow excused his actions. I went to pieces on the stand, which didn't help. Are you sure you wouldn't like a drink, Inspector?'

'No, thank you. Don't let me stop you.'

'I already have one.' She sipped at the coffee, found it cold and put it down again.

'I'm sorry to ask you this...but what makes you so sure he's responsible for the note?'

'Because, he said that after he had finished sodomising me, he was going to rip out my cunt.'

Darrow pretended to jot that down in his book. Throughout his police career, when faced with hysterical and incoherent witnesses, he had prayed for a direct, plain-speaking witness such as the one before him now. Confronted finally with the answer to his prayers, he couldn't help but feel a little disconcerted.

'Could you tell me about the phone calls, Christine?'

She sighed. 'There's not much to tell. The first was on Sunday-'

'The eighth?'

'Yes. It was about half eleven at night. I was reading a magazine in bed when the phone rang. There was no-one at the other end. I might have heard breathing, but I couldn't swear to that. I can't explain how I knew it was him, a gut feeling I suppose, and when I said his name...he hung up. The second call came on Monday at work, about twelve fifteen. I checked with the switchboard and the call didn't go through them. I have no idea how he got my number and no, he didn't say anything again. I received no more calls. The note was waiting for me when I got up this morning. That was around eight. My alarm went off at seven-fifteen, but I stayed in bed. I didn't hear anyone post the note, so it must have been posted before then. I opened the envelope with my finger and spent the next hour crying on the stairs. If I receive any further correspondence, you can rest assured that I shall not touch it.'

Darrow nodded; her comprehensive review had answered almost all his potential questions. She was a tough one, of that he had no doubt. 'Well, *you* can rest assured, Miss MacNeil, that I shall make visiting this Gary Jennings my number one priority. Have you any idea of his whereabouts?'

'He lived in Leeds before he was sent to prison; I assume he would have returned there.'

'Do you have an address?'

'I'm sorry, I don't.'

'That's okay. Why do you think he has waited so long to contact you?'

'After the attack I spent six months in the YWCA before moving to Newcastle to finish my degree. Economics. After that I travelled for a year through Europe before finally settling in Liverpool. The only explanation I can offer you, Inspector is that he has had difficulty in tracking me down.'

'I see. Do many people know about the attack?'

'I have absolutely no idea. There was some media coverage, but nothing more than a few lines in the local papers. It wasn't exactly headline news. Other than myself and you...there's only Janine. My parents don't even know.' Her eyes widened. 'There's no reason that they should be told?'

Darrow held up a hand. 'None whatsoever,' he assured her. 'There is one more thing, Miss MacNeil. And I hope you can appreciate that I have to ask this...is there anybody else who could have sent you this note?' he wondered if it was in anyway related to the Pamela Bell. Did Jennings know her?

With a soft sigh she leaned back in her chair, eyes cast up to the ceiling. 'As I said, the only person I have told, other than those who were involved in the case, is Janine. And I didn't go into details. She wouldn't have been able to write that note. She wouldn't have *wanted* to write that note. I met her at the YWCA after the attack. She helped me get through the ordeal more than anyone. She'd been through something similar, you see.'

'Mm,' he nodded sympathetically. 'Do you remember the name of the investigating officer involved in your case?'

'DS Townsend. Paul.'

'Good.' He flipped his notebook shut and placed it back in his pocket. 'Thank you, Miss MacNeil, you've been more than helpful. I shall begin making inquiries as soon as I leave here but, other than that, there's nothing much else we can do at the moment. I'll take the note with me.' He placed it in a small clear plastic bag. 'In the meantime, you should be extra vigilant. Be on the lookout for any signs that you are being watched or followed. Get in touch with the phone company and register with the nuisance caller service. Is there anybody who can stay with you?'

'Well, there's my boyfriend...but he's in bed with the flu.'

'Perhaps you could stay with him. Here's my card. If Jennings contacts you again I can be reached at that number night or day.'

'Thank you,' she said.

Darrow stood up. 'I'll get in touch the moment I have any news.'

Christine thanked him again, and followed him to the front door, closing it behind him without any further words.

She picked up the cordless telephone and strolled into the living room, dialling the number for Price's house. His framed 6x4 photograph stood on the fireplace. It was taken three weeks earlier in her back garden. A spur of the moment thing that had captured his jocular essence and handsome features perfectly. She loved that photograph almost as much as the man. She traced the outline of his chin with her finger. 'Dammit, David!' she hissed, when he failed to answer.

Chapter Twenty-one

What are you doing?
'Getting dressed, what does it look like?'
Are you sure you've got rid of all the blood?
'Damn sure,' he spat. He'd spent the best part of an hour, soaking, scrubbing, showering, scrubbing again. There was still a faint red on his knees that was proving difficult to remove completely. But his jeans would conceal that.
At least stand in front of the mirror so I can give you the once over.
'What do you mean by that? I thought you said that you were me and I was you? So therefore what I see you see, and vice versa.'
I wasn't paying attention.
'You weren't paying attention!'
Well I can't be expected to give you my full, undivided attention every second of the day, can I?
'Why not?'
Because it's boring.
Price closed his eyes and sighed. 'Look, I would really appreciate it if you didn't talk to me anymore. Okay?'
If that's the way you feel about it?
'I do, yes.'
Fine.
Price hesitated before pulling up his jeans, but the voice remained silent. He could sense it pouting. Passing his belt through the loops on his jeans he moved to the window. He had to find some way of making this right. He had to get away. He had to go

to see Dr Mason. Had he said it was inoperable? They might be able to cut the worms out of him. Oh yes. Kill the worms, kill the problem.

Kill all the fucking bitches.

'I thought I told you to be quiet.'

You have no authority over me.

'*Would* you *please* be quiet?'

In a minute. First, I would like to say something. Two things, actually. One: you are quite clearly deranged and suffering from delusions. And two: please see number one.

'Bollocks.'

Really, David. 'Bollocks,' may indeed be a highly satisfying response to your predicament but it's hardly conducive to an intelligent discussion.

'There is nothing to discuss. You are a by-product of them. They made me do it?'

Them?

'The worms, who the fuck do you think I'm talking about? They've poisoned my mind. Made me see things that aren't there, made me hear things that aren't there, made me...do things.'

I still believe that The Voice of God is a far more plausible justification for the courts.

'I'm not interested in what you *believe*. I know what I know and that's the end of it.'

Really.

'Yes, *really*.'

Price closed his eyes and thought of Christine. He pictured her face as they made love in the Palace.

For a start, you should stop thinking of her. She's no good for you. I hardly think that your plan to grow old with Christine is a viable one now that you are a practising homicidal maniac. Besides, you're going to die. That's like a get out of jail free card. Ok, you'll be dead but what the hell at least you won't be getting bummed in prison by Mr Big.

'But I'm not going to go to prison. Because if I go, so do you. I'm sure that you would have ensured that I was careful enough not to leave any evidence of my presence behind.'

Yes, well. I do pride myself on being rather thorough. But I would advise you to be a little more courteous towards me...I could suddenly become very remiss about that side of things.

'You can be as careless as you like.' he said defiantly. He buttoned up his shirt, and then tugged on his Caterpillars.

Is that so?

'Yup.'

And what has brought on this ill-founded bravado?

'You don't need to ask me.' He tied the laces and walked down the stairs to the kitchen.

I think that you are mistaken if you think that I am a product of your tumour.

'What else are you, then? Anyway, it's a start, isn't it?'

In the wrong direction, I'd say.

He filled the kettle and switched it on. 'Then what do you suggest?'

Me? Where's the fun in that?

He dumped a tea bag and two sugars in a mug. 'You're short of an opinion all of a sudden.'

I don't see why I should do all your thinking for you.

'But you do know what is going on?'

I haven't the faintest idea.

Interesting. 'I find that really difficult to believe.'

It's the truth.

'So you can't explain what's happening to me?'

No.

He was on to something. He could feel it. 'You're lying.'

If you say so.

'I do, I do.' he said, rifling through the scrapbook of images in his mind. 'I know you aren't me. Oh, you might sound like me but that's as far as it goes. I know the names of people I haven't even met, where they live and even the name of one of their daughters. How is that possible? Unless...unless someone told me. And that someone was you.' He poured the boiling water into the mug. 'So, that would indicate that you are an external...*whatever*...put inside my head.'

You know nothing of mental illness. Or of brain tumours and disorders.

'Now it's you that's clutching at straws. How could I know? Even if I was a schizophrenic or suffering from a similar psychosis, how could I? Answer me!'

Silence.

'Well, I'll answer for you. You told me. And the only way that *you* could have known it is through the worms. Don't ask me how because I haven't the foggiest. All I know is that it's true. *Quod erat demonstrandum*. Put *that* in your pipe and smoke it.' He stirred the brew triumphantly.

Very good. The voice sounded less than pleased. *But it doesn't help you.*

'Oh, but it does. It means all I have to do is cut out the worms. If I can't do that, then I will imprison myself in the bedroom. Board up the windows and door, nail them, put padlocks on everything, do anything that will prevent me from getting out and committing more atrocities. I'll handcuff myself to the bed and throw the key away. I'll nail my fucking feet to the floor if I have to. Then, you can suggest all you like for the rest of my life and I won't budge an inch. Hopefully you will lose interest and go and find someone else.'

You'll make them very angry, David.

'What the fuck do I care?'

They'll make you care.

'We'll see.'

Yes, David. We shall.

*

The ghouls were in full force outside the Bell residence by the time Darrow pulled up. PC's Fletcher and Davis, the replacements for WPC Parr and PC Rawlins, were trying unsuccessfully to convince them that there was nothing to see. Darrow set the alarm for his car and walked briskly over to DC Jay who was taking a statement from an elderly lady three doors down.

'Anything?' he asked when he had finished.

'Not really, Sir. There is one bloke...' He flipped through a few pages. 'A Mister James Doonan at number sixty-two. That's directly opposite.' His pen identified the residence. It was identical to Bell's except the door was a dirty yellow. 'He reckons he heard something last night. He's a bit of a misery. I thought you might have a bit more luck than I did, Sir.'

Darrow nodded. 'Did you have any luck finding a diary?'

'Haven't had a chance yet, Sir. SOCO are taking their time with this one.'

'Understandable.'

'How was the threatening letter?'

Darrow reported the details of his conversation with Christine. A PNC check had revealed Jennings's last known address and, after Control had located the number for him, he had spoken to the now Inspector Townsend, who assured Darrow that he would send someone to visit as soon as possible. 'Hopefully, we should know by this afternoon what the score is,' he concluded.

Darrow's gaze returned to the ghouls, where he noticed a woman jotting frantically into a notebook. 'See if you can get rid of that reporter,' he ordered. His voice was sharp and failed to conceal his loathing.

'I think the Super would prefer you to make a statement, Sir.' Jay smiled nervously.

But Darrow just shook his head thoughtfully. 'What would we tell them? No, until we've something the press can help *us* with, we tell them nothing.' An incident room was already being set up and DS Lambert and DC Mills were already bringing in all known sex-offenders for questioning. Then there was the post-mortem and the SOCO report. No, it was far too early to involve the press.

Jay, who knew better than to argue with the Inspector, moved purposefully towards the reporter. Darrow crossed the street, taking in the neat rows of modern houses that seemed crouched in reverent silence. Even the air was still. The leaves and litter lay lifeless in the gutters. He rapped his knuckles on the door of number sixty-two.

Mumbles from inside. The unbolting of locks. A muffled expletive.

The door opened.

The security chain snapped tight. A wrinkled and rheumy eye appeared, and a musty smell drifted through opening. 'What do you want? More bloody questions I shouldn't wonder.' The man coughed phlegm, gurgled it for a moment then swallowed it with an audible gulp.

'My name's Detective Inspector Darrow, Eastern Road CID-'

'I told your dogsbody all I know so bugger off and leave me be.'

Darrow couldn't quite place the accent. Burnley, maybe. 'I'm sorry to disturb you again, Mister Doonan-'

'No you're bloody not.'

'A young woman has been brutally murdered-'

Doonan was unimpressed. He blew air through his teeth. 'Young tart more like. Men coming to and fro like a brothel, dirty scrubber. Probably riddled with the pox or that AIDS stuff, I shouldn't wonder.'

'You say that there were a lot of men coming from Pamela Bell's house-'

'I 'aven't got wax in me ears son, you don't have to tell me what I said.'

Darrow bit his tongue. 'Did you see or hear anyone last night?'

'I did, yes.'

'Go on...'

He released an exaggerated sigh. 'It was about six this morning. I heard her door slam shut. I knew it was hers because it goes like a privy door in the wind, and the letter box rattles. Bloody racket. Banging away at all hours. I think she was a prostitute, trying to get a bit of pin money. Student nurse, you know. Can't be very hygienic, mucky bint. I didn't pay it no mind, though. I turned over in my bed, praying to the

Lord that the girl get knocked up, then went back to sleep. The end.'

The door closed in Darrow's face. He hammered his fist against the wood. It opened again. 'Look, I told you all I know, now leave me be.'

'If you don't co-operate with me Mister Doonan I'll have you down the station. Do you understand me?'

Doonan considered arguing, but the policeman's tone was more than enough to cast that from his mind. He nodded.

'May I come in?'

'No. And there's no law that says I has to let you in either. Anything you want to ask me, you is quite capable of askin' me from the doorstep.'

'Very well. Did you hear anything else last night? Possibly Pamela returning in the small hours.'

'Nope.'

'Are you certain?'

'`Course I am, son. I might be an old bugger, but that don't mean I'm stupid, does it?'

'No. Did you ever see the men leaving her house?'

'A few times.'

'How many? Two? Ten?'

'I don't bloody know, do I?'

'Please Mister Doonan, it is important.'

Another theatrical sigh. 'I'd say it was more like twenty. And before you say anything, I'm no peeping Tom or nothing. I don't get as much kip as I'd like these days, so I read in bed. I hear voices and her door go at four in the morning and I has a look to see what's going on. There's no law says I can't. Neighbourhood watch you calls it.'

'I understand perfectly, Mister Doonan. Would you recognise any of these men again?'

'Nope. They was just blokes.'

'Were they similar in any way? Did they all have blonde hair, or were they all well built..?'

'I suppose you could say they was all tall.'

'How tall?'

'I don't know, I'm not a bloody undertaker, am I?'

'Please, Mister Doonan.'

'I'd say they was all no smaller than six foot, but I wouldn't swear on my mother's grave on that one.'

'Good. Can you remember anything else about the men?'

'Er...none of them was darkies.'

'You mean none of the men were of ethnic origin?'

'That's what I said. You should get your ears tested, son.'

Darrow's tongue was in danger of being bitten clean through. 'Were all of them white?'

'As far as I could tell.'

'And they had nothing in common apart from their height?'

'Nope.'

'Did they all dress the same? Were they wearing suits? Or was it more casual?'

'I never saw any ties if that's what you mean. Shirts, pants, that sort of thing. No jeans.'

'Now I want you to think about this carefully...where any of the men you saw there more than once?'

'Nope.'

'And you're certain of that?'

The red eye rolled heavenwards. 'I just said so, didn't I? Look is that it? Can I go now?'

'Thank you Mister Doonan, you've been most...helpful. If you-'

But the door was closed. Darrow considered knocking again then decided against it.

It was something, he supposed. If Doonan was to be believed, Bell preferred taller men. It might prove useful, but then again it probably wouldn't.

He ventured back into Bell's bedroom. It seemed much larger now that it contained only DC Jay. The body had been removed along with the bed.

'If that bastard was thirty years younger, I'd have him down the station. Nasty piece of work.'

'It doesn't look as if she kept a diary, sir. No PC or mobile either, so no email or texts.' He moved to the dressing table and opened a drawer. 'She kept any post here. Only one piece of personal correspondence: a post card from Lanzarote. It's signed Cathy.' He offered it to Darrow who motioned his disinterest. 'The rest are all bank statements and a few pieces of unopened junk mail.'

'What about the rest of the house?'

'Although they shared the kitchen and bathroom, most of the personal items were confined to their respective bedrooms, Sir.'

Darrow glanced around the room. 'Not much to leave behind is it?'

'No-one to leave it to, Sir.'

The Inspector sighed. 'I suppose we should pay a visit to the *Inferno*.'

'I've already checked, Sir. There's no-one there until one, and then it's only the cleaners. I spoke to the owner, he said that he would meet us with the names of all the staff who were working last night at half-past.'

Darrow consulted his watch. Just gone midday. 'He seems very keen.'

'I don't think there's anything to read into that.'

'You're probably right. I'm starving. Time for some dinner, I think.'

*

Janine leapt from the taxi and ran down the small path to Christine's front door. Had her employer witnessed this dash, he would have wondered how a woman with agonising period cramps could have executed such an action without collapsing to the floor. Janine hammered on the door. 'Chris, it's me!' she shouted unnecessarily.

The sight of Janine's concerned expression was enough to release the flood of tears that Christine had been choking back.

Janine threw her arms around her and held her tightly. 'Are you all right?' she inquired softly. The question tore a heart-stopping sob from her friend and she shushed her, patting the back of her head softly. 'Come on,' she soothed. 'Come one, I'm here now. It's all right. Shhh.'

Janine gently nudged her into the kitchen.

She pulled away and plugged in the kettle without really knowing why. Christine was in a terrible state; her hair was a mess and her eyes were red and puffed through crying. She had sounded calm enough when she had phoned her at work. Now it seemed as if the shock was in control. Janine removed her cigarettes from her handbag, extracted two and held them in her mouth, lighting them both simultaneously. Stuffing one between Christine's lips, she said, 'God bless nicotine. And period pains.'

Christine's head snapped up. 'Period pains?' she asked. She drew deeply on the cigarette and coughed. She hadn't indulged in over a year. But it felt good.

'My excuse for getting the afternoon off. Good job Mrs Moore wasn't in today, I don't think she would have bought it. Poor Mr. Fraser. You should have seen the look on his face.' She stretched her features in an exaggerated expression of shock and horror.

Despite everything Christine smiled.

'Then he touched my arm, like this...' Janine placed her hand just below Christine's elbow and gave it a gentle squeeze. The shocked and horrified expression was replaced by one of deepest sympathy. 'I understand completely,' she mimicked and burst out laughing.

'Poor Mr. Fraser,' said Christine.

'I'm a bitch, aren't I? Give it to me straight I can take it.'

'Janine...you're a bitch.' A brief flash of the true Christine.

'I knew I was.' Christine dragged on her cigarette again and looked down at her bare feet. Janine, lost for a distracting subject, told her to get dressed. 'Let's go and get tanked up.'

'I need to phone David,' she said as if Janine hadn't spoken. And with that she moved to the phone. Janine stayed where she was, listening to the bleeps as Christine dialled. There was a lengthy pause then Christine said, 'Damn.' Janine heard the phone being slammed down.

'Problem?'

'His phone is still unplugged. He was really sick last night. I put him to bed, and he asked me to unplug the phone. I need to know he's all right.'

'We'll stop by on the way to the pub,' suggested Janine.

'I don't want a drink!' She pulled the cigarette from her lips, 'And I don't want *this*.' She hurled it in the sink. A faint hiss as the water extinguished it.

Janine shuffled awkwardly, unsure of what to say next.

'I'm sorry. It's not your fault.'

'Hey, don't worry about me. If I can take a ten-inch penis I think I'm tough enough to take anything.'

Christine smiled again. But Janine could see it was forced. Janine decided to stop trying to be funny. 'Look we can call round to David's if you want,' she suggested softly. 'I just thought you could do with a drink. Hell, I know I would.'

Again, it was as if she hadn't spoken. 'I'm going to get dressed. I won't be long. Help yourself to tea and coffee.'

And then she was gone.

Janine lit another cigarette and awaited her return.

Chapter Twenty-two

Never had the world seemed so dreary. The sun had slinked behind a clump of dull clouds and looked as if it was never going to venture out again.

The voice in his head had fallen silent. It had said nothing since he informed it of his plans. Initially he had been relieved. Now, he felt sure that it was up to something.

He was worried.

The only other person sat in the bus shelter was an elderly woman, bus-pass in gnarled hand and an empty shopping bag at her feet. Price smiled a greeting when the woman glanced up at him. She seemed to age as their eyes met and her lined features sagged despondently.

'Kill me,' she breathed.

Price swallowed hard. 'Excuse me?'

'Kill me,' the old woman repeated, her eyes drooping.

'No,' he hissed and stepped away.

The old woman returned her attention to the road. 'If you change your mind...I'll be waiting.'

'I won't,' he said.

'Please yourself. Don't say I didn't offer.' She hummed to herself softly.

Price left the shelter intending to walk to the next stop. A bus turned into the road. He squinted to discern the number. It was a 40d. His bus.

The old woman tipped him a tired wink. Price shuddered. If she got on the bus, he would wait for the next one.

The bus groaned to a halt and the doors opened. When the old woman made no move, he skirted around the shelter then boarded the single-decker.

He paid his fare. The doors closed noisily behind him. Snatching his ticket from the machine he turned to find an empty seat.

He stopped; his breath coming in low, irregular gasps.

All the passengers were dead.

On every seat he saw slashed throats drooling blood and gore. Heads lolled back tearing the wounds further. Blackened tongues protruded from blue lips. Bloodied eye sockets writhed with worms. Flesh hung from cheeks in long moist strips.

The bus began to move, jerking Price forward. He stumbled and grabbed the handrail for support. His clammy palm slipped down the metal bar and he almost fell onto the cadavers in the front seats. He threw himself backwards, falling into the baggage area. As the bus gathered speed the heads jiggled precariously on the ravaged necks and Price closed his eyes, scrunching the lids so tightly that white stars danced in the dark, willing the apparitions away.

He opened them again.

The passengers were all looking at him.

They were all still dead.

The wounds in their throats began to move. Trembling slightly at the edges at first, then rippling like waves. The movements began to follow a repeated pattern. Blood bubbled as the wounds became obscene mouths struggling to articulate the word.

'Da...Da...vid...Da-vid.' Soon others took up the lamentation, dribbling congealed gunge as the words left the jagged wounds.

Price raised both his hands to his head and sucked in a sharp breath. He almost retched on the cloying stench of coppery blood and decay. 'No! I know what you're trying to do,' he shouted to the voice in his head. But he received no reply.

The driver of the bus shouted for him to shut up and sit down, but Price heard only the repeated gurgle of his name.

A corpse at the rear of the single-decker tried to stand. Rotten hands gripped the rail in front and pulled the body up from the seat, a tongue slicking the wound as if it were a pair of lips. As it did the head toppled backwards. There was a terrible tearing sound as the head tore itself free from the neck and fell. The corpse sat down again; the putrid hands comically probed the empty space above the shoulders trying to locate the missing head.

'Stop the bus!' he screamed.

The driver stole a quick glance at Price then returned to the road. 'Sit down! I won't tell you again!'

Price thrust his face up to the window of the driver's compartment. 'Listen to me.' Spittle flew from his mouth onto the plastic. 'You have to let me off!'

Other cadavers struggled to their feet, balancing their heads delicately on their necks. The throats continued to call his name. 'Da-vid...Da-vid...Da-vid.'

'Please,' he begged.

The driver boiled. 'That's it!' He slammed on the brakes and Price fell forward, hearing more severed heads thud to the floor.

The doors hissed open. 'Get off!'

Price didn't need to be told a second time.

'Tosser!' snarled the driver as he closed the doors.

Price forced himself to look at the bus's passengers.

Shaking heads and pitiful expressions. A few smiles of sympathy.

No headless corpses. No sliced throats.

He could hear the passengers murmuring as the bus pulled away, sniggering as they discussed his antics.

It grew louder. Louder.

It was in his head.

'You bastard!' He glared at the heavens shaking his fist. 'Leave me alone!'

I'm not up there, David.

'What do you want from me?'

That's it, Davie boy, make a scene. Draw attention to yourself.

The words cut through his heart.

A round face appeared before his eyes. It was completely blank save for a pair of bloated, peeling lips. 'Could you kill my wife for me?' asked the smooth orb of flesh.

Price took a horrified step back.

'Please,' beseeched the lips. 'She's a dirty, *dirty*, little *whore!*'

Price broke into a run.

'She's asking for it!' the lips shouted after him.

*

Jay thumped on the blue metal door of the *Inferno* again. No-one came to answer. Darrow reclined nonchalantly against the side of his car crunching a spearmint. It was his third in a minute and he still couldn't remove the taste of the fish from his mouth. Well, the menu had claimed it was fish. He had his doubts. 'Leave it,' he said.

It was twenty-five to two.

Jay returned to the car slightly relieved. Darrow had informed him that he would be leaving the questions to him. The idea of being the subject of one of Darrow's disparaging investigative critiques while wrestling with a gutful of dodgy steak and kidney pie was not an appealing one. 'He said he would be here at half past.'

Darrow took out his mobile phone and asked for the number of the owner. He had tapped three digits when a black BMW pulled up behind his car. Snapping the mobile shut he motioned for Jay to investigate.

The man who exited the vehicle was middle aged, bald, about six foot and powerfully built. He was dressed in a grey tracksuit and the fingers on his right hand were covered in sovereign rings. Jay stood back to allow the door to open fully. 'Mr. Brown?'

'That's right.' The man's size may have afforded him considerable menace, but his face was soft and rotund.

'I'm DC Jay, Eastern Road CID. We spoke on the phone earlier.'

'Who's your friend?'

'DI Darrow,' he flashed his warrant card. Jay groaned inwardly and did the same. Cursing himself for forgetting something so basic, he decided not to dwell on the pleasantries. 'May I see the list of employees, Mr. Brown.'

'I haven't got it on me. It's inside.' He slammed the door shut, set the alarm, and after wrestling with a cluster of keys opened the door. 'Bleeding cleaners. Never on time. Well, they'll get a shock when they find me waiting for `em.'

Brown led the two detectives behind the bar to a small office which made no attempt to match the chrome splendour of the rest of the establishment. He pulled a sheet of paper from a cluttered notice board and handed it to Jay. 'The duty roster,' he explained.

Jay scanned the list of names, ten of which were down to have been working last night. He handed it to Darrow.

'Were you here last night, Mr Brown?'

'I'm here every night, son,' came the terse reply.

'I don't suppose you have ever seen this woman at your club?'

Brown ogled the photograph. 'Yeah, I've seen her. Tasty little bit of arse. Her name's Judith, Mary, Deb. Take your pick.'

'She was here often, then?'

'Only every bleeding Wednesday. What's she done, rolled some poor sod, has she?' He chuckled.

'She's dead,' said Jay.

'You're joking.' He leered at the photograph once more. 'What a waste, what a waste. What happened?'

'She was murdered.'

'Bleeding hell! The poor cow. All right, she was bit of a snob but-'

'You knew her then?'

'Oh, yeah, I mean. I'd spoken to her a few times but...wait a minute. You don't think-'

'What did you speak to her about?'

Brown became bashful. 'Well...I tried to get her into bed, didn't I? But she wasn't having none of it. Too old. She said she preferred the younger man.' He made a tutting sound. 'She'd have had no complaints,' he adjusted his track-suit trousers, pulling them higher up his waist.

'And you accepted that?'

'Too right I did. Granted, she was a tasty morsel but I ain't running after no bird. I can get a bird like *that*,' he snapped his fingers. 'They all want to get to know the manager of a club. I could look like the Elephant Man and they'd still try it on.'

'I see,' said Jay, delaying the proceedings to write in his notebook.

Nicely done, thought Darrow.

'Did you see her last night?' asked Jay finally.

'Yeah, I saw her.'

'Was she alone?'

'When I saw her, she was at the bar.'

'And she was alone.'

'As far as I can tell, yes. I tend to keep my distance. She's got a sharp tongue, that one.'

'What time did you see her?'

'About eleven. She was dressed exactly like the photograph.'

'So you wouldn't be able to tell me if she was with anyone last night.'

'Like I said: I noticed her and didn't give her a second thought. Do you think that somebody she picked up in my club killed her?'

'We have reason to believe that could be the case, yes.'

Brown ran his heavily adorned hand across his bald head. 'Shit...this could be terrible for business.'

'I doubt it was any less damaging for the lady's health, sir.'

Took the words right out of my mouth, thought Darrow. He's learning.

Brown conceded the fact. 'I apologise, that was in poor taste. I take it back.'

Jay decided not to labour the point. 'Have you any contact numbers or addresses for the names on the list you gave us?'

'Yeah, sure.' he moved to a small, dented filing cabinet. Opening the drawer he pulled the files forward, taking the last file and handing it to Jay.

'Can I take this with me?'

'Just as long as I get it back before tonight. If someone don't turn in and I've got no numbers, I'm knackered.'

'Thank you for your time, Mr. Brown. I'll ensure that I have this file back to you by the end of the day.'

Darrow cleared his throat. All eyes shifted to the Inspector. 'There is one other thing, Mr. Brown. I noticed that the roster doesn't include the doormen.' He raised his eyebrows.

'Er...yes, ah, that's right.'

'They *are* all registered and above board?'

'Of course...well, no as a matter of fact.'

'Ah,' said Darrow, adopting the tone of Jay's 'I see.' He paused for effect then snapped his fingers. 'Names.'

'That's the thing, they sort the days out among themselves. I have nothing to do with it.'

'Well, give me them all, then.'

Brown reeled off a list of about twelve names and Jay inscribed them in his notebook. Darrow recognised a few of them as petty thugs, with previous convictions for burglary, GBH, ABH - nothing that sent his pulse racing. He would have a word anyway. It seemed unlikely that Doormen would have let a treat like Bell leave the club unnoticed.

'I suppose they'll all be down the gym?'

Brown nodded. 'Just left there myself.'

'Johnny's?'

Another nod.

'Good.'

*

'You did well, Simon,' Darrow informed the anxious looking DC Jay as they drove to Johnny's gym. 'You did well.'

Jay tried his best not to beam his own praise. 'Thank you, Sir.'

Darrow stopped at the lights. He turned to Jay with a smile of his own. 'But I think it would be best if I dealt with the gym.'

*

At roughly the same time Darrow, Jay and Mr Brown entered the *Inferno*, the black cab that contained Janine Taylor and Christine MacNeil pulled up outside 57 Winterburn Road. Janine told the driver to wait.

Christine rapped her knuckles on the door. When the summons went unanswered, she stepped back, straining her neck to see if his bedroom curtains were open. They were. 'David!' she called. 'Open the door!'

She knocked again, hard enough to redden her knuckles. She flipped up the letterbox and shouted through it. Although the draft excluder prevented her from seeing inside, she knew she was wasting her time. The house was empty. She needed him. Why wasn't he there?

A hand touched her shoulder. She jumped and spun round.

Janine pulled her in to the embrace. Christine allowed herself to be smothered in her friend's arms gratefully. She wiped away a tear. 'Why isn't he home?' Her words were muffled by Janine's chest.

'He might have gone to the doctor's,' offered Janine, hopefully. 'Why don't you leave him a note?' She took a letter from her handbag and removed the credit card statement from the envelope. Shoving the statement back into the bag she fumbled for a pen and handed them both to Christine. 'Here, use this. I'll be in the cab.'

Christine began to write. She managed to inscribe the letter D before the ink ran dry. 'Shit.' Shaking it vigorously she scribbled impotently for a few seconds before the ink transferred itself to the paper.

Dave
Call me when you get in.
URGENT!!!
Chris xxx

With some difficulty she pushed it through the letterbox, feeling with her fingers to ensure that it had passed all the way through to the other side. Satisfied that it had, she plodded despondently back to the cab. 'I want to go home and wait for him to call.'

Janine told the driver the address.

Christine leaned forward. 'Could you stop at the nearest off-licence, please,' she asked the driver. She turned to Janine. 'How much money have you got?'

'Enough to ensure we'll never walk again,' she grimaced.

*

Price could run no further. His lungs burned and he was drenched in sticky sweat. He leaned against a lamppost, his body shaking and heaving in an effort to regain his breath. Things were getting out of hand. He wasn't going to make it to the hospital. Besides they wouldn't have any spare appointments anyway. Even if they did, what would they do in an afternoon? He would have to go with his other plan.

He darted out into the road to hail the cab, stepping back onto the pavement as it pulled over.

'Edge Lane retail park, please,' he gasped as he slumped in the back.

The cabby started the meter and drove off.

'You know what I think?' she asked.

Price could have cried with relief. A normal conversation at last. 'What?' he asked.

She leisurely shifted the cab down into second gear and steered it around a bend. 'I think you should drag me in the back, beat the shit out of me, viciously rape me, slice me up a bit then leave me to bleed to death.'

Price moaned.

'Or if you prefer, I've got two daughters. Stacey, she's fourteen and Dana, who's sixteen. I think you'd like a bit of fresh meat. Don't worry I won't be offended if you do them instead of me. I've been had a thousand times. I'm filthy. A dirty, dirty, *dirty*, little scrubber, is what *I* am. It's much better to defile the innocent, don't you think? Of course you do. Not that that's what they are. I've been teaching them my sordid ways since they were born. But their little snatches are fresh like flowers.'

Price listened in silence staring out the window, praying that she would end the conversation if he didn't respond.

The woman continued regardless. 'I keep nagging at my auld man to molest them, but he won't have any of it. What they need is a real man to give them what for. Stacey's still got a bald cunt. Can you believe that at *fourteen*? In this day and age. If my bread was buttered that way, I'd have a go myself. I tried but I can't. I hate the smell of minge, see. Knocks me sick, it does. Hey, if *your* bread's buttered that way I've got a mate with twin boys, only seven.'

Price's head was reeling. 'Could you be quiet, please. I'm not feeling very well.'

'I didn't think you looked the type. You're a *real* man. No, I agree. It's the foul sluts like me you should be concerned with. I'm insatiable. Even talking about it has made me wet. I can feel it dribbling all over the seat. It's like Niagara-bleeding-Falls, it is. I'm surprised you can't hear it.'

Then, to his horror, he could. A sickening squelching sound; like heavy boots treading on sodden soil and leaves, the water squirting underfoot. His stomach rolled. 'Oh my God.' He covered his mouth with his hands.

'See?' The woman appeared to be pleased by his revulsion. 'I told you I was a dirty bitch. Asking for it I am. If I promise not to enjoy it will you kill me?'

'I know what you're up to,' Price informed the voice in his head, 'and it won't work.'

Me? It said innocently.

The woman shifted her body at an angle, enabling her to steal quick glances at her passenger and keep an eye on the road. 'I'm only asking for what I deserve. Nothing fancy. A few minutes in the back, that's all.'

'Could you let me out here, please?'

'Stick it up my arse. Make me bleed. We could get some salt - the ASDA's just around the next bend - rub it into the wound. Oh, yes. The sting. That's what I'm after.'

'Could you let me out here, *please*?'

'Don't be a spoil sport.'

The cab stopped. Price stuffed a ten-pound note through the gap in the glass. The woman took it. She licked her lips and scratched her fingernails down the left-hand side of her face, from temple to chin, leaving four deep trenches of red. 'I'm begging you,' she moaned, her eyes rolling back into her head.

Price fumbled with the door handle. It wouldn't open. The red safety light was still on. 'Let me out.'

The woman tore at the scratches, digging her nails into her cheek and removing thick clumps of flesh. She tore open her shirt with her free hand and began massaging the bloody flesh into her cleavage. All the while her tongue twisted and lolled lasciviously over her lips. '*Please*,' she groaned.

Price jerked at the handle, tugging with his entire body. 'Let me out!'

The red light blinked off. Price threw himself through the open door and slammed it shut with a powerful kick. 'Fucking psycho!'

The cab driver leaned forward and stuck out her tongue. It stretched, thinning as it did, and smeared the inside of the windscreen with saliva.

For the second time that day Price ran as if his life depended on it.

But it wouldn't be the last.

*

Even if there had been no sign outside the building, thought Darrow, the nature of the premises would have immediately become apparent to anyone once they stepped inside. The unmistakeable odour of stale sweat, the peeling posters of bulging, baby-oiled bodies, the sounds of clanking metal.

'Can I help you?' asked the receptionist. She was wearing a pink leotard over a small grey support top that failed to keep her ponderous breasts from resting on the surface of the desk as she leaned over it. Her skin tone suggested that she was no stranger to the tanning beds advertised on the wall behind her.

Without a word Darrow flashed his warrant card and pushed open the double doors to the sparring room.

Darrow scanned the busy room. The punch-bags were all in use as were the weights. He watched the two men in protective headgear sparring in the ring for a few moments, taking in the grey-haired chubby man shouting encouragement to them. The owner.

Darrow pointed over to a punch-bag in the far right-hand corner of the room. 'Dean Burrows and

Michael Tandy,' he explained, and promptly marched towards them.

Burrows supported the bag while Tandy, a pony-tailed hulk, beat the living daylights out of it.

'Hello, Mickey. Letting off a little steam?'

Tandy stopped his pounding and turned to the Inspector. His face was red and dripping with sweat, yet he appeared not to be short of breath. 'Mr. Darrow. Nice of you to drop by. And I see you've brought your little monkey.'

Jay fixed Tandy with unblinking eyes. Tandy snorted his derision at the DC's efforts at intimidation. 'What do you want?' he asked the Inspector.

'Working last night were you, Mickey?'

'So, what if I was?'

'Still claiming dole?'

Tandy snatched a towel from his bag and mopped the sweat from his face and chest. 'That would be dishonest, Mr Darrow,' he said angelically as he wiped his armpits dry.

Darrow produced the photograph. 'Did you see this woman last night?'

He glanced at it. 'So, what if I did?'

'She's dead, Mickey. Murdered. Know anything about it?'

'Behave yourself!'

'Not your thing, then? Fancy the boys these days, do you? We could go down to the station. Introduce you to a few.'

'You should try stand up, you're so funny.'

Darrow's glare prompted the pony tailed man to elaborate on his earlier admission. 'I can't remember what time she left. It was before the big chuck out, though.'

To Burrows: 'Did you see her?'

'Nah. My night off, wasn't it?'

Back to Tandy: 'Was she with anyone?'

'Not that I saw. If she'd have asked nicely, I'd have took her home, though.'

'I think she would have preferred to be murdered, son. Did you say anything to her?'

Tandy shrugged. 'Just the normal. You know, wolf whistles...a bit of smutty talk. No harm in that. I expect a stunner like that has had her fair share of all that.'

'Fancy her, did you?'

'Of course I did, yes. But that don't mean I killed her, does it?'

'So she didn't call you a big, fat, greasy pig and tell you to fuck off, then?' Darrow's smile was infuriatingly benign.

Jay thought he could see the veins in Tandy's neck jut out. 'No, she didn't,' he replied calmly.

'Are you sure? As you said: she was a stunner. Even I wouldn't have taken no for an answer. I'll tell you what I think happened, shall I? You and your fellow baboons started rubbing your steroid shrivelled pricks together and gave her the come on. She called you an ugly bastard and told you to get lost, so you followed her home.'

'No-'

Darrow cut sharply across his protests. 'One of your mates, then?'

'No.'

'She left all on her own. A 'stunner' like that. Come on, Mickey.'

The former arrogance was now entirely evaporated. 'I swear, Mr. Darrow. Straight after she left, a group of young scrubbers came out beggin' for it. We was occupied with them. I didn't see nothing, I swear.'

'Who else was working with you last night?'

'I can't remember.'

'Get your things. We're going down the station,' Darrow said without hesitation.

Tandy held up his hands. 'Okay, okay. Frank McDougal, Andy Gore and Scott Lloyd.'

'Four. No-one else.'

'That's it.'

Darrow narrowed his eyes. 'You wouldn't be lying to me, Mickey, would you?'

'On my mother's life.' He spat on the floor.

'I don't suppose you would have any idea where they would be?'

'No.'

'I didn't think so. We'll be in touch.' Darrow spun on his heels and left the gym as swiftly as he had arrived.

'Fucking pig bastard,' muttered Tandy when the two detectives were safely out of earshot.

*

As they walked to the car Darrow asked Jay what he thought.

Jay shrugged. 'He seemed genuine enough. Fancied himself a bit, but he doesn't strike me as the kind of person we're looking for. And if he did see anyone, I think he would have been glad to mention it. Even if it was just to get rid of us.'

Darrow agreed. 'Well, if I know McDougal and Gore, they'll be in the bookies on Porter Street. I'll pay them a visit myself. Then Lloyd; that lazy bastard will still be in bed. You can call on the bar-staff.' He tossed Jay his car keys. 'Take the car, you'll need it more than me. If I don't hear from you by the time I'm done, I'll be back at Bell's.'

Jay nodded, aggrieved that the lengthier of the two tasks was left to him.

Chapter Twenty-three

Price's body screamed for him to rest but he ignored it. His initial sprint had slowed to a painful, shambling jog but he forced himself on, finding stamina he never thought possible. The muscles in his calves were tight and aching, his lungs wheezed and burned. But he couldn't stop. To stop would be to surrender. To lose.

The streets were crowded with the walking dead. Everywhere he ran dead grey eyes were upon him. He shambled past a man walking a golden retriever. He heard the man ask if he would like to watch the dog in bed with his three-year-old daughter. Price shook his head in horror and found a fresh burst of energy.

There's nowhere for you to run to, David.

He turned into Edge Lane, his mouth dry and tacky. Ahead was a newsagents and upon seeing it his thirst intensified. He pictured himself gulping an ice-cold can of something and his body ached for him to make real the mental image. He found himself slowing down, steering towards the newsagents.

'No,' he roared, angrily wiping sweat from his brow. The DIY store was less than five minutes away. All he had to do was concentrate and he would make it. Once he had purchased the things he required and was home again, then he could drink all he wanted. Not far now. Just let me make it. Please God, that's all I ask.

God? I'm disappointed in you. God is the refuge of the weak and spineless. Julie was right; you have no backbone.

Ignore it. It's trying to distract you. Focus. On anything. His eyes settled on a lamppost about three hundred yards further up the road.

Almost immediately a naked woman crawled on her hands and knees before it. Even at such a distance he could see that she was nothing more than skin and bones, her thighs no thicker than his own forearms. As he drew closer, he could see that she was almost completely bald, only a few gossamer strands of dirty brown hair remained on her scalp. Her scabby nose sniffed the base of the post with interest.

With considerable effort he dragged his eyes from her emaciated form as she scooped a coil of dog shit from the pavement and devoured it eagerly.

'Nice try...but no...cigar,' he panted, allowing himself a wry smile.

The voice screamed in his head. *YOU'RE MAKING THEM VERY ANGRY, DAVID!*

'Fuck them....and...fuck you.'

He staggered into the DIY superstore carpark and stopped.

'No,' he moaned, and fell to his knees, his head in his hands.

I warned you.

'No,' he repeated. There was nothing more to say. His way was blocked. As far as he could see the ground writhed with millions of worms.

With a triumphant screech, the worms crawled towards him.

*

Christine sipped her vodka and lime, the glass trembling slightly as she brought it to her lips. She was drunk. Initially they had drank in silence; Christine lost in a world known only to herself and Gary, Janine staring awkwardly at the TV unsure of what to say. When Christine had finally spoken it was a frank and lurid outpouring, darting from the attack to the court proceedings and back again in the space of a few words. Janine had not interrupted, content to piece together her own picture and knowing Christine needed to release the information in her own time and her own way. When Christine wept, she held her. When she became enraged, she soothed her. But mostly she just listened. And when it was over, there were no tears, anger or self-castigation, only a lengthy exhalation. The burden was unloaded. That was all that mattered. Christine had talked for the best part of an hour, stopping occasionally to leave the room and phone Dave. At first, she was frustrated and hurt that he wasn't home. Gradually that faded into a grim acceptance.

'If he doesn't get back to you, I'll stay with you,' said Janine as she poured herself another vodka. She drowned it in lemonade. Whenever she got drunk she was apt to say something insensitive. She couldn't help it. As the booze flowed the part of her brain that warned her to keep certain comments to herself went on holiday. If there ever was a time that that couldn't happen, then this was it.

Christine patted the phone nestling in her lap. 'He'll call.' Of that she had no doubt. They were in love. He wouldn't allow her to come to any harm.

'He's a good man.' She said, certain that it was what Christine wanted to hear.

'The best thing that ever happened to me.' She raised her glass as if to toast this fact then slurped down a mouthful.

'I wish I could find a good man.'

'What about Roland?'

'How could anyone marry a man with a name like *Roland*?'

Christine frowned in concentration. 'You know, I don't think I've ever come across that name before.'

'*Tears for Fears*,' said Janine simply.

'What?'

'There was a guy in *Tears for Fears*...Roland Orzabal, or something.'

'Oh, yes. And there was that chubby kid in *Grange Hill*.'

'The one who's in that chef thing on the BBC...er...*Chef*.'

'That's right. I take it back, then.'

'What?'

'When I said I'd never come across that name before. I take it back.'

'Oh.'

Christine pressed the *re-dial* button. She closed her eyes, listening to the ringing, her head spinning slightly as she became immersed in the sound. It rang and rang.

She began to cry.

*

Walking into the bookies was like walking into a thick blanket of fog. Almost every person in the place was smoking. Darrow sniffed for marijuana, yet another habit he found impossible to shake. Even if he had detected a scent, which he hadn't, he wouldn't have done anything about it. There were more important things on his mind. He scanned the room's occupants, all of whom were male, except for the two cashiers. To his right, hunched over a copy of *Sporting Life*, were Frank McDougal and Andrew Gore. Gore was the younger of the two men, only twenty-one, but with a juvenile record for burglary and assault about ten foot long. As far as Darrow was aware, he had kept his nose clean since his release from Risley two years ago. McDougal was thirty and as honest as they came. His main failing was that he was easily led. And also that he was as thick as they came.

Darrow leaned over Gore's shoulder and whispered in his ear. 'What do you fancy in the two-thirty at Chepstow?'

'Who the-oh, it's you. What do you want?'

'Just a few minutes of your time.'

'I'm straight, now, Mr. Darrow.'

'I believe you Andrew. Really I do.'

McDougal casually turned and made for the exit.

'Not leaving us, are you Frankie?'

McDougal smiled nervously. 'Just going for some cigs, Mr. Darrow.'

Darrow shook his head. 'Try a mint, Frankie.' He offered the packet. When both men declined, he popped one in his mouth and returned the packet to his pocket. McDougal made to leave again. 'Sit down, Frankie.'

With a sigh McDougal complied. 'What are you hasslin' us for? We haven't done nothing.'

Darrow ignored his question. 'You were both on the door at the *Inferno* last night. Yes?'

The two men fidgeted uncomfortably.

'Relax. This isn't a DSS probe. I just want to ask you a few questions.'

'What about?' asked Gore.

'Last night a woman left the club before closing. She was blonde, wearing a short red dress. Ring any bells.'

At their innocent blank faces, he added, 'I've already spoken to Mickey and he says he saw her.'

'Oh, yes now I remember. Quite the looker.'

'That's the one. Was she alone?'

'I think so,' said McDougal.

Gore shrugged.

'This is important. Try and remember.'

'We gave her a bit of chatter, but she wasn't interested,' explained Gore. 'Then these birds came out who were. All over us like a bleeding rash they were. Prick teasers. Ran a bleeding mile as soon as I tried it on.'

Darrow shifted the spearmint to the other side of his mouth. 'Anything else?'

'Like what?' asked Gore.

'You tell me.'

'I dunno, do I?'

McDougal lit a cigarette with a match.

'I thought you didn't have any?' asked Darrow.

McDougal grinned sheepishly. 'Last one,' he said.

Darrow glared at him. 'Can you add anything?'

He looked to the ceiling. 'Er...no.'

Back to Gore. 'Who left before the girl?'

'Just some lads.'

Darrow groaned. 'How many, Andrew?'

'I dunno...six, seven. Look, Mr Darrow. If they're not birds or causing trouble I don't give them a second look-'

'How old would you say they were?'

'Mid twenties, maybe.'

'Wait a minute. I think I remember now....' interrupted McDougal.

'Careful, Frankie. You don't want to give yourself an aneurysm,' jibed the Inspector.

'Them blokes what Andy said. One of them stayed behind.'

Darrow's heart skipped a beat. 'What do you mean?'

'Well, they left and walked up the street but one of them hanged around by the corner.'

The Inspector sucked hard on the mint. 'What did he look like?'

'I couldn't say Mr. Darrow. As he said,' he nodded to Gore, 'them birds came out. When they give us the knock back, he wasn't there no more.'

'Let's keep it simple, Frankie. How tall was he?'

'About as tall as me.'

Darrow nodded. About six foot two. 'What did he look like?'

'I couldn't say. I only saw him for a second. Less probably. He just looked like a bloke.'

'Was he white or black?'

It was Gore who answered. 'They were all white.'

He kept his eyes on McDougal. 'And what was he wearing?'

'The usual clobber. Shirt and kex.'

'And you're sure the man you saw left the club.'

'I think so. I can't remember.'

'If I told you she was murdered last night and, other than the person who killed her, you were the last people to see her alive would that jog your memory.'

'Shit,' hissed McDougal.

'Bleeding Hell!' exclaimed Gore.

'Well?' encouraged Darrow.

'I wish I could help, Mr Darrow, but I didn't see him.' Gore seemed genuinely repentant.

McDougal looked pained. 'The shirt wasn't tucked in; I remember that much. They all wore the same gear. I think it might have been white or cream or yellow...It wasn't black or nothing like that.'

Darrow decided to leave it for the time being. 'Any idea where Lloyd is?'

'He didn't see nothing,' blurted McDougal.

'What made you say that?'

The two doormen exchanged a look. Gore sighed. 'He was tongue wrestling with some tart in the back, Frankie's not a very good liar,' he grinned ruefully at McDougal. 'He's worried in case Scott's Missus finds out, that's all. He's sentimental like that is our Frankie.'

Darrow slapped a hand on McDougal's shoulder. 'Don't worry, Frankie. I'll be very discreet.'

McDougal sighed with relief. 'She's a good woman, his Missus. I don't know why he does it.'

Darrow's mobile warbled for attention. 'Darrow.'

It was DC Jay. 'I'm with the glass collector, Martin Fletcher. He recognised Bell but knew her as Anne. He saw her talking to someone last night. Unfortunately, he only saw him from behind. About six foot two, short dark hair, white shirt, possible black or dark blue trousers. Nothing else.'

Darrow told him to wait a moment. He turned to McDougal. 'This man you saw; white shirt, dark trousers, short blonde hair?'

McDougal shook his head. 'No, it was definitely dark hair.'

'But the rest is right?'

He thought about it. 'Yes.'

Back to Jay. 'The description tallies with someone spotted by one of the doormen. Apparently, a group of men in their mid-twenties left just before Bell did. It looks like he was one of them. Good work, Jay. Keep at it and meet me back at the station when you've spoken to the rest of the staff.'

'Will do.'

Darrow snapped the mobile shut, thanked McDougal and Gore for their assistance, and left for the station.

*

I told you there was nowhere for you to run, David. Doesn't it make you proud? Don't you feel special?

He dropped to his knees. 'What's the point,' he moaned.

That's the idea. Soon you will wonder why you ever thought to resist. Soon you will understand.

He stretched out his arms either side, a gesture of grim acquiescence. The DIY shop might as well have been a million miles away.

His body twitched as the worms crawled over him. He could feel them burrowing into him, nudging their way through his flesh. Price felt no pain only tingling warmth that spread pleasure through his body like a shuddering orgasm of realisation. It rocked him and he gasped, ejaculating into his trousers. He toppled back, feeling like everything was happening in slow motion.

His vision danced with a kaleidoscope of twinkling light more beautiful than he could have ever dreamed.

Price remained on his back, hypnotised. The light slowly began to fade.

He rose smoothly to his feet, feeling invigorated, alive. Powerful.

He understood.

He knew what was expected of him.

He smiled.

Chapter Twenty-four

The neck of the bottle clinked against the rim of the glass as Janine poured. 'Say when.'

Christine waited until the vodka filled half the glass before raising her hand.

Despite her best efforts to stay sober for her friend, Janine was rolling drunk and Christine was the same. Christine's head periodically lolled from side to side as consciousness deserted her. Whenever this happened, she would snap her head up, eyes staring wildly as she tried to collect herself, then pick up the phone and dial Price. He had yet to answer.

Janine was feeling uncomfortable. Christine was a good friend, probably the best she had ever had, but Christine's unwillingness to accept her support was wounding. She had lied her way into the afternoon off, followed her round to Dave's and back, bought the booze, listened to her, and now that was all out of the way she was beginning to feel as if she was surplus to requirements.

'Roland Rat!' shouted Christine, words slurred, eyes half closed.

'What?' asked Janine in much the same fashion.

'Roland Rat...another Roland.'

'Oh, yes,' she agreed finally.

'What was the name of his mate?'

'Roland Rat?'

'Yes,' her head dipped forward, chin almost resting on her chest.

'Oh...erm...oh!' She snapped her fingers as if this would aid her remember. 'It was a gerbil, I'm sure.'

Christine grinned, the vodka turning it into a leer. 'Kevin the gerbil.' She laughed.

Janine laughed, too. 'Kevin the gerbil, oh yes. I remember now. Don't you reckon that Roland Rat sounded like Blakey off '*On the Buses*'?' She launched into a less than accurate impression, shaking her fist. 'I'll get you Butlaaaaar!'

Christine, however, responded as if it was the funniest thing she had ever heard, and her face flushed red with laughter.

'I'll get you Butlaaaaar!' repeated Janine, eliciting a fresh bellow of laughter from her friend. She was about to attempt the impression a third time when Christine, now choking on her own mirth, fell backwards. This in itself was no cause for alarm, she was sitting on the floor, but as she toppled the telephone slipped off her lap, receiver separating from cradle. The laughter ceased immediately, replaced by an inhalation of horror, and Christine scrambled for the receiver and slammed it back into position. 'What if he was trying to call?' she gasped, her cheeks no longer red but deathly pale. 'What if he was trying to call when the phone was off the hook?'

'Phone his house and find out,' suggested Janine.

'But what if he was phoning from the hospital, what if he's been in an accident?'

'What could he possibly have been doing in a hospital?'

'He went for a scan the other day-'

'Scan? What for?'

'He said he'd been getting headaches and that the doctor sent him for a scan but that it was nothing to worry about, but Dave never goes to the hospital unless it's something serious.' She sucked in a deep breath. 'What if he's got a brain tumour?'

Janine placed her hands on each of Christine's shoulders and held her firmly. 'Stop panicking. Stop It!' She shook her. 'He didn't phone. Nothing's happened to him. If there was something wrong with him, he would have told you. Don't you believe that? Don't you think that if he had a brain tumour, you would be the first person he would tell?'

Christine nodded slowly. 'You're right. Of course, you're right. I'm sorry.'

'Phone him again. You'll see that he's not in yet and that you've nothing whatsoever to worry about. Knowing that man of yours he's probably down the boozer supping ale.'

Christine's eyes lit up. 'Do you think we should check?'

Janine shook her head. 'I don't think that would be a good idea.'

'Why the hell not!' shouted Christine. 'He's my boyfriend and I can see him whenever I want to!'

'Think about it,' breathed Janine, desperately trying to keep her own quiet. 'What would he think if we rolled in there blind drunk and embarrassed him? Look at the state of us, we're as pissed as farts and I know the moment you set eyes on him you'll burst into tears and bawl the place down.'

The phone rang.

Christine snatched up the phone. 'Dave?'

'No dear, it's your mother. Why aren't you at work? Is everything all right?'

*

Darrow sat on his chair with his feet resting on his table. This was what he referred to as his contemplative posture. Those who knew him well enough, or had worked with him in the past, knew that it was really a euphemism for forty winks. Today, however, sleep eluded him.

He saw Bell's vagina on her dining room table and wondered at the hatred required to execute such a mutilation. Darrow had despised a great many people during his life, a considerable number of which were women, but he had never experienced the kind of all-consuming detestation that would be necessary for that kind of violence.

Certainly, he had killed people in his mind's eye on numerous occasions and he often sympathised with those individuals who had succumbed to a moment of fury and actually taken a life. To a certain degree he also understood those who planned their killings, whether the motive be revenge or financial gain, or at least he understood the reasons for them committing murder. Understanding the reasons behind the nature of Bell's death was not as simple.

The inevitable answer that would spring to the minds of his more unimaginative colleagues was that the killer was a psycho. Undoubtedly this was, in a sense, true, but in their eagerness to pigeon-hole the perpetrator of such a foul act they failed to answer the most intrinsic question: Why?

That was what it always boiled down to. One question. *The* question. Why? The lifestyle appeared to be the most likely reason. Her... (he groped unsuccessfully for a less offensive word) ...promiscuity was well documented. Not only by her neighbour, Mr. Doonan, and the owner of the *Inferno*,

Mr Brown, but by her friends. This was a reasonable enough motive for her murder; if not one he could readily understand. However, it was, in his experience, those who were unable to pursue similar lifestyles for themselves that were promiscuity's most fervent denouncers.

The problem with that lay in the description of the men who left before her, and of the man who allegedly loitered behind.

McDougal suggested that they were in their twenties, and Mr Brown had also said that Bell preferred younger men. If indeed this mystery man was responsible, his young age meant he was unlikely to hold casual sexual encounters in any great disdain. Unlikely but not unthinkable, of course.

If not him, then who? Although it was procedurally correct to interview all known sex offenders after the discovery of such a crime, he doubted that the killer would be among them. It was such a distinctive M.O. and aside from the obvious hatred of women, the nature of the dismemberment suggested a first attempt. It was elaborate and time consuming but also clumsy. It also intimated that the killer was familiar with Bell's routine. He knew Smith would be out at her friends and that she wouldn't be home until the next morning. Yet both Smith and Jarvis claimed that Bell never saw any man more than once so how could he have obtained this information? Surveillance? There was another possibility, and one that he hoped would not be the case. It was possible that the killer had met Bell for the first-time last night, knew next to nothing about her - except that she was 'easy', say - and killed her and cut her up with no thought to whether or not he would be disturbed. If this was indeed the case - and the more he thought about it, the more it felt right - then there would be more deaths.

The door opened and DC Jay entered. 'Anything?'

Jay shook his head. 'Fletcher was the best of the bunch. A few recognised Bell but none had seen her last night.' He tossed Darrow's car keys on the table.

Darrow scooped them up and slipped them in his pocket. 'Well, it looks as if you were right about the Super.'

'Sir?'

'He's arranging a press conference as we speak. In his element, he is. Apparently, our clear up rate is not what it was and 'we should all try our utmost to rise to the challenge.' His words.'

Jay didn't know whether he was meant to comment and so opted to remain silent.

The Inspector rubbed the back of his neck. 'Get yourself down to the incident room, we need copies of the photograph.'

'Will you be speaking to the press, Sir?'

'Unfortunately, yes. It seems my head fits better on the chopping block than the Super's.'

Again, Jay did not respond and left for the incident room.

Darrow returned to his previous train of thought.

It wasn't as easy as it used to be. People were too clued up. They stayed at home in their millions tuned into *The Bill, CSI:NY, A Touch of Frost, Law & Order, Crimewatch UK*. They know all about the police holding back specific details of crimes to prevent hoaxers wasting their time, they know the standard investigative procedure, the lines of inquiry, the type of clues forensics scanned the crime scene for.

They're aware of DNA profiling, psychological profiling and are familiar with terms such as *corpus delicti, modus operandi,* and *rigor mortis.* He had even saw a book called *'The Encyclopaedia of Forensic Science'* on sale in his local bookshop. Flicking through the pages he had saw a comprehensive guide to forensic investigative techniques and case scenarios detailing how specific criminals had been apprehended. Darrow believed the book, although intended as a reference guide for the crime enthusiast, was probably used as a *'How not to get caught'* book by the average nut job.

Armed with the failures of TV murderers and a knowledge of what the Soco's would search for at the scene, the average nutter was becoming more and more difficult to catch.

It was an unfortunate truth that often the successful apprehension of a criminal lay not in the competence of the investigating officer but in how careless the criminal had been. So far, the killer of Pamela Bell had left no trace and if no further witnesses came forward and he didn't kill again, the odds were heavily against him ever being found.

*

It was like being asleep but awake at the same time. Previously, the world had seemed weary but now it was as if a veil had been lifted from his eyes, revealing the world as it really was. A world where the unworthy hung flayed from barb-wire, the streets awash with rivers of bloodied, limb-less monstrosities and women turned inside out stalked the land, their wombs sewed to their backs.

The end of all things was coming. And it was greeted with open arms.

As Price made his way to the DIY store information rushed through him with frightening clarity and speed; thoughts, names, ideas, aspirations. It was as if he were connected to an inexhaustible database.

Price watched a man dressed in soiled coveralls deliberating over a selection housing screws. The man's sharp, narrow face with his pointed nose possessed a furtive quality, accentuated by restless grey eyes that darted in all directions as he browsed. His grey hair was short and spiked in places adding to the scruffy mien his coveralls and dirty stubble proclaimed. Price knew the man's name was George Browning and that it was his fiftieth birthday in two days time. He lived alone having murdered his wife a year ago and burying her in the cellar of their three-story house in Kensington. Price was suitably impressed, more so when the details of her dispatch were made clear. George had wanted to kill his wife for years but had bided his time in order to eliminate any chance of capture. His wife's sister was dying of cancer (*aren't we all*) and as she was his wife's last living relative, he reasoned that her disappearance would be less suspicious if after the tragic death of her sister his wife had left him in a fit of grief. So, he patiently endured their lacklustre marriage until her emaciated sister finally surrendered her last breath.

Unfortunately for Mrs. Browning she had complained a few days previously about the living room ceiling. George smoked a great deal, forty a day, and the white of the ceiling had become nicotine brown.

When his wife ventured into the room to criticise his painting, he had smashed in her skull with a claw hammer, wrapped her up in the plastic sheeting and then buried her in the cellar. No mess, no evidence. Whether or not he was caught was of no consequence, he was fifty and smoked like a chimney he was aware he hadn't long to go himself. But at least he could now watch the football in peace without her squawking down his ear.

'Best thing I ever did,' he said, his lips remaining firmly closed. Price said nothing, the admiration on his face saying enough. George shambled away into another aisle.

Turning his attention to his own requirements Price perused the selection of screws before dumping a couple of packets in his trolley then moving on. As he strolled through the aisles of the DIY superstore his eyes grew wide like a child in a Christmas grotto.

Ignoring an emaciated middle-aged woman masturbating with an adjustable spanner in aisle three, Price filled the trolley with everything he believed was essential for his purpose: hammer, nails (various lengths and head sizes), Stanley knife, masking tape, plastic sheets.

The woman masturbating was reaching a noisy climax and her shrieking gasps were beginning to grate on his nerves. Her name was Valerie Jones, mother of three children, all of whom were no longer living at home. Her husband, Guy, was having an affair with his secretary, Bridget Flaherty, twenty-five, and had been for three years now. So Valerie had taken to self-gratification. Too embarrassed to visit a sex shop she had found pleasure in household items. Nothing drastic at first; leaning against the handle of the vacuum cleaner as she worked the living room carpet, pushing herself up to the corner of the washing machine as it roared and vibrated on full spin.

On one occasion she had even allowed the cat to suckle at her genitalia. This had disgusted her - but only after reaching a climax and she had been so ashamed she'd contemplated suicide.

In a brief flash of empathy, he remembered his own suicidal contemplations after Julie left.

She loved her husband and couldn't bear to leave him. A lover wasn't the answer. The one man she had taken to her bed since her husband's infidelity - Harry Joyce - although endowed with a considerable organ had failed to satiate her desire or assuage her despair. She was for her husband only. No-one else. And that was her particular pain.

Price pictured himself snatching the hammer from the trolley and smashing the teeth from her sweaty face.

They were all without hope and meaning. But if they were patient, waited their turn, he would give them meaning. He would show them fear, but not in a handful of dust, he would hold up their still beating hearts to incredulous eyes.

As he paid for the goods, he removed the Stanley knife from the packaging and opened the veins of the cashier's neck with one smooth slice. The blood leapt from his body in a steaming jet, drenching Price's jacket, soaking the counter and the money in the till.

With one hand clamped to his throat to staunch the bleeding, the cashier thanked him for his custom and asked him to come again. Price smiled his own thanks and nailed the cashier's hands to the checkout before departing.

Chapter Twenty-five

Price scrunched up Christine's note into a tight little ball and kicked it down the hall. 'What the fuck does she want?'

Don't ask me.

'I wasn't. It was a rhetorical question. Well, she can wait. I've got far more important things to do than waste my time pandering to the likes of her.'

It would be better if you phoned.

'And since when have you been interested in my love life?'

Just take my word for it and pick up the phone and call. And remember to sound normal.

He closed his eyes, searching for the discarded voice of his previous self. It was a difficult task now that he was throbbing with knowledge and power.

Price opened his eyes, looked at the numbers on the phone for a few moments, and began to dial.

*

Christine was asleep when the phone on her lap began to ring. Janine, who was drifting off on the sofa, sat upright upon hearing the ringing. 'Chris,' she called, rubbing her eyes. She looked down at the snoring form of her friend, and after casting the idea of answering the phone herself from her mind, shook Christine's leg.

Christine groaned and shifted position but did not wake. 'Chris! Phone!'

Her eyes opened and grew wide and she snatched up the receiver and jammed it to her ear. 'Hello! Hello, Dave?'

'What's up?'

'Oh, thank God. Where have you been?'

'I went to the doctors. I didn't have an appointment, so I spent all day sitting around waiting for someone to cancel. Is everything all right? I was a bit worried when I read your note.'

She was crying now. There was nothing more to worry about, Dave was here. He would see that she came to no harm. 'No, Dave, everything is not all right. Someone has sent me a death threat.'

*

'What?' he said, covering the mouthpiece with his hand to muffle his laugh. Once he had composed himself, he said, 'Tell me everything?'

'When I got up this morning...' her voice was trembling, it was a delicious sound, like the sound Pamela Bell had made when he cut her throat. Intoxicating. '...there was this note.'

'What did it say?' He was masturbating leisurely, the fear in her voice increasing the pleasure of each stroke.

'*It said he was going to rip out my cunt!*' she screamed before breaking down into hysterics.

'Oh my God!' he exclaimed, jetting semen over the telephone.

'Hello, Dave? This is Janine, can you come right over? She's in a terrible state.'

'I'm on my way,' he said urgently and put the phone down. He wiped at his ejaculate with a bored finger. He regarded the cloudy fluid for a moment before sucking it clean and strolling to the kitchen to make a cup of tea.

*

Janine took the telephone from Christine's lap and placed it on the floor. 'Let's get you to bed.'

Christine shook her head. 'I want to wait up for him. He won't be long.'

'I know you do but it won't make any difference if you're here or in bed will it?'

Christine's blank expression confirmed that bed was the best place for her.

'Don't worry, I'll stay with you until he comes. Come on.' Janine stood up and offered Christine her hand. Christine stared at it for a moment, pausing for her eyes to focus then allowed her friend to guide her up the stairs.

Chapter Twenty-six

North West Tonight, BBC One, 9:36 p.m.

'Police in Liverpool are hunting the killer of twenty-four-year-old Pamela Bell, a student Nurse, who was discovered murdered in her home this morning. The officer leading the investigation made this public appeal for any witnesses who may have seen her at a local night club the previous evening to come forward.'

CUT TO TAPE.

CAPTION: **Detective Inspector Brian Darrow.**

'This was an extremely vicious and horrific attack and speed is the key to apprehending the man responsible. Pamela was last seen at the *Inferno* club on Kenworth Avenue-'

CUT TO PHOTOGRAPH OF PAMELA BELL.

'-and we would urge any member of the public who was at the *Inferno* club on Wednesday the eleventh of October, or anybody who knew Pamela, to come forward. We are particularly anxious to speak with a group of men in their twenties who left the club immediately before Pamela at around one o'clock to eliminate them from our enquiries.'

CUT TO STUDIO

'The hot-line number for any information-'

*

Darrow switched off the television satisfied with the broadcast.

'What do you think?' he asked Sapphire who was curled in his lap purring contentedly. He tickled behind her ear. 'That good, eh?'

Darrow hated sitting around the house when he was on a case like this. It somehow seemed insensitive. But the Super had taken him to one side after the press conference, told him he looked like a bag of shite and ordered him to get some rest. Grudgingly he had agreed but not before briefing Jay thoroughly and instructing him to call him the moment there were any developments.

His eyes weighed heavy and he allowed them to close, comforted by the grumbling of his cat. Sapphire, which was the closest thing he had to a friend, was originally bought as a method of relaxation. Chief Inspector Shaw, now retired, had sworn that animals were the only way to relieve the stress of the job. He argued a woman could cook, fuck, and wash your shirts for you but only a pet could truly listen without chipping in an unwanted opinion, or complaining that you never took them out anymore.

If you failed to do something right for a woman, they usually let it stew for six months before throwing it back in your face one Saturday morning while you were eating breakfast. If you annoyed a cat you knew about it there and then.

Shaw had also lived alone and claimed that his clearest thoughts came to him while watching his tropical fish move gracefully about the tank. Darrow, who had never understood the appeal of fish, had opted for a kitten instead and was pleasantly surprised to discover that there had been some truth to the Chief Inspector's claim. After a hard day, and recently there seemed to be a shortage of easy ones, he would sit in his armchair stroking Sapphire and everything would gradually fall into perspective. Quite often it was while he was doing just that he would remember something he had omitted to do. Like now.

'Shit,' he hissed, and Sapphire jerked at his exclamation. Townsend hadn't got back to him about Jennings. Damn, he would have to make sure he called him first thing in the morning.

No doubt Chief Superintendent Ackroyd would instruct him to devote his full attention to the Bell case, expecting him to hand his workload over to that fool Glover. If that happened, he would keep the McNeil case for himself knowing that Glover would simply file it away without a second thought.

It was unusual for the authors of poison pen letters to carry out what they threatened but not unheard of. Only this time something told Darrow that the author would carry the threat out word for word.

Chapter Twenty-seven

The casual observer would have been forgiven for thinking that the four young women huddled in the booth at the *Havana*, chatting and sipping from bottles of blue *WKD*, were simply that: four attractive, well-dressed women enjoying a night out. However, had the casual observer stepped a little closer the illusion would have come into question. To start with, the group seemed to be arguing. Not shouting and screaming, but the level of gesticulation and pointing suggested that it was heading swiftly in that direction.

That in itself was not an unusual sight in the *Havana*.

But if our hypothetical observer had stepped close enough to eavesdrop on the argument, he would have been shocked to discover that the four women occupying the booth were no more than children.

That in itself was not an unusual sight in the *Havana*.

'I can't go home. Me mum'd have a fit if I came home at this hour reeking of booze,' Lucy Eliot glanced at the Silk Cut between her finger, 'and ciggies.' Lucy was only sixteen and remembered the hiding she had got from her mother the last time she had come home late with the smell of cider on her breath.

'Then come somewhere else with us, then,' suggested Jane Doyle, also sixteen.

'We were lucky to get in here,' countered Lucy. 'You saw the way those bouncers were looking us over. We were dead lucky.'

'This place is shite!' declared Anne Doyle, Jane's twin sister.

Jane was in full agreement. 'Who the hell wants to listen to Abba and all that seventies stuff?'

Anne nodded emphatically. 'What this place needs is a bit of bouncy techno. Liven things up a bit. God, it's like a pensioner's disco in here.'

Clare Gordon, fifteen, was running out of patience. 'But me and Lucy haven't got enough money to go anywhere else. It's only a pound a bottle here. So what if the music's crap, the night's what you make it.' Ordinarily, Clare wouldn't have cared less if the twins went home. Tonight, however, it was important that they all stayed together. 'Anyway, you can't go home yet, me and Lucy told our parents that we were staying at yours tonight.' Mr and Mrs Doyle played bridge at a friend's house until the early hours every Thursday. The plan was to be tucked innocently up in bed before they arrived home. She knew that if the twins went home now, Lucy wouldn't go with them and then they were all in trouble.

'What? We're meant to hang around this dump until you feel like coming back to ours?' asked Jane.

'You haven't even given it a chance,' complained Clare.

'We don't have to. Look, you can always make your way to ours after here, we'll wait up until one.'

Clare consulted her watch. 'It's ten to eleven. You won't get in anywhere else at this time.'

'Then we'll go home,' said the twins in unison. They giggled to themselves.

'At least stay for another drink,' beseeched Clare.

Lucy let them squabble amongst themselves. This was her kind of place. Not too full, not too empty and the DJ was playing her type of sounds. Tunes from the seventies and early eighties. Such songs had been the soundtrack to her early life, thanks to her music loving mother, and she was filled with the urge to dance the night away.

Clare warned Lucy that it would be unwise to draw attention to themselves. 'Just because we got in, doesn't mean they can't throw us back out again,' she had said. Lucy agreed with her, but the urge was difficult to resist. Another thing in the club's favour was the bloke at the bar. He'd been giving the eye ever since she'd come in. At first she thought he was looking at Clare, like they always did, but when Clare and the twins had gone to the toilet, he had tipped his bottle towards her and smiled.

Clare finished her drink and told the others she was going to the bar. Clare always bought the drinks because she looked and sounded at least twenty-one.

The three girls dipped into their identical *Next* purses and removed a pound coin each.

Clare passed her open palm around the table to collect the money. 'Same again?'

'Can I have a *Mule* this time?' asked Jane, slightly aggrieved.

'What's one of them?' asked her sister.

'Vodka and something. It's quite nice.'

'Get me one as well,' said Anne.

'Same for you, Luce?'

Lucy, who was busy singing along to *Dancing Queen,* nodded. The man had tipped his bottle towards her again, this time mouthing a silent 'Hi.'

Lucy turned away, knowing that this would only serve to increase his interest. He was a big bloke and well built - exactly her type - and well turned out. D & G shirt, Versace jeans, and it looked like he had a pair of Paul Smith shoes. He had nice hair and a strong jawline. Perfect. All she needed now was for him to have a bit of cash and want company for the night and she was sorted. The twins could piss off home if that was what they wanted to do. Miserable cows. They were never happy unless they got their own way. She felt bad about Clare, though. She wouldn't stay if the twins went home.

Clare wasn't into going back with blokes, said she was waiting for someone special. Lucy had nothing against that, but she argued that if she had only been with that 'special' someone how did she know he was special? In her opinion it was better to try a few first, then make an informed judgement. Also, she had told Clare, it was better to learn about sex with strangers because they didn't expect much and never hung around to remind you of the mistakes you made. Clare hadn't been impressed with that. To her, love was the most important thing and sex came as a result of that love. Lucy had shrugged, everyone was entitled to an opinion, and hers was that sexual compatibility was everything. What if you loved someone, waited until you got married or engaged or lived together, and then you found out he had a small willie or he didn't like oral sex, or sex at all for that matter? Clare said that it wouldn't matter if she loved him. Lucy had shuddered at the thought. Life without sex. No, thanks. She had yet to experience an orgasm with a man, but she had come close.

Clare handed Lucy her bottle. 'What are you going to do if the twins go home?' she asked quietly.

Lucy frowned. 'Well, I'm not going home with them if that's what you mean.'

'You're going to stay here?' she asked, trying to sound surprised.

'Too right, there's this well fit bloke over by the bar who's been eyeing me up - *don't look!*'

Clare snapped her head back to her friend. 'Where is he?'

'He's looking over at me now. Wearing the D & G shirt.'

Clare turned and asked Jane the time, stealing a quick glance at the man at the bar. 'He's too old,' she concluded.

'You're never happy. If it's not a daft footy player, you're not interested. Well, I like a man to look like a man and not a girl, someone who can gather me in their arms-'

'Lucy you're only sixteen-'

'I'm nearly seventeen!' she declared defiantly. 'And besides what difference does it make how old I am? I can do just as much as any woman twice my age.'

Jane, who had followed this conversation, decided to voice an opinion. 'My mum says that you shouldn't be in a hurry to grow up 'cos you spend the rest of your life trying to recapture your youth.'

'Oh well, if your mum says so then it must be true,' said Lucy sarcastically. She appraised the three faces at the table and frowned. 'What am I doing with three virgins, anyway?'

'I'm not a virgin!' complained Anne.

Lucy laughed. 'I don't think that Kevin Waters counts. He can hardly walk in a straight line let alone get it up.'

'He did, he did.'

'All right, then, what was it like?'

'It was wonderful, brilliant...'

'Don't talk daft. The first time I did it, my fanny felt like it was on fire...'

'But mum says that all women are different and-'

'God, everything's your mum this, your mum that. She's got twins so I reckon she's done it at least once.'

'Don't talk about our mum like that,' chorused the twins. There were no giggles this time.

'Why, what are you going to do about it?'

'You'll find out,' said Jane.

'Oooh, I'm peeing my pants. Please don't hurt me.'

'You're just a slag!' said Anne.

Lucy laughed again. 'I might be but at least I never went round saying I shagged Kevin Waters. Even if I had shagged that mong, I would have kept it a secret until the day I died. Even then I probably wouldn't tell anyone.'

Clare was shifting her attention from Lucy to the twins and back again; increasingly concerned that at any second words would no longer be the preferred method of attack. 'Look, calm down. There's no need for all of this.'

'Isn't there?' barked Lucy, her frown now more pronounced. 'It's not me anyway, it's the virgin sisters giving me the green eye.'

'Us?' gasped an incredulous Jane. 'Why would we be jealous of some slag who would go to bed with anyone who bought her a drink?'

'Do you want a smack?' snarled Lucy.

'I don't know, do you know anyone who's got one to give?' goaded Anne.

Lucy dived across the table, knocking bottles and the ashtray over, and grabbed two fistfuls of Anne's hair. Anne shrieked as Lucy tugged her head forwards and back lifting her from her seat, Lucy smiled as she felt the hair tear itself away from the scalp.

'Stop it!' shouted Clare, pulling at Lucy's arms. 'Stop it before we get thrown out!'

'Get off her you bitch,' cried Jane as she helped herself to a handful of Lucy's hair.

Lucy cried out, more a roar of rage than of pain, and after releasing her hold on Anne, swung a punch at Jane. She only managed to connect with Jane's shoulder blade, but the force was enough to knock her back into her seat.

'Stop it!' The twins slumped back in their seats glaring at Lucy ready to lunge again but Clare was now standing between them. 'Pack it in now, before we all get thrown out!'

'What do I care if we get thrown out of this dump?'

Clare refused to be distracted. 'Now, make up and let's finish our drinks.'

The twins turned their heads away, arms folded.

'You can all go and fuck yourselves,' panted Lucy, 'Because no-one else would do it to a bunch of dogs like you.'

Clare was hurt. 'Come on, you don't mean that.'

'Don't I?' she spat, and her eyes warned Clare not to push it further.

Jane turned to Anne. 'Come on, let's get out of here.' They both stood up, Anne asked Clare if she was coming with them.

Clare glanced anxiously at a pouting Lucy. 'I'll wait for you outside school tomorrow to give you your uniform. Meet me at half eight by the newsagents.'

'Don't bother.'

Clare, realising that only a National Lottery jackpot win would break her friend's mood, resigned herself to a sigh. 'Well, I'll be there all the same,' she said and followed the twins as they huffed their way out.

Lucy watched them leave, her mood mellowing as they disappeared from view. She straightened her skirt and hair, swallowed the dregs of her bottle, unleashed her most dazzling of smiles, and made her way to the man at the bar.

'Buy me a drink?' she asked.

He handed her a bottle. 'I bought you one already.'

She took the bottle and swigged from it. He was good-looking, strong.

'I was hoping you would come over.'

'Really?' she hid her rising excitement.

He nodded with a slow deliberate movement that indicated a man of confidence.

'And why was that?' she asked, eager for the compliment that she knew would follow.

'Because you're the only real woman in here.'

'That's true. This place is full of kids. It ruins the night sometimes when the only people in here have to get to bed early because they've got school in the morning. How can you party in a club filled with children?'

'Exactly.'

'So,' she put on her most seductive mask. 'Do *you* have to be up early for school in the morning?'

'Not me.'

'Nor me.' she lied, drinking from the bottle again.

'I know,' he said evenly.

He really did have a nice smile. It was sort of a smirk, mischievous. It was a clear sign of someone who was no stranger to fun. And providing he didn't say anything to upset her, fun he would have. 'So, do you think we could have our own private little party?'

'Oh, I think that could be arranged.'

She bit at her lower lip; a gesture she had been informed was demurely sexy. 'My name's Lucy.'

He offered her his hand. 'Pleased to meet you,' he cooed, but instead of shaking her hand he drew it up to his lips and kissed it. Her eyes twinkled and her cheeks flushed. 'My name's David.'

*

My consciousness reached out to her and was distressed by the disorder it discovered within.

She smiled when I suggested we leave, as wide and bloody as a caesarean scar that refused to heal.

In an attempt to prolong the game, she declared something coy and strutted off to the Ladies.

When she returned, she swayed her hips in that pronounced and unnecessary way, and oddly was thinking of her mother. The image wafted from her mind on a thousand invisible wings and into me.

The guttural gasping screams that her unenlightened mind mistook for pain. She didn't know what was happening. She was sure of only one thing; that the man on top of her mother was not her father.

No doubt any number of psychologists or social workers would have cited this incident as the cause of her voracious sexual appetite, but they would be wrong to do so. Although the girl carried this alarming image, and no small amount of ill feeling towards her mother, with her for years she now understood why the stranger was invited to the marital bed. She truly understood the need that had eaten away at her mother, and the desperation that had caused her to seek the embrace of another.

*

'Shall we go?' asked Lucy, sneaking an arm around his.

'In a moment. First I need to ask a favour...'

'What?'

'I'm already seeing someone, and her brother works on the door here. So, if you wouldn't mind, I would like to leave first, say my good-byes to him, then meet you around the corner in about five minutes. I'll buy you another drink while you wait.'

Lucy was almost breathless with excitement. She was the other woman. She hoped he was married; his wife sat alone with the kids wondering where her husband was.

'But aren't we going back to your place?'

'We don't live together.'

'You're not married, then?'

'No.'

No matter. He was still someone else's man; the thrill of taking something that wasn't hers remained. 'Where shall I meet you?'

'On the corner of Rybek Road, but make sure there's no-one about. Okay?'

She nodded her agreement.

'What would you like to drink?'

She bit her lower lip as she decided to keep his interest. 'A Bacardi and coke.'

Price ordered the drink

*

There were three men on the door all bulging out of black clothes.

Price walked slowly, hands in pockets, head up, enabling his features to easily be recalled. As he approached the exit one of the bouncers leaned forward and opened the door for him. 'Night,' he said gruffly, with the barest hint of a smile.

Price returned the farewell with a nod, conscious of not drawing too much attention to himself.

Better than I had hoped; eye contact and a verbal goodbye. Excellent.

Outside the wind chased the sweat from his skin and he enjoyed the chill.

He heard the distinctive grumble of a black-cab and after seeing that it was occupied flapped his arms to catch the driver's attention. As anticipated, it sped past.

Good. Just another lonely drunk searching for a ride home.

He shambled around the corner.

*

The noise of sex drifted to him from an alley. It was guttural and pig like. He heard the oink of each thrust and the tearing of her flesh as worms pounded into her.

There was no need for him to look. He had seen such a scene countless times. He knew there would be a skirt hoisted over bloated hips, knickers around fat ankles, the man's state of undress nothing more than an open zip. There was no need to look, but he couldn't help himself.

She was holding his bag of chips in one hand while he grunted, the other held his neck for support. Her snout sniffed at the chips wondering if it would be ok if she pinched one. She decided it would be better to wait until he was finished. It wouldn't do to look common. Thick, silky streams of piggy drool fell onto the chips.

Lucy wriggled her way around the corner all smiles and drooling sex. Price pretended to look for a cab to hide his revulsion.

'We can walk?' she said. 'Is it far?'

No.

They walked in silence, but her mind was babbling like a garrulous child. Images of sex flashed from her repertoire briefly into his mind before being replaced by another, then another. Her first time invaded him with a fiery pain, then the image of a cheeseburger with fries and a coke, next a snippet of some loud superhero movie.

With considerable effort Price closed himself to her but not before he caught a scream of questions from her convoluted consciousness: 'What, is it time? Am I making a mistake? Should I be afraid?'

He answered yes to them all.

*

Lucy was hungry. She could murder a portion of chips and possibly manage a couple of sausages, too. But food would have to wait. There was another hunger within her now. Tonight could be the night. He was big and strong and silent. He was a real man, not like those pretty boy footballers Clare was always dreaming of. If there was any man who could make her come, then she was walking next to him. She squeezed his arm and found it hard and muscular and wondered if he worked out. She wondered at the size of his penis. She hoped it wasn't too big; that could be a pain. Average was all she needed. That, and that he knew how to use it. She glanced up at him; strong jaw, the merest hint of stubble, and felt herself weaken. He lowered his head to share a smile and it answered all her questions. Yes, tonight would be the night.

*

'This is me,' I declared as we reached my front gate. She glanced at the house then back to me, smiling all the while. It astounded me how easy it had been. All the planning, the script meticulously researched, rehearsed and memorised, the lines baited and ready for casting, and none were required. She had no idea. Shame? A waste? All a matter of opinion in the end, really.

Opening the gate I ushered her through. A proper Gentleman.

The girl shivered on my doorstep and muttered something inconsequential about the weather. I smiled in agreement feeling like a redundant Cheshire Cat. Not long now before my facial muscles could enjoy a well-earned rest.

216

I opened the front door and once more displayed my impeccable upbringing by allowing her to enter first.

She had time enough to ask the location of the light switch before I smashed the hammer into the back of her skull.

Chapter Twenty-eight

Janine waited an hour after Price had said he was on his way before phoning him again. Twenty-five rings without answer and she had hung up, reasoning that he was in transit. Half an hour later she had tried again, counting the unanswered rings up to thirty before slamming the receiver down in disgust. It only took half an hour to walk and about ten minutes by cab so there was no reason why he shouldn't have arrived already (or at least none that sprung to mind). She wasn't worried for him. Christine had said he was sick, and he claimed to have spent the day at the doctors waiting for an appointment but for some reason Janine didn't swallow that. It was more likely that he was acting the big man by letting her wait, showing her who's boss. Janine had never taken to Price, there was something about him that she wasn't sure of. Recently she had re-evaluated that opinion; he was making more of an effort and Christine positively glowed whenever he was near or his name was mentioned in conversation. But his failure to show up when Christine needed him the most had forced her to revise her opinion of him again. Thank God Christine was out cold, she would be distraught if she knew he wasn't here.

As time crept on and there was still no sign of him or an answer at his place, she had phoned Roland to cancel their night out. Naturally he was disappointed, but there had been little complaint once she explained the circumstances. She had sketched the details for him deciding that the full picture wasn't really any of his business. He managed to fill in the blanks for himself, offering to come around and stay with her. She'd told him that it wasn't necessary and besides she doubted that Christine would have welcomed an unfamiliar face and it was hardly the most fitting of scenarios for an introduction. She could tell he wasn't very happy about her staying there alone, but she had assured him that she could look after herself and was planning on getting a big knife from the kitchen the moment she hung up.

She toyed with the idea of calling Liz, Christine's mother, but as Christine hadn't mentioned anything about Gary or the note when she had phoned earlier she had decided that Christine wouldn't have appreciated it. Instead she took a wickedly sharp meat cleaver from the kitchen - and a rolling pin for good measure - and settled down on the living room sofa allowing the vodka to drag her down into a heavy slumber.

She had awoken with a start, grimacing at the sourness in her mouth and checked the time. Her phone claimed it was two in the morning. She dialled Price again knowing that there would be no answer.

'What is he playing at?' she snarled. Missing the date with Roland and staying here wasn't the problem - she loved Chris and would do anything to help her - but explaining to her that her boyfriend couldn't be arsed to come and see her *was*. And one that she could do without. When that good for nothing bastard finally showed his face he was going to get an earful and no mistake.

A yawn became a stretch and she sat up. She was thirsty. Picking up the lemonade bottle she discovered it was empty and annoyed that she would have to go into the kitchen she threw it to the floor.

She didn't know why she glanced at the front door on her way to the kitchen and when she saw the small brown envelope on the mat, she wished she hadn't.

There was no doubt in her mind what the envelope contained.

After glancing up at the stairs to check Christine wasn't there, she picked it up. It was exactly as Christine had described; sealed with no address. Drawing a deep breath, she opened it.

I See YOU'VE iNvited A FRIEND tO OuR LITTLE PARTY
Good.

She stumbled backwards as the words knocked the breath from her, collapsing on the bottom stair as Christine had done when the first note had arrived. Her eyes fastened themselves to the front door half expecting it to burst open and Gary to rush in and hack her to pieces. With trembling hands, she read the note again.

Immediately she thought of Roland and felt foolish for seeing a man as her salvation. She wouldn't call him. How could she be his equal if she went running to him like a fainting forties film star every time trouble reared its head? No, she would deal with it herself. When the policeman returned with the information on Gary's whereabouts, she would take him to one side and show it to him. He wouldn't judge her; it was his job. The note was evidence and he needed to see it. It wasn't weakness on her part, she was merely fulfilling her duty to Christine as a friend and to the police as a citizen.

Placing the note back in the envelope she folded it once and put it in the breast pocket of her blouse. There was no need for Christine to know about it, the less she knew the better. The poor girl was already close to breaking point as it was, and this could topple her over the edge. Better for her to think that nothing happened. Let her rest.

Janine slipped soundlessly back into the living-room and sat upon the sofa once more, her fingers caressing the sharp blade of the cleaver.

Chapter Twenty-nine

There wasn't as much blood as I had anticipated. A blow to the base of the skull with a hammer, although the most effective manner in which to immobilise a victim, is hardly the most spectacular.

A single dull thud and she crumpled to the floor. The end.

She was lying face down, her left arm folded under her stomach, the other stretching out in front of her as though she were trying to reach something. Her skirt had lifted to reveal bare, firm buttocks separated by a red thong.

It is this that disturbs me the most.

When I was sixteen the girls I knew wore jeans and tracksuits and played rounders and sometimes football; they rode bikes or spent endless summer days roller-skating. This thing before me would have laughed at their innocent use of time and probably have done her utmost to corrupt them. 'Lighten up. It's the twenty first century!'

It's the new millennium and because of that it was perfectly acceptable for people to behave like animals? Girls barely out of puberty swallowing ecstasy and semen as readily as my generation swallowed sweets, giving birth between classes at school, reading magazines that twenty years ago would have only been available under the counter in Soho.

But I digress. After removing her clothing, I dragged her to the living room where everything was waiting. I lay her on her back in the closest approximation to the letter X as I could then secured her to the floor with leather belts. I nailed one end of the leather to the floor then stretched the leather snugly over her extremities, fixing the free end to the floor with another nail.

Once this was done, I screwed down either side as an extra precaution. This effectively simple method of restraint was employed on both wrists and upper arms, both ankles and knees. The straps across the forehead and stomach were not as satisfactory as I had hoped but I employed them all the same.

There was one moment where the girl gave the impression that she was gaining consciousness, so I stamped on her forehead a few times. I did so tentatively at first, until I remembered the line from The White Peacock *by* DH Lawrence; *'Be a good animal, true to your instincts' and soon I found myself stamping for all my worth.*

With some reluctance I curtailed my enjoyment - after all it wouldn't do to kill her just yet - and continued with the task at hand.

I began the purification process. Even when her genitals morphed into different shapes, I remained focused while removing her contaminated pubic hair. I saw Julie's thick pouting lips, then Christine's trim smile, the dry lifeless flesh that belonged to Pamela Bell, and the hungry, drooling mouth of Margaret Henderson.

I removed the eyebrows next, then the hair on her head. It was thick, naturally curly and as black as the mind upon which it sat.

The second stage of the purification process was less enjoyable. I poured the bleach into a bowl containing a sponge and stainless-steel wire wool. Snapping on the marigolds I soaked the sponge with the bleach and scrubbed her body liberally with the fluid, paying particular attention to the shaven areas.

This bleach will force the poison back into the body and allow me to work on her more delicate areas without risk of infection. It took twenty minutes of cleaning before I was certain the poison had retreated within her.

It was only then that I took the wire wool and scrubbed out her vagina.

There was considerable bleeding although I was relieved to see that it was red and not black. If it were black then I would be lost for certain and there would be nothing I could do about it. Ensuring that I had thoroughly disinfected the vaginal cavity up to the neck of the cervix I cleared away my things and retreated out of view and waited. Waited for the glorious awakening...

*

The first thing Lucy noticed was the stinging between her legs. It was hot and maddeningly itchy. The second thing she noticed was that she was naked, she could feel goose-bumps on her arms and legs. The third thing she noticed, and this was the most alarming of the three discoveries, was that she couldn't move.

She opened her eyes and was rewarded with a jolt of pain. She closed them again. What on earth had she been drinking last night? She hoped it wasn't brandy and coke. She always puked when she had that, and her mother would tan her hide if she puked anywhere other than the toilet, and then tan her hide for drinking.

She smacked her lips to try and locate an after taste. Her mouth was rough and dry. Why was she hurting down below? Whoever she'd shagged last night must have been hung like a donkey. She tried to sit up, but nothing happened. Was she paralysed?

Ignoring the pain, she peeled back her lids and stared at an unfamiliar ceiling. White and bare. Where the hell was she? A smell assailed her nostrils. Bleach?

Fear chilled and burned her at the same time. Oh my God, I'm in a hospital. I've had an accident and I'm paralysed and I can't move.

But that wasn't strictly true. She could feel her fingers moving, and she could lift her elbows slightly. What was going on? She moved her eyes to the left and saw her arm stretching out. When she looked to the right she saw the same. Waggling her fingers she was relieved to see them respond. But what was that on her wrist? A strap? She listened carefully as she tried to raise her arm. The strap creaked. Leather? Whatever it was, she was secured fast. If only she could see her legs. Are those floorboards I'm lying on? What is going on? A small spark of unease was suddenly fanned to a flame. Oh my God, that bloke I went back with he must have hit me and then tied me up.

'Help,' she croaked instinctively, unsure of who she was actually calling to.

A laugh. Somewhere behind her. She strained to move her head. 'Hello? Is anybody there?'

More laughter. Low. A snigger.

'Please...is there anybody there?'

'Please, is there anybody there?' mimicked a voice. High pitched. Almost childish. Then a snigger.

She screamed; a hoarse wail that failed to communicate her terror. She swallowed and tried again.

Stars danced before her eyes. A blow from something had cracked the side of her face.

'Any more of that and I'll sew your lips shut,' barked the voice.

'Who are you? Is that you, David? Where am I? What am I doing here? What do you want from me? Please-'

The voice made a prolonged shushing sound. 'So many questions, such an inquiring mind, but you failed to ask the most important question...'

'What?' she sobbed.

The owner of the voice towered over her, feet either side of her hips, and the thin alcohol smudged impression of the man whom she had gone home with fleshed out. He was naked. His penis dangled without life between his legs and somehow that alarmed her more than if it had been erect.

'Well, considering the type of society you and I are compelled to exist within, with its designer violence, recreational violence and let us not forget good old violence violence, I thought that would have been quite obvious?'

Lucy said nothing. Her mind was numbed and unresponsive. He offered her a ghastly smile. The kind of smile that meant you were in deep trouble. It reminded her of the deranged grin Jack Nicholson gave his wife in *The Shining*. Watching it, half drunk on cider, with her friends on TV, she hadn't been frightened. On the contrary she had laughed hysterically, joining in as her friends threw peanuts at the screen. It was over the top and stupid, they had all agreed. But now she understood the madness he was trying to communicate to her. It was a dangerous smile. Deadly. Only there were no friends to hide behind here. No opportunity to change the channel.

Price lay down on his side to her left, his head propped up on his right hand so that he was facing her. 'No?' he traced his fingers around her nipples, tweaked them gently then sucked them lovingly. 'I think the question you should be asking - and correct me if I'm incorrect - is how long have I got to live?' Her body stiffened beneath his lips.

'Personally, if the roles were reversed, that would be the first thing on my mind. I mean you might have thought that rape was my motive but - again correct me if I'm incorrect - I was under the impression that you were here for sex...so rape probably wouldn't have the desired effect. On my part at least. I took the liberty of shaving your rude bits, I do hope you will excuse that, but I had to clean you up a bit. Normally I would say something along the lines of 'because I don't know where you've been,' but the thing is, I do. Know where you've been, that is. It's quite alarming that a girl three months shy of her seventeenth birthday should have partaken in sexual congress with six men, don't you think? I see from your alarmed expression that you agree. It's such a shame, if you weren't a filthy whore you really would be most attractive. I mean that, really I do. But anal sex, tut-tut-tut Lucy; that really is too much to forgive. I'm relieved that I had the foresight to resist your siren song and prevent myself from becoming number seven.'

He stood up and disappeared from her limited view. He returned holding something black in his left hand, and a roll of grey tape in the other. The man stood astride her again, bending over her chest. 'Open wide,' he said.

She closed her lips tight when she realised it was a sock he was holding. There could only be one reason he would need her to be gagged.

'Open wide,' he repeated.

She tried to shake her head and succeeded in moving it a little.

Price sighed and pinched her nostrils shut. She opened her lips slightly, sucking in precious air through gritted teeth.

Price let go of her nose and sighed. 'It's entirely up to you,' he disappeared from view again. When he returned one hand was concealed behind his back. 'We can either do this the easy way,' he leaned forward and opened his mouth, then brought the sock up to his lips to demonstrate the simplicity of his request. 'Or we can do it the hard way.' He produced the hammer from behind his back. He weighed the sock and hammer in both hands. When the sock was highest, he said, 'easy?' When the hammer was highest, he said, 'hard?' He raised his eyebrows. 'Easy or hard, the choice is yours. Either way suits me. If you're worried about the sock, I can assure you it is clean. Now what is it to be?'

Lucy opened her mouth.

'Good girl,' he said, smiling that gruesome smile again, as he stuffed the sock into her mouth. She felt his fingers brush against her teeth and she toyed with the idea of biting them, crunching the bone and leaving the bastard with bloody stumps. But then what? She couldn't go anywhere, and he would more than likely beat her face in with the hammer for her trouble.

The sock was secured in place with a length of the grey tape. He patted the side of her cheek. 'There. Now that wasn't too difficult was it?'

He returned to his previous position at her side. 'Violence is such a terrible thing, don't you agree? In a lot of ways it's like sex. Nobody really wants to do it but there's this compulsion that is almost impossible to resist. Something I'm sure you know an awful lot about.' His face lit up. 'Yes, they *are* similar. Both are very messy and there's usually a great deal of cleaning up to do afterwards. Also, both activities, if things are done correctly, should leave the participants in a state of exhaustion and occasionally, and I mean occasionally, in a state of relaxation and possibly bliss. I've only experienced the latter a few time's myself and between you and me I find the whole sex thing intensely disappointing. So I think it'll be safe to assume that you won't be afforded the honour of my loving tonight.'

He pinched her breast, turning the pale flesh pink. Lucy struggled against her restraints. Price's expression clouded. 'Come to think of it, I think that what I've just said doesn't really bear up to a close examination. That's the problem with associative thinking. One minute it's there, the next...well, the next minute you're wondering how on earth you ever came to such a ridiculous conclusion.'

He kissed her nipple again, rolling his tongue around the erect flesh nipping it with his teeth. Lucy closed her eyes, hoping that if she imagined someone else doing it she wouldn't be sick. Mel Gibson from *Lethal Weapon* teased her nipples expertly, his long hair caressing her breasts as he moved about her. The fantasy was working and for a moment she was elsewhere; a penthouse in Malibu, the sounds of distant crashing waves lulling her to dreaming. Mel clamped her nipple firmly between his teeth then with a swift jerk of the head he tore it from the breast. Lucy screamed, the sock muffling the sound, and her body tried to thrash against the restraints. She scrunched her eyes against the pain, tears ran down the side of her face and into her ears. She heard Price spit and felt what could only be her nipple drop on her stomach.

'I expect that hurt considerably,' he said. 'I would explain my reasons behind it, but somehow I don't think you would understand.'

The voice faded. Now there was only the dancing pin-pricks of blinding white pain and the ringing in her ears. The whiteness flared as fresh agony ran through her and she screamed.

'A touch of seasoning,' Price said as he rubbed more salt into the bloody hole. 'Would the young lady care for some vinegar?'

No, please! But all she could do was scream and shake her head from side to side.

'Maybe later, then. You will let me know if you change your mind, won't you?'

Lucy felt his hands on her head and she froze, forcing her eyes open.

'Don't panic, little Lucy, I'm just removing the head strap. It wasn't as effective as I'd hoped. So rather than leave it there to remind me of my inexperience I have decided to remove it. There,' he held the strap of leather before her nose. 'Is that better?'

She nodded.

'Well, I'm glad to hear it.' He began to whip her stomach with the belt. It slapped against the soft flesh leaving thick red stripes. Lucy tried to relax her body, a distant voice telling her that a limp body was less likely to sustain injury, but it only increased the pain. Choking on her screams, all she wanted to do was rub her stomach to ease the maddening agony. Again and again Price brought the belt down, grunting with the effort. Then as suddenly as he had started, he stopped. Lucy heard him panting.

'I'm sorry about that,' he said, and Lucy found herself believing him. There was a sorrow in his voice totally at odds with his manic smile. If only he would take this gag off. She could talk to him, reason with him. She had seen enough films to know the type of man she was dealing with. He was probably abused as a child or had been treated badly by women and was taking it out on her. If only she could tell him that the world was on his side, that she was better than those that had hurt him. Then he would let her go and she would run. Run until she was a million miles away, until her feet bled and her lungs collapsed.

'I tend to get a bit carried away sometimes. Dreadful habit. Although I hope you can understand that it is not entirely my fault. I can only imagine what you must think of me; pervert, loony, psycho, sicko, etc. However, you must understand that sickness in the individual is an amplification of sickness in the system...or is that the other way around. I'm not sure. I can't even remember who said it.' He waved a dismissive hand. 'Anyway, that's beside the point. Sickness is in the eye of the beholder. I'm differently tuned, that's all. I see things in a different light to people like you. On a grander scale if you like. I realise that's a terribly portentous thing to say,' He gestured airily with his hand, 'but there it is.'

Lucy shook her head from side to side, raising it from the floor as far as she could, grunting and lowering her eyes down to her mouth in the hope that he would remove the sock and tape.

Price cupped his hand to his ear and leaned his head close to hers. 'What's that, Lassie? Timmy's fallen down a well and we should go and fetch him?'

Lucy began to cry, bubbling snot from her nostrils.

'Don't cry, Lassie,' moaned Price, his face contorted with mock anguish. 'Timmy had a good innings, he won't mind...' He stroked her bald head, 'There, there, don't worry.'

She called him a bastard.

He wagged a reprimanding finger. 'Now, now, Lassie. Remember that this is a U certificate. We can't go upsetting all the little kiddie-widdies, can we? That's my job. But listen to me babbling on and I haven't even told you why you're here. If you'll bear with me a moment while I fetch my cigarettes...'

He moved behind her again, her eyes strained to follow him, but it hurt so she gave up.

'It's a filthy habit as I'm sure you're aware, but we are all slaves to something,' he said still behind her. 'It just so happens that the dreaded weed is one of mine. I gave up once,' he settled alongside her sucking on a *Regal*, 'but soon found myself drawn to the sweet stench again. Some might cite that as a weakness. I, however, see it as an indication of a man who knows what he likes and is brave enough to throw caution to the wind and indulge. You see there are an awful lot of unhappy people in this world and I believe it is because they resist everything they enjoy. Women who refuse chocolate because it will make them fat even though it brings them pleasure, men eating salad instead of burger and chips to keep cholesterol levels down even though it is the sweaty beef they truly desire, or people who stop smoking or drinking for fear of premature death. This strikes me as odd, it always has, that a population forced to endure a miserable, hopeless existence should so readily surrender the few things that make that existence tolerable. And for what? To trudge the same path to work and back home again for another ten years, to bring another wailing mouth into the world and teach it to wail on the inside for the rest of its life because no-one will listen, to watch another twenty thousand episodes of their banal soaps, living life through the misfortune of others safe in the centrally heated knowledge that the same will never happen to them. And why will it never happen to them? Because they never set foot outside the house, that's why. How many people do you think there are in the world who have mistaken a conversation they have heard on television for one they had with a friend? Mmm? I've done it myself a few times and I doubt that I am the only one.'

He flicked ash absently onto Lucy's stomach. 'It's insidious. Every day the idiots are instructed how to do things; magazines tell them how to look, television tells them how to act. I expect that you are already trying to understand the type of man I am. Piecing together psychobabble from *Cracker* or *Seven* or *The Bill* and God knows what else to aid your comprehension of my mental state. Well let me assure you that not everybody who forces his opinion on the world subscribes to the neat Hollywood formula, leaving biblical references at the scene, or punishing those who adhere to the seven deadly sins.' More ash landed on Lucy's quivering stomach. 'Most are just average blokes who have had enough, bored with life and looking for something different. Granted some claim to hear the voice of God or have a genuine hatred of those they maim...but as I've said, people like me simply see things in a different light...wasn't that a song by *The Bangles?*' he asked taking a final drag on the cigarette, then putting it out in Lucy's navel. Price ignored her screams and listened to the crackling sound her flesh made as it burned. 'Now there's a bodily function I was previously unaware of. The built-in ashtray.' Price frowned. 'Stop whining!' he barked. 'If you don't cease that racket, I shall fetch the vinegar.'

Lucy managed to lower her scream to a shuddering whimper.

'Good. Now that I've discovered a practical use for you, I may delay your dispatch for a while. Until I become bored or you become full, whichever comes first. Then again there are other orifices which would do just as well...

'I can't really blame you for trying to find similarities in your current predicament with that of films and the like. After all, it's the only exposure one has with that sort of thing until one actually encounters it, and I do believe that if it is handled correctly it can be extremely effective, but there hasn't been such a portrayal for a considerable time, not since *The Vanishing* - and by that I am referring to the original Dutch version and not the happily ever after drivel with Keifer Sutherland. I did so enjoy serial killer films, but they've lost their edge. The makers of such films, in an attempt to outdo the previous year's drivel, think that by offering us more bodies and more elaborate modus operandi, we will leave the cinemas satisfied. They couldn't be further from the truth. You see it's not the graphic nature we crave -

and by 'we' I mean the enlightened and discerning patrons of the genre - nor is it a higher body count, but it is originality we crave. Yes, Joe Bloggs from Northampton may have killed thirty-three women, but if all he did was stab them a few times then it's hardly worth the effort. But the obverse dilemma is how to avoid making your art convoluted. I mean here I am ranting and raving about filmmakers incessantly trying to outdo each other and I am guilty of much the same thing myself. I mean, I ask you, what kind of psychopath does it take to hack out a woman's naughty bits and use it for a flower vase?

'And before you start, I am well aware that the mutilation and murder of women is nowadays considered trite, except of course if you're pretty. Then the tabloids will be falling over themselves to plaster your photograph over the front pages, along with headlines as subtle as GET THIS MONSTER and WHY? all that type of nonsense. *Why?* If that doesn't illustrate the ignorance of the press, then I don't know what does. *Why?* I'll tell you *why*, because the dirty little bitch was asking for it! That's *why*! I mean, for fuck's sake what are they on?

'Oh dear, there I go again,' Price giggled covering his mouth with the back of his fingers. 'Up on my soap box trying to put the world to rights, you really must inform me when I go off on tangents like that, but just allow me the courtesy of finishing what I was saying.' He took a deep breath. 'Granted if I was devoted to the mutilation of small boys or even heterosexual men, then that would probably be newsworthy. But that's not really my forte. There. I've finished, as my baby brother used to call when he'd done his business so mother could come and wipe his bottom-'

Price's eyes expanded to the size of dinner plates, his teeth shining like polished china. 'There. Do you see?' he exclaimed excitedly. 'I don't even have a brother. I probably picked up that memory second hand from some God-awful sitcom or 'poignant' family drama.' He sighed contentedly. 'Ah, the satisfaction of being proven correct.'

For reasons she couldn't understand, Lucy found herself relaxing. She was still frightened, but it wasn't the overwhelming breathless terror she had experienced upon gaining consciousness. It was almost as if an unknown part of her mind had already accepted the fact she was going to die. Part of her still clung to the hope that if she co-operated, he would let her go. She wouldn't tell. Not ever. She'd swear on the bible, her mother's life, her father's grave, anything that would persuade him to let her go.

'Now, if you'll excuse me for one moment...' said Price as he stood up.

Lucy heard him open a door, the door closing and then footsteps descending or ascending stairs. When the ceiling above her creaked she determined that she was downstairs, either in a cellar or on the ground floor of his house. She turned her head to the left. Drawn blue curtains, a fireplace, stripped walls ready for papering. A living room? Study?

Lucy tried to raise her left wrist. The leather creaked and groaned but refused to budge. She tried pulling her hand through the bond but was unable to summon enough strength. What if she stretched the leather? She twisted her wrists, the friction made her wrists burn, but she persevered hoping the heat would relax the leather.

At the sound of returning footsteps she froze.

'I see you've decided to stay for the festivities...excellent!' He dumped a holdall on the floor.

Price came to her side, winked, and lay a white towel beside her, smoothing it out with his hands. 'Working area,' he explained, then rummaged through the bag. Clinking sounds, metallic.

'Tools of the trade,' he announced and began neatly laying out objects on the towel. 'Stanley knife, tweezers, scissors, lighter, matches, stapler, drawing pins, hole puncher - I don't know why I brought that, but I'm sure we'll discover a use for it - razor blades...' He appraised the selection before him and after stealing a quick glance over to the door, said, 'Well, I think that's enough for starters. Right,' he clapped his hands together and rubbed them eagerly. 'Time to begin.'

Lucy screamed.

'Hush, now,' he said with surprising compassion. 'The quicker we get down to it then the quicker it will be over, okay? But first an explanation. This may wound your ego a little, but you are not the real focus of my hatred.' He held up his hands, 'I'm sorry to break it to you but this is what you would call a dry run. An opportunity to practice before I pay a visit to another special young - well, youngish - lady by the name of Julie. This lady holds a special place in my affections and when I call on her, I wish to create a lasting impression. Therefore, I must have some idea of what I'm doing. I mean, imagine how embarrassing it would be for all concerned if I turned up on her doorstep all ready to torture and maim and all I managed to do was cause her some minor discomfort. I'd be a laughingstock, wouldn't I? Of course I would. But with your help all that unpleasantness can be avoided. One moment.'

Price moved out of her line of sight and Lucy strained her ears to hear what he was doing. The sound of a plastic jar being unscrewed and the lid tossed to the floor, a rustle of something, possibly a sheet or clothing. 'I'm just getting into character, be with you in a tick,' he said.

He stepped into view, beaming a dazzling smile. His hair was slicked back tightly against his scalp with gel, and he was wearing a white chemists coat with three pens (blue, black and red) clipped to the pocket. Clutched to his chest proudly was a thick blue book, A4 size. 'Nice, isn't it?' he said, referring to the white coat. 'Lends me an air of respectability.' He leaned forward, looking furtively from left to right, then whispered, 'Between you and me I used to be an apprentice butcher many moons ago and this was my smock,' he winked and straightened. 'But try and see it as an indication of authority if you could.' Price cleared his throat and began speaking crisply: 'Excuse me madam, I'm conducting a survey on pain responses for a personal thesis and I was wondering if you could spare me a few moments of your time to take part...you would? Excellent, thank you.'

Price sat cross-legged behind the towel, opened the notebook on his lap, selected the black pen from his pocket and placed the top on the rear end. 'Name?' he paused a few moments before writing. 'L-u-c-y E-l-i-o-t. Address?' Another significant pause.

'One-oh-seven-D-u-g-d-a-l-e L-a-n-e. Liverpool!' He tapped the pen triumphantly against the paper.

How does he know my name and address?

'Now. To start with, Miss Eliot I would like to ask you a few questions. I have taken into account your inability to speak and let me assure you that it is not a problem. To answer yes simply close your right eye, answer no by closing your left eye. Okay? Good. Question one,' he cleared his throat and read from the book. 'Laid out before you are a number of household items that have been selected for the purpose of our survey. Could I ask you if there are any of these items that alarm you in any way?'

Lucy eyes remained open.

'I must warn you that failure to answer any of the questions I have will result in a forfeit,' he said earnestly.

Lucy closed her right eye. *Yes.*

'Splendid. Now I shall run through the list and I want you to tell me which of these objects in particular alarm you...Stanley knife.'

Yes.

'Tweezers.'

Yes.

'Scissors.'

Yes.

'Lighter.'

Yes.

'I hope you do not intend to answer in the affirmative for every item. That too can result in a forfeit.'

Lucy shook her head.

'*Answer yes or no!*' roared Price.

Lucy closed her left eye. A tear squeezed from under the lid.

'Lighter.'

She hesitated. What was the right answer? Did a positive mean that he would use them on her, or did it mean he would discard them as too obvious and experiment with the ones she gave a negative answer to? They all frightened her. However, if she answered half yes and half no then there was the possibility that he would discard some at least. She closed her right eye.

'Matches.'

No.

'Stapler.'

Yes.

'Drawing pins

No.

'Hole puncher.'

No.

'I think you're are absolutely right on that one. In striving for originality I failed to see what patently lacked any aura of menace. Razor blades.'

Yes.

'Thank you. Now there are a pre-determined set of responses to the next set of questions. For example, in a few moments I am going to perform a little exploratory surgery with one of the items laid out before me. This may cause you some discomfort or none at all or maybe it will be the worst pain you've ever experienced. At the moment I have no idea which item will do what exactly and that is where you come in. There are six possible responses for you to choose from: a) Excruciating, b) very painful, c) painful, d) mediocre, e) not painful, and f) I think you should come up with something better than that, Davie Boy. Considering your predicament I can understand your reluctance to respond with d, e and f. But let me assure you that I won't be offended if my efforts are deemed, how shall I say, lacklustre, and no forfeit will be administered. Understood?'

Lucy closed her right eye.

'Splendid!' He picked up one of the razor blades. 'To begin with I would like to stick with the obvious targets, forgive my predictability but one must master the basics before one can progress to the more elaborate areas. Therefore I intend to slice your remaining nipple off with this shiny sharp blade.' He shifted to his knees and leaned over her chest.

Lucy thrashed against her restraints, screaming and spluttering through her nose.

He paused. 'Interesting,' he said thoughtfully. 'Is it more effective if I let slip my intentions rather than go straight to it?'

Please, don't, she muffled.

'Never mind all that. Answer the question!'

She shook her head.

'*Answer yes or no!*'

She closed her left eye.

'Well, that's a bare faced lie if ever I saw one. Just for that I'll add a dash of vinegar to the wound.'

Fucking Bastard!

'Charming!' he said in an indignant Kenneth Williams' voice.

Price sat on Lucy's stomach facing her. Lucy felt the breath robbed from her lungs and her head grew hot with the strain. Price took her remaining nipple between finger and thumb and lifted, pulling the breast up from her chest creating a fleshy pyramid.

With his other hand he brought the blade horizontally below his fingers and began to saw through the flesh from left to right. As soon as the steel made contact Lucy started to buck wildly and Price was surprised at her strength, but he held firm until the nipple was severed. He dangled it before her eyes. 'Success!' he cried. 'Say hello to mister Nipple, little Lucy. He's come to visit.' He jammed it in his nostril.

Lucy passed out.

Price's face fell. 'The youth of today,' he sighed, 'no stamina.'

*

The telephone began to ring.

You know who that is.

'Yes,' said Price wearily.

What do you intend to do about it?

'I suppose I should go round...'

What about this one?

Price pinched the bridge of his nose and sighed. 'To be honest, it's not as much fun as I'd envisaged.'

Really? I was enjoying myself.

'I suppose it's because I'm eager to visit to Julie.'

Ah.

'This,' he nodded to Lucy, 'is all well and good but I'm finding it difficult to focus knowing that whore is still drawing breath.'

You mustn't let it distract you.

The phone continued to ring; its shrill call echoing through the house. 'Well the bloody phone going at all hours doesn't help.'

As if responding to his complaint the ringing ceased. The house suddenly felt utterly empty. 'What now?'

As I see it, we have several options: one, we kill the girl and go to see Christine; two, we leave the girl, go see Christine then resume our experimentation; or three, we ignore Christine and continue with our work.

Price remained silent for a while. 'I think we should kill the girl and go and see Christine...'

Are you sure?

'Not a hundred per cent, no, but I've lost my enthusiasm for this one and...'

...there's plenty more where she came from.

'Exactly! The streets are brimming with similar creatures, there is no need for me to dwell on her; one is very much like another.'

Except one.

'Yes,' said Price with a grave nod of the head.

Price turned as a low groan drifted to his ears. 'Sleeping Beauty awakes.'

Excellent. I think we should skin her alive.

'Not just yet. Watch me, I think you'll enjoy this. One thing, though: Are you quite sure the poison has been cleansed from her and there's no risk of infection?'

Quite sure.

'There's nothing at all I can do that will infect me?'

Except if you ate the heart.

'Good.' Price sauntered over to Lucy and knelt beside her head. 'Lucy,' he whispered softly.

Her lids flickered open and shut several times in quick succession. She flinched. Price hushed her. 'Don't be afraid, Lucy.' He hung his head, staring shamefaced at the floor. 'What can I say? I got a little carried away. I really didn't mean for things to go that far. You have to believe me.' He looked at her. 'Do you believe me?'

Lucy closed her right eye. *Yes.*

'Bless you, child there's no need for that,' he said endearingly, blushing slightly. 'I've treated you quite appallingly. It was my intention to teach you a lesson regarding promiscuity. It pained me to see one so young and beautiful and fresh reduce herself to a common whore, pardon my French. You have your whole life ahead of you, don't waste it in the embrace of those who don't respect you. Men are governed by their genitals, sad but true, and your ignorance to the fact that men saw you only as a vagina on legs was something I couldn't allow to continue unchecked. I hope you can understand that?'

Lucy nodded frantically.

A smile curved on Price's lips. 'I'm glad. No doubt this experience has, how shall we say, lowered your opinion of men considerably and I expect you won't be rushing into another sexual liaison for quite some time.'

Lucy nodded her agreement with such fervour Price felt she was in danger of breaking her neck.

Price halted her with a raised palm. 'But here's the problem...I want to let you go...'

Agitated muffled pleas.

'Calm down,' he soothed with a grin. 'I understand that you're excited. Bloody hell, I would be, but you must wait until I've finished, okay?'

More nods.

'As I said, I want to let you go, however, I'm a tad concerned that you will dash off to the nearest police station and tell them everything...'

Lucy shook her bald head violently from left to right *'I won't, I won't, I promise.'*

'That's all well and good, little Lucy,' his voice that of a patronising uncle. 'But I have only your word on that and as you are under considerable duress I would wager that you are likely to agree with anything I told you...'

Her head told him that she wouldn't.

'So, if I told you that black were really white and vice versa, you would tell me I was wrong?'

A nod.

'Really? That is refreshing; I've been worried sick ever since you passed out. When that happened I knew that I had gone too far, and I hope you will accept my sincere apologies.'

Another burst of nods.

'And before I let you go I shall attend to your wounds, we can't have you getting all infected. Explaining away your shaven head is, I'm afraid, less easy to remedy. The best I can come up with is that it's a teenage rebellion thing. Agreed?'

A sock full of affirmatives.

'And you'll tell no-one of our one-night stand?'

Lucy shook her head.

'Promise?'

Her 'yes' was surprisingly intelligible.

'Splendid!' He remained silent for a while, as he constructed his next sentence. 'Here's the catch,' he said darkly. He could almost hear her heart thrashing against her ribs. 'Unfortunately, I'm an arrogant man, and also a man that values his time. So, before I let you go, and don't fret for I shall release you, I have to ensure that you will carry this night with you forever.'

The beat picked up speed. Her eyes grew wide.

'As we concluded earlier you will be unlikely to leap into bed with another man for some time and, dare I venture, possibly may never do so again. If this is indeed the case, and this is where my insufferable arrogance comes into it, I would very much like to be the last man to ever use you for his own gratification. Therefore, with your permission of course, I would very much like to make love to you.'

Lucy nodded her consent after a few seconds of confusion.

'Thank you,' said Price. 'And when it is over, I shall honour my word and let you go.' He moved between her legs and slipped off his white smock. Lucy stared fearfully at him. 'Close your eyes, beautiful,' he whispered, and when he had he massaged himself to an erection and gently lowered himself into her. Her body warmed him and he released a grunt of pleasure. He felt her body stiffen but that only added to his delight, her muscles tightened on his penis as it moved. Already he could feel his climax and he slowed to delay his release and prolong her discomfort.

The burning between her legs reminded her of the time she lost her virginity. His name was Barry Adams. She had let Barry do it to her behind the youth club and even to this day she had no idea why; he wasn't much to look at, didn't wear the right kind of clothes and most people thought he was a bit of a weirdo. But he was besotted with her; always following her around asking her out and telling her how beautiful she was. It was difficult not to be flattered by his persistence and in a way she felt sorry for him. When he came, he cried. Looking at his flushed, blubbering face she wondered why she was unable to match his emotion; the only things she felt were soreness and relief that it was finally over.

'Lucy,' whispered Barry through the pain. 'Lucy?'

She opened her eyes and looked into Price's shining orbs.

'I lied,' was all he said.

She caught sight of the Stanley knife just before it opened up her throat.

Bravo! Bravissimo!

Price stood and bowed, his face alight with pride, his blushes lost beneath her blood.

Lucy twitched and gurgled.

Encore! Encore!

Price permitted himself a second bow. The applause was deafening. A small girl in the front row threw a single red rose. People stood on their seats, clapping frantically.

The fountain of blood began to lose height. Her twitching slowed.

'And for my next trick...' beamed Price.

Yes?

'I shall attempt to create something from this lifeless husk.'

What?

'Patience...all shall be revealed.'

An expectant hush descended over the theatre.

Chapter Thirty

Thoroughly bathed and refreshed, I stepped out into the crisp morning air.

As I walked down the path to the gate I felt as though I weighed nothing at all. It was as if a burden had been lifted from my shoulders. A cliché I know, but one that describes the sensation perfectly. The act of murder is an exceptionally liberating one; with a single clean slice of the knife one transcends the drudgery of everyday life and becomes something more significant. Who would believe something so simple could send you a step up the evolutionary ladder?

Man has long claimed to be at the top of the food chain (based entirely on his ability to create weapons of destruction that allow him to venture into other creature's domains unchallenged) but it is the man who kills another who is truly at the peak of that chain. People strive to label such men 'barbarians', 'thugs', 'scum' and most comically of all 'animals'.

What are we if not animals?

Yes, we are so very respectable now one can be arrested for urinating in the street, or we have amended our speech so the weakest rejects of 'our society' no longer feel oppressed or are reminded of their inadequacy. How proud we are that this insignificant majority, unable to protect their family and property have the 'law' on their side to condone their spinelessness and punish those strong enough to take from them what they desire...

I think not.

It always amuses me when I hear the declaration that we are living in a free world. If this is so, then why can I not choose to walk the streets without clothing, or sleep in the street? Why am I unable to decide that I shall build a home on the side of a mountain, without officious clerks and lawyers throwing pieces of paper in my face threatening imprisonment?

The only freedom is the freedom of thought and even this is not without external influence. Only those brave few who make their thoughts a reality without fear of consequence can dare claim to be alive.

As I approached Christine's house, I wondered how she would react to my recent personal growth. It would be foolish of me to expect her to react with anything but horror. But if she found my newfound zest for life appealing, I will ask her to join me.

Perhaps.

*

A black shape moved behind the glass of the door. As it drew closer Price could see that the slender form belonged to Janine. She pushed her face up to the glass.

Bolts were snapped back. The door swung angrily open.

'Where the fuck have you been?' Janine's words were hushed but the anger in her voice was unmistakable.

'Keep your hair on,' hissed Price.

Who does she think she is?

'Fuck knows.'

'What did you say?' snarled Janine.

Price pushed past her. 'Nothing that is any concern of yours.'

Janine closed the door quietly and swung round at Price, jabbing her finger at him. 'Just who the hell do you think you are? Christine's been in a dreadful state, crying and on the edge of her nerves. The poor cow waited up for you-'

'Well, I'm here now so what's the fucking problem?' he said over his shoulder as he walked into the kitchen and began making himself a cup of tea.

'What's the fucking problem?' She could hardly believe her ears. 'I'll tell you what the fucking problem is. The problem is that I've spent the whole night waiting up for you to show, phoning you and hoping to God that Christine didn't wake up and find out that you weren't here...'

'No-one asked you to. What do you want, a medal or something?'

'I stayed for Christine,' her voice was gaining volume. 'Have you any idea what it would do to her if she found out that you couldn't be arsed coming round to see her?'

Price shrugged. 'Don't tell her then.'

Janine was speechless. Each time she attempted to reply her anger and incredulity choked the words in her throat. 'Listen, you little prick. Let's get one thing straight; I've never liked you. You're not good enough for Christine and the first chance I get I shall be making my opinion of you quite clear.'

Blah, blah, blah.

Janine noticed Price's thin smile. 'I don't see what you've got to smile about.'

'Just listen to yourself blabbering on and you will.'

Snappy comeback.

Janine flushed with rage. 'If it wasn't for Christine, I'd smack you one right now.'

Price slammed his cup on the unit. 'Jesus Christ, woman, give it a rest. Anyone would think we were married...'

Janine snorted. 'I wouldn't marry you if you were the last man on Earth.'

'At the rate you get through men I wouldn't be surprised if I was the only man on Earth you hadn't shagged.'

Touché.

'Thank you.'

'You cheeky little shit!' Janine swung a slap at Price who stepped back, caught the blow and twisted her arm behind her back, drawing her body to his.

Price licked the side of her neck in a long slow manner. 'But if you like we could get to know one another.'

Janine stamped down on Price's foot and tried to break free. Price yelped but held her firm, grabbing her hair with his free hand.

'Let me go you twat!' She dug her nails into the hand that gripped her hair.

Price sighed. 'I really didn't want to kill anyone else today. Too much of a good thing and all that...but you're like a broken record...'

Hear, hear.

'...and if I have to listen to your nasal whine of a voice for one second longer, I'm afraid my ears will start to bleed.'

Price shuffled an awkward waltz with Janine over to the wall.

'Janine this is Wall, Wall this is Janine,' said Price and smashed her head against it. Her body buckled but remained upright. Janine pushed against the wall with her free hand, preventing Price from doing it again.

With a growl he swung her to the left; her nine stone build unable to provide any resistance and smashed her into the refrigerator. Dazed, her knees gave way and she fell limp in his grasp. Undeterred he dragged her back to the wall and thumped her head against it again. As he pulled back her head for a third strike, he noticed a smudge of red on the beige wall. 'One for luck.'

When her head hit the wall, he felt the fight slip from her body and let her to drop to the floor. Price spat on her and delivered a vicious kick to her ribs. 'All you had to do was mind your own business, that's all. I think there's a lesson for us all there, don't you agree?'

I would say so.

'I knew you would...Now, how shall we rid ourselves of this tiresome female? Your choice.'

Evisceration.

'Under normal circumstances I would concur. However, I have to say hello to Christine and I think that wearing her best friend's guts on my sleeve would be a little insensitive.'

Er...just stab her then.

'Any particular area?'

I've heard that a knife wound to the anus is quite a horrific way to die.

'Anus it is then.' Price appraised the selection of steak knives hanging on the wall beside the microwave.

Make sure it's a long one.

'I know, I know. How about this?' He held the knife up before his eyes; the fluorescent lighting glinted on the blade.

Perfect.

Crouching down, Price rolled Janine on her stomach, and then hoisted her skirt up over her hips, revealing black panties. She moaned. A blow to her temple with the knife handle silenced her. 'Do you think we should gag her?'

Superb idea. If I remember rightly there should be some masking tape in the third drawer down under the sink.

Price investigated. 'So there is! What would I do without you?'

Stop, you're making me blush.

Price wrapped the tape three times around her head then bound her ankles and wrists together. 'Not exactly a hundred percent secure but it will suffice.'

Using the knife he slashed open her underwear.

Ugh!

Price laughed. 'I see she's got the painters in. Well,' he remarked as he examined the blade, 'Let's see if we can give her something to take her mind off it, shall we?' He straddled her legs and opened her buttocks with the thumb and forefinger of his left hand. He lined up the knife, the tip of which touched her rectal opening.

With a swift powerful jerk of his shoulders he plunged the knife deep into her body. Janine stiffened, her limbs taut with agony, and she unleashed a scream that seemed to go on forever. There wasn't as much blood as his fantasy with Christine had suggested (there never was, he concluded), only a steady, but disappointing, seeping of red from between her clenched buttocks.

Eventually her scream juddered to a soft gasping as her life twitched away.

'What's with all this twitching business? That's all they seem to do,' He pranced about the kitchen mimicking Janine's death throes. 'Twitch, twitch, twitch.'

Stop it! You're killing me! Laughed the voice in his head

Price jerked his way in circles around Janine's dying light. 'Twitch, twitch, twitch.'

His enthusiasm waned and he landed a kick to her ribs. 'For fuck's sake woman try and do something more original!'

The twitching continued. 'Can you hear me? Not so fucking cocky now, are you? Well, what have you got to say for yourself?' He cupped his hand to his ear. 'Nothing? Talk about breaking the habit of a lifetime.'

Price gripped the knife handle and began to twist. 'Perhaps if I do this, you might think of something to say.'

Janine squealed.

'Goodness!' exclaimed Price, grinning. 'It's one of the sows from the *Inferno*. Maybe if we sliced off some of her rump we could have a fry up. I'm quite sure Chris will have some eggs in the fridge.'

His smile was lost in a snarl, teeth clenched and burning with hot drool. He pushed the knife further into her body, spittle spraying from his tight lips. 'You really have no idea how much I despise you, do you? The way you swan around thinking that you are so much better than everyone else. Is this what the emancipation of women was all about? Mmm? All those women fighting and dying for equality just so you can run around rubbing your crotch against the biggest dick you can find. Do you honestly believe that Mary Wollstonecraft and Emily Pankhurst would be pleased with the monsters they have created? If they could only see what women have become...'

Price removed the knife from her anus, as it came free it made a loud sucking sound. He sniffed the blade cautiously; a pungent mixture of copper and faeces. He wrinkled his nose in disgust. 'I always thought the whole point of equality was that although women were capable of acting as sexually indiscriminate as men they considered themselves above such triviality. It appears I was wrong...'

He slammed the knife between her shoulder blades. Janine fell limp.

Price stared at her back, fascinated by the widening circle of blood. 'I think I've broken her,' he said like a guilty school-boy.

Shame.

'What now?' he asked, eyebrows raised.

Christine?

'Ah, yes. The delectable Christine...'

Price went upstairs.

Chapter Thirty-one

Room 14a at Eastern Road Police Station was reserved for major investigations. It was large enough to seat twelve people around two small rectangular desks that up until yesterday had been gathering dust. Today, every inch of their surface was covered with papers and files, ashtrays filled with chewing gum and plastic cups of congealed coffee and tea. Slumped on top of these items was a sleeping DC Jay who, after successfully obtaining the overtime, had spent the previous thirteen hours in the room reading and re-reading the files of local sex offenders in between answering calls to the hotline. Opposite him, also sleeping was DC Mills. Mills was in his late thirties and losing the battle against baldness. He had grown a moustache in an attempt to pull eyes away from his shiny dome. It only accentuated his lack of hair.

The stench of sweat and sly overtime fags caught the back of Darrow's throat as he opened the door. He swallowed down a cough and reached for his spearmints and popped two. After staring at the snoring men for a few moments he slammed the door behind him. Jay snapped his head up, wiped drool from his chin and the file he had been using as a pillow, and bid the Detective Inspector a good morning. Mills remained undisturbed. Jay gave him a nudge.

'W-what?' Mills took in Darrow's displeased expression. 'Oh, sorry, Sir.'

Darrow ignored his stammering apology and asked Jay if there was anything he should know.

Jay stifled a yawn. 'We've had twenty calls from people who saw Bell at the club, but no-one saw our man with her...and no-one saw her after one o'clock. So far none of the men you mentioned in your statement have come forward.'

Darrow removed his trench coat, hung it beside the door and sat down between the two constables, crunching his mints noisily. He wrinkled his nose at the ashtray to his right and pushed it behind a mountain of files. 'Anyone who knew her call?'

DC Mills answered. 'If they did, they didn't say. The majority of callers were women, and they seemed more concerned with asking us if they should stop going to night-clubs. Apparently, a young girl was assaulted on her way home from the club on Cotton road on Tuesday night. *The Echo* picked up on it and linked it with the Bell murder.'

Darrow groaned. 'That's all we need. Did you know about this?' he asked Jay.

He nodded.

'And you didn't think to call me?'

'Er...'

'Never mind,' snapped the Inspector. 'This assault, who's on it?'

'Rawlins and Parr answered the call, Sir,' replied Mills.

'Have you spoken to them?' he asked the two men.

Blank faces. Did he have to do everything himself? He stood; his displeasure clear. 'You,' he pointed angrily at Jay, 'Get hold of DI Townsend for me and ask him what's going on with Jennings.' He scribbled the number on a scrap of paper, and then turned to DC Mills. 'And you...tidy up this pig sty.'

'I'm due off in a minute,' protested the constable.

'You can go when I say you can go.'

Darrow slammed the door behind him.

Jay sneered at Mills. 'I told you we should have phoned him.'

*

Darrow caught up with WPC Parr just as she was leaving the building.

'Kate, can I have a word?'

Parr turned to the Inspector and disguised her tiredness with a broad smile. 'Certainly, Sir,' she said pleasantly. Darrow appraised the woman before him with an approving eye. Out of uniform her features lost some of the severity it lent her, the smile on her lips seeming more inviting than any he received whilst on duty, but she was still a formidable sight. Six-foot-tall but every aspect of her was toned and in proportion.

'It won't take a moment,' Darrow assured her as he directed her back into the station. 'Tell me about this assault on Cotton road.'

'Cotton road...' Parr searched for the memory.

'On Tuesday,' prompted Darrow.

The penny dropped. 'Oh, right. Susan Lally. She was on her way home from Cotton Road, but the assault actually took place in the Maldern Estate.'

'Did you pick anyone up?'

Parr shook her head. 'The girl's father was certain that her boyfriend was responsible, but he was still in the club at the time of the assault. When we called on him, he was in bed with another girl.'

'Nice,' he commented coldly.

'We questioned the doormen and his story checks out.'

'Did Lally give you a description?'

'Not really. Male, IC One, about six foot four, no accent, knew her name...'

Darrow nodded thoughtfully. 'Have you read the brief on the Bell murder?'

Parr said that she had.

'What do you think?'

About what?'

'Do you think that it could be the same man?'

Parr considered this. 'It's possible I suppose...but we don't know enough about either to compare.'

'Well, the *Echo* thinks they do. They linked the two incidents and already clubbers are beginning to get worried.'

'I could call round tomorrow; see if she's remembered anything new...'

'That won't be necessary, Kate. Thank you for your time.'

'Good night, Sir.' she said before she left.

Darrow nodded and watched her walk into the early morning sunlight and wondered if there was anyone waiting to share her bed.

Chapter Thirty-two

Price pressed his ear against the door of Christine's bedroom and held his breath. She was snoring like a piggy.

That'll be the drink.

'No,' whispered Price. 'She's lying on her back again, I can tell. I've lost count of how many times I've had to turn her over in the middle of the night.'

Do you remember that time you held her nose and covered her mouth until she couldn't breathe?

Price suppressed a giggle. 'I do.'

Will we be treated to a repeat performance? Perhaps with a less happy ending?

'Who can tell? I shall do what the situation dictates.'

That's what I like about you...such an open mind.

Price opened the door and sneaked a look. Through the gloom he saw the duvet on the Queen-sized bed rise and fall steadily. The smell of stale booze, bad breath and a night of flatulence crept into his nostrils.

What a stink!

'Shhhh.'

Don't be a pillock. She can't hear me.

'Sorry,' breathed Price. 'I forgot.'

He stepped into the room and closed the door gently behind him, holding the handle down until the door was in place then slowly allowing it to lift.

Stealthily he moved to the vacant side of her bed and began to undress. As he bent down to untie his Caterpillar boots the snoring stopped. He froze, his breath catching in his lungs, as she mumbled and turned on her side. Only when her rhythmic breathing resumed did he release his breath in a long trembling exhalation.

That was close.

Price nodded and smuggled himself under the duvet. Even without physical contact he could feel the heat from her body. It was inviting; irresistible, and he shifted himself onto his side and shaped his body to hers, sighing at the sensation of skin on skin. The stale odours of the room were replaced by the sweet scent of her perfume and the intoxicating aroma of her body. His erection pressed against the soft flesh of her buttocks. God, how he ached for her. Everything seemed so perfect when she was near.

Steady now.

Price ignored the voice and ran his hand over the smooth curve of her hip and down onto her stomach, enjoying the movement of her breathing. She seemed so much more real than anyone else he knew. Shuffling down he manoeuvred his penis between her buttocks and pushed gently. There was a brief moment of dry pain before he gained entry to the moist pleasure within. He forced himself deeper, opening her, desperate to bury himself further. As he moved he heard the air push from her in time with his own subdued grunts. Gradually her body capitulated to his invasion and his thrusts met with less and less obstruction until the object of his desire was as slick as if she were awake and consenting. He increased his speed, gripping her hip for purchase, his grunting becoming louder and less restrained. His fingers dug themselves into her flesh, preparing for his climax, and when he came he almost called out. It was so much more than ejaculation; it was a release.

He withdrew and rolled on to his back, his body trembling. If he were to stand, he knew his legs would fail him. He was drained. Unusually so. Had he really needed her so much? He supposed that he had.

I'm sorry to interrupt this wonderfully poignant moment but I feel I should remind you that the corpse of her best friend is slowly decomposing in the kitchen.

'And?'

And I don't think that we have the time for this.

'I'm thinking.'

No you're not. The only image I can determine is a man drowning in his own sentimentality.

'Give it a rest.'

I will when we are far from here.

'Okay, okay.'

Wake her up.

'I intend to,' complained Price, rapidly losing patience with his internal critic. He lightly pushed her hip. No response.

He shook her more forcefully. A low moan of displeasure. He shook her again. Another moan followed by a barely intelligible complaint.

He whispered her name in her ear. Again.

Her head jerked to face him, her eyes wide and bloodshot. Price thought he saw the fading clouds of a dream in their grey but before he had a chance to comment she threw her arms around him and hugged him hard enough to squeeze the air from his lungs. She was crying. He tried to say something comforting but only succeeded in choking on a mouthful of tangled hair. With a cough he drew away.

At her tearful and wounded eyes, he said, 'There's nothing to be afraid of, I'm here. I won't let anything happen to you.'

'Where have you been?' She sounded like a petulant child.

He answered her question like a weary parent. 'I've already told you, at the doctors...'

'I was so frightened...'

'Well, there's no need for you to be any longer,' he interrupted, hoping it would signify the end of the matter. 'I've been here all night and there was nothing to worry about.'

'All night?'

'Yes.'

Christine yawned. 'What time is it?'

'Morning.'

'And you've been here all night?'

He couldn't understand her suspicion. 'Well, not here in this bed but in the house, yes. I spent a couple of hours talking to Janine...'

She groaned. 'Oh God, Janine. I was such a pain in the arse last night.' She made to sit up; Price pushed her gently back on the bed.

'I sent her home.'

'Oh.'

'How much did you drink?'

'I have absolutely no idea...' she said, massaging her temples, '...but judging by the pain in my head I would say a lot more than I should have.'

Price kissed her forehead. 'Poor baby.'

I think I'm going to retch.

Price chose not to respond. Instead he pulled a loose strand of hair from her eyes and told her that he loved her.

'I love you, too,' declared her sparkling smile.

A lengthy, relaxed silence followed.

It was Price who brought it to an end. 'Can I ask you something?'

'Sure.'

'What would you say if I asked you to live with me?'

Christine, who had braced herself for a barrage of questions about the note, was momentarily taken aback. 'Move into your place, you mean?'

'No. Get somewhere together. A new home that we could call our own. Somewhere outside of Liverpool...'

She looked into his eyes to see if he was serious; it took less than a second to see that he was. 'Outside of Liverpool?'

Didn't you just say that?

Price nodded to them both.

She frowned. 'Where?'

'I don't know. Anywhere. Just as long as it's far away from here. I can easily get a transfer-'

Christine sat up; her frown more pronounced. 'That's okay for you but it's not as easy for me. It would mean me giving up my job and trying to find another, which might take some time. And there's my family and friends...'

What's left of them.

'...you can't expect me to drop everything just like that.'

He took her hand in his. 'Look, Chrissy. I've never felt about anybody the way I feel about you, I've not even come close. Whenever I'm with you everything is perfect...but this city holds too many bad memories for me, it's choking the life from me. There are days when I can't even face getting out of bed and going to work. The filth, the streets crammed with the walking dead, the same grey faces, the same diseased places.'

'What are you talking about?'

See how she fails to understand?

'Don't you ever feel that way?' he asked, his eyes searching hers for agreement.

There was none. 'What way? I'm sorry David but I have no idea what you're talking about.'

'It's everywhere. The world is suffocating on promiscuity; children are singing songs that ten years ago wouldn't have obtained air-play on the radio, dressing like common whores-'

'David, you're scaring me.'

He gripped her arm, his eyes wide and feral. 'But don't you see? That's the first step to solving the problem.'

Christine pulled her arm free and left the bed. Price noticed his semen dribbling down the back of her leg. His penis twitched.

'Where are you going?' asked Price.

'To the toilet, if that's all right with you?' she replied.

'Come back to bed,' he requested with a smile and patted the rapidly cooling area of the bed she had just vacated. 'I want you.'

'Judging by the stuff dripping down my thighs I would say you've already had me,' she responded sardonically. 'Now, if you don't mind I would very much like to clean myself up.'

'Whatever.' Price watched her stride out the room, his face displaying his disappointment more successfully than his words ever could. He began to dress.

You're a fool if you think she will go with you.

'I don't recall asking for your opinion,' he said, buttoning his jeans.

Tough. This is not just a bad idea, it's a terrible idea. So she loves you, that's wonderful, but you are forgetting the most important factor...

'Which is?'

She's a woman. And by her very nature she is perfidious, insalubrious, duplicitous and every other pejorative adjective that ends in ous. You cannot rely on her and you certainly cannot trust her to understand your recent flourishing. Besides, is there really room in your life for a partner? The key to your success is freedom of movement and she will only restrict that freedom. If you're honest with yourself you will realise that the only thing she can offer you is a good fuck, that's all.

I allowed you to fool yourself up until now because it was making you happy and wasn't interfering with our work. But what you are suggesting is madness. If being in love means that much to you then I'll arrange for the worms to make the woman of your choice fall head over heels for you. Christine is ridiculously easy to replace.

'I suppose you are right.'

Of course I'm right.

A scream from the kitchen tore its way through the house and up to the bedroom.

Price jumped. 'What the-'

I think she's found Janine.

Chapter Thirty-three

When Darrow returned to the incident room he found Jay on the telephone and Mills beaming expectantly at him. The room smelled better, the windows having been opened and the ashtrays emptied.

'On your way,' he said gruffly to Mills and sat in the seat the constable speedily vacated. He opened the report on the Lally assault.

Mills deliberated at the door, unsure if 'Good morning' could be used as a farewell.

Darrow absently waved him away, more interested in the fact that Jay was bringing his telephone conversation to a close. When he replaced the receiver, Darrow raised his eyebrows to the constable.

'I don't know whether this is good news or not, Sir...'

Darrow silently seethed at the delay.

'...But DI Townsend says that Jennings hung himself in prison three months into his sentence.'

Darrow sighed. 'Never an easy path...'

'Sir?'

'Nothing.' He tossed the Lally file over to his colleague. 'Do you think that could be our man?'

Jay refrained from replying, not wanting to give an unqualified opinion which would inevitably provoke a scathing response.

'Well?' prompted Darrow as he fumbled in his pockets for his mints. They were all empty.

'I would say it wasn't our man.'

'Why?' asked Darrow, trying to remember if the canteen still sold his preferred brand of mints.

'It's a completely different MO. There's no evidence of sexual molestation or anything to link it with the Bell murder.'

'You're right, of course, but I can't shake the feeling that they're the same man.'

'Why?'

The Inspector shrugged 'I think it's what police dramas class as a gut instinct. Although,' he admitted, 'it's probably not the case here.'

Jay looked at his superior and thought that he looked almost disappointed with himself that he had even mentioned it. Darrow prided himself on the methodical accumulation of data before engaging in speculation. However, over the short length of time he had worked with the Inspector he had already come to trust his theories more readily than he did anyone else's facts.

'It's possible...' ventured Jay.

'Go on,' encouraged Darrow.

Jay cleared his throat. 'He could have intended to take her back with him and perform the same ritual as he did with Bell and decided against it. Maybe he was disturbed.'

'Which means?'

Jay's expression changed from one of thought to one of realisation. 'Somebody might have seen him!'

'Exactly,' said Darrow rising from his chair. 'Right. We'll pay a visit to Lally and ask her if she saw anyone else about on the night she was attacked. On the way we'll call in and tell McNeil the news about Jennings, although I doubt she'll be too thrilled.' He shrugged himself into his trench-coat. 'But first...I need some mints.'

Chapter Thirty-four

Christine was still screaming when he reached the kitchen. He stood on the threshold incredulous; was this the woman whom he had believed was the answer to his pain only moments ago? She struck him as a ridiculous figure; naked, breasts wobbling, hands clawing at her cheeks, eyes boggling like that insufferable Macauly Culkin on the *Home Alone* posters. Gone was the strong feminine creature with her grey inscrutable eyes. All that remained was a woman; weak, corrupt and lacking the capacity to comprehend the work of art before her.

Price stuck his fingers in his ears. 'For heaven's sake be quiet, woman. It's only Janine!' he shouted above her grief.

The screaming stopped and bloated, watery eyes turned in alarm toward him. He heard the rusted cogs of her mind working to understand his words. Price waited patiently while she grappled with what had happened.

In an attempt to alleviate his growing boredom he decided to emulate her expression; he dropped his jaw, opened his eyes wide and clapped his hands to his cheeks and squealed in a strident feminine voice, 'Oh dear Lord, who could do such a thing?'

Christine didn't appear to notice his lack of concern and pointed with a shaking hand to the bloody mess that was once her friend. 'G-Gary.'

'What?' said Price in disbelief. 'Gary?'

Christine's ashen face forced a nod.

'Correct me if I'm incorrect, but I think you'll find that's Janine,' he said sarcastically.

'Gary,' she repeated. 'He's killed her.'

Price shook his head. 'Guess again.'

The cogs almost ground to a halt and her eyes became greyer that ever. 'I-I don't understand.'

Price looked heavenwards, his lips pursed impatiently. 'I said,' he enunciated his words slowly as if he were talking to a dim child, 'Guess again.'

'I don't understand.' She was shivering now, and all the colour had drained from her skin.

'It's quite simple,' he said with a sigh. 'Janine dead, Gary no kill...now is that so difficult to understand?'

Dead eyes stared, unblinking.

'It was me!' he shouted, tired of her blank expression. 'I tied her up and stabbed her in the arse!'

His admission received absolutely no reaction. He leaned forward searching for a flicker of understanding; a narrowing of the eyes, a twitch of the cheek, an involuntary swallowing. Nothing.

He pinched the bridge of his nose wearily. 'This was not how I had imagined it would unfold. I can't tell you how disappointed I am, really I can't.' He stepped towards her and gripped her upper arms, they were cold to the touch. When she failed to register his presence, he gave her a shake.

'Earth calling Christine, Earth calling Christine. Come in Christine.'

He succeeded in provoking a faint frown.

'I...killed...Janine...I...stabbed...her...in...the...arse... with...a...big...knife.'

Her eyes narrowed almost imperceptibly. 'I-'

'If you say I don't understand, I swear I'll kill you where you stand.'

'I-I...I-'

'Spit it out, lover.'

'Janine.' She uttered her friend's name in a delicate moan.

'A sign of life at long last. Are you finally with us?'

She didn't respond.

'I'll tell you what we'll do,' he said, putting an arm around her shoulders and leading her to a chair. 'We'll take you through it. Think of it as an explanation in pictures. Like a movie. You like going to the cinema, don't you?'

She gave a little nod.

'Splendid. First a confession.' He made the sign of the cross. 'Bless me father for I have sinned; it has been...a long time since my last confession.'

Continue, my son.

Price fell to his knees, his hands clasped before him in a penitent gesture. 'I don't know where to begin, Father.'

Begin at the beginning, my child.

'That would take forever,' he said with a wicked grin.

Then you must start where you feel is most appropriate.

He closed his eyes and bowed his head. 'My girlfriend Christine, Father. I sent her a...bad letter.'

In what way?

'Spelling, punctuation,' he choked on his own mirth. 'It was painful to read.'

Is that all?

'Not quite,' he opened one eye and kept it on Christine who was lost in a world known only to her. 'I said I was coming to rip out her cunt, Father.'

Go on.

'And then I slaughtered her best friend...'

Was it in a manner fitting her moral corruption?

'Oh yes, father. I shoved a steak knife up her anus.'

Then as far as I am concerned there is no sin to confess. Go in peace, my child. But if it worries you that much just ask for forgiveness on your death bed, that usually does the trick.

'Thank you, Father. I will.' He rose to his full height and examined Christine for any indication of life. 'There's nobody home.'

Try knocking on the door.

'Good idea,' he said and slapped her face hard enough to cause his palm to sting. A moment later a red impression of his palm appeared on her cheek. Nothing. He pushed her knees apart and groped her crotch, clawing at her labia. Her eyes continued to stare blankly ahead. He forced his fingers roughly inside her, digging his nails into her softest flesh. Still nothing.

He removed his hand, wiped her moistness on her thigh and sighed with frustration. 'This is boring.'

I couldn't agree more.

He shrugged and further articulated his bafflement by waving his hands airily. 'I'm at a loss.'

I hope you realise that she must be dealt with.

Price fell silent for a while. 'Yes,' he said finally.

May I select the method of dispatch?

'No.' he said firmly. 'I am well aware that her feelings for me disgust you. But that doesn't alter the fact that I care for her a great deal.'

I really can't keep up with you. One minute you're all slushy, the next you're slapping her in the face, then you're all slushy again.

'Back off,' he growled. 'You have no idea how I feel.'

But that's the point. I know exactly how you feel. Think of it logically, if you let her live then sooner or later she will tell them you are responsible for the death of her promiscuous friend. But if you kill her, your anonymity is assured and there is the added bonus of saving her from the despondency years ahead. Think about it. If you let her live what has she to look forward to? Prostituting herself to men in search of the happiness we brought to her. Is that what you want for her? Is it? Hmm?

He closed his mind to the voice and examined the vacant husk slumped in the chair and knew nothing at all. All of his convictions, all the things he had witnessed were of little comfort to him now. He had robbed her of everything. *It's not your fault,* the voice in his head said softly.

'It isn't?' mumbled Price distantly.

Of course it isn't. All of this was thrust upon you by another.

'Who?'

Julie.

The name cut through his introspection with startling severity. Then there was no longer sorrow and regret, only anger and fatigue. He felt his hands clench into a fist and his knuckles crack under the strain. His origins were staggeringly clear, Julie. Without the pain she had brought to him he would not be here now; would not have become the man he was. A smile curled on his lips. So, something good had grown from bad soil after all.

And it is only polite that you should extend your thanks...

'And so I shall,' he said pulling the knife from Janine's back and wiping it clean on her hair. 'But first let us do something that will require us to be especially grateful.'

Rubbing his chin thoughtfully, he considered his options. After a few moments a decision was reached. He tucked the knife underneath his armpit and spread Christine's legs.

*

Darrow, sucking his recently purchased mints contentedly, pulled up outside Christine's front garden and turned off the engine. He wasn't looking forward to this. MacNeil had convinced herself that her ex, Jennings, was responsible for the note and experience told him that she was unlikely to react well when he told her that this was not the case. The last thing he needed was to waste a morning comforting a hysterical woman, especially now that he had found a new line of enquiry (admittedly a tenuous one). He was itching to see where it would lead him and even the steady grinding of the spearmints beneath his teeth failed to alleviate his anticipation.

'Stay here,' he instructed Constable Jay who turned to the Inspector expecting him to issue further instructions. He didn't and was half-way up the garden path before Jay replied his understanding.

*

Price delayed his killing blow, momentarily distracted by the sight of her vagina and the memory of how good it felt to be inside there. He marvelled at how something so simple could purge him of his mental grime.

What are you waiting for?

There was a loud knock at the door.

Price snapped his head to the direction of the sound, snatching the knife away from her genitals as he did.

See who it is.

Price moved to the kitchen door and, after getting down on all fours, peered around the door frame. Through the glass of the front door he distinguished a large shape of a man. The man's hands cupped his eyes and tried to see through the glass. A grey suit jacket, white shirt and grey tie pressed themselves against the door and Price quickly withdrew his head.

'I think it's the police,' he breathed.

You idiot! I warned you not to send those notes.

'I thought it would be a laugh. How was I to know the silly bitch would run crying to the police?'

There was a squeak as the letter box was opened. 'Miss MacNeil? It's Detective Inspector Darrow!'

Quick! Kill the slut and get out the back door! Now!

Price clambered to his feet and grabbed a handful of Christine's hair, lifting up her head to expose her pale neck.

Dead eyes rolled up to face him.

In one fluid and determined motion he opened up her throat.

He continued to hold her head, oblivious to the blood as it jetted over his shirt and face, utterly absorbed in her fading light.

Move it!

He released his hold and Christine's head slumped down to her chest and she slipped from the chair sprawling untidily on the linoleum. The knife fell from his hand and landed silently and unnoticed on Christine's back.

'Forgive me,' he said softly.

He ran to the door.

*

Darrow banged on the door one final time and waited to the count of ten. There was nobody home. She must have taken his advice and stayed with her boyfriend. He would call back later. He had taken three steps towards the front gate when he stopped. Something was bothering him. Nothing in particular just a general sense of disquiet. He signalled to Jay that he was looking around the back. Jay exited the car and took up position by the front gate.

*

Price landed on the other side of the garden wall at the same moment Darrow opened the back gate. Adrenaline pumping Darrow tensed when he found the kitchen door ajar and swinging slightly. Someone had only just left. Immediately the Inspector's eyes flashed to the six-foot wall at the rear of the garden. He was about to investigate further when instinct told him to check the house.

He saw a naked female body lying face down on the floor, a rapidly increasing pool of red spreading from underneath her head. Without hesitation he ran into the kitchen and in his haste almost tripped over Janine. He steadied himself and automatically felt her neck for a pulse even though his experience told him he wouldn't find one, her body already tainted by the unmistakable aroma of death. When this was confirmed he moved to Christine and repeated the process. He was about to give up when he felt a faint tremor beneath his fingers. Snatching a tea-towel from a nearby radiator he pressed it to the wound and held it firmly to staunch the bleeding and reached inside his jacket with his free hand for his mobile phone. 'Hang on, Christine,' he shouted, hoping she could still hear him. 'Hang on.'

The emergency operator asked him which service he required.

'This is Detective Inspector Darrow of Eastern Road Police Station. I need an ambulance at 52 Laburnum Street immediately. Knife wound to the throat. There's a faint pulse but she's lost a lot of blood.' He let the phone fall from his hand. 'Jay! Get in Here!' he bellowed. Then to Christine, 'Stay with me, love. Help is on its way.'

Jay appeared in the doorway.

'Check the alley!'

*

But Price was no longer in the alley. Once over the wall he had sprinted to its end, strolled across the road nonchalantly and headed into another alley opposite and ran the length of that before turning left into yet another alley. He had now slowed to a saunter and was regaining his breath.

You know you can't go home again?

'Yes,' he replied as he unbuttoned his shirt and pulled it off, using it to clean his face and neck. The blood had not soaked through to his T-shirt as much as he had feared. There were a few barely visible spots about the chest which resembled more a clumsily eaten Indian meal than blood. Hopefully it would not draw much attention. However, the fact that he was

wearing only a thin cotton T-shirt on a freezing
October morning would and he needed to get some
clothes soon. He crumpled up his shirt and stuffed it
in a bin.

Muddy up your boots and clothes.

'Why?'

*To create the facade of a builder or someone of a similar
trade.*

Price was impressed. 'Once again you are my
salvation.' As a precaution, he cut down another two
alleyways before stopping at a puddle and smearing
mud over his Caterpillars and clothes. 'What do you
think?'

*Daub a little on your face. Just a tad, nothing extreme.
You don't want to look homeless.*

Price rubbed two small fingers of dirt on his brow
and smeared them with the back of his hand.

Now wipe your hands on your T-shirt.

Price did so.

*Excellent. To complete the illusion buy a tabloid, fold it up
and put it in your back pocket.*

Price nodded. 'What now?'

*The first thing we need to do is draw out as much money as
we can from the nearest cash machine.*

'Right,' agreed Price. 'There's one around the
corner.'

*Well do it quickly. We have to see Julie and get out of here
as quickly as possible. Within the hour would be the best. You
can change your clothes there. Have you any idea what method
of dispatch you shall employ?*

Price smiled smugly. 'I have.'

What is it?

'Wait and see.'

Go on, tell me.

'Be patient, my friend. All will be revealed.'

*

Darrow knew he was losing Christine. The towel was now soaked red and her pulse was growing fainter. 'Christine? Can you hear me? Who did this to you?'

Her lips began to move.

Darrow leaned closer. 'Who did this to you?' he repeated.

The lips continued to move but he could make no sense of the shapes they formed. He lowered his head to try and listen to her words. His ear was in place to catch her last breath.

'Damn!' Darrow felt her blood drenched neck for a pulse. He held his fingers in place for a full minute before giving up. In the distance he heard the wail of a siren. Too late. He was always too late.

'Don't you worry, love. I'll get the bastard who did this to you,' he promised.

Jay, panting slightly, entered the kitchen. 'No sign,' he gasped. 'There's some blood on the wall. He definitely went that way.'

Darrow snapped his head to the Constable. 'Cancel the ambulance and get SOCO and the Police Surgeon down here. Then get on to the neighbours.'.

Jay nodded and stepped over Janine.

Darrow stood and stared at his sanguine hands numbly. How many times had he been here? Drenched in the life of strangers. Always too late. He had stopped counting years ago. Numbers equalled faces and faces equalled unwanted sleeping partners. His mind taunted him with the fact that he had seen more naked women who were dead than alive. He closed his eyes and willed the blank staring eyes and violated sexes away, but they lingered. He crossed the kitchen to the sink, swaying slightly, and turned on the hot tap and began to scrub his hands clean. The water scalded his flesh, but he kept them under the steaming torrent using the pain as a distraction. He followed the clear liquid as it turned red and gurgled its way down the plughole. Three murders in a week, two involving incised knife wounds to the throat and all employing a household carving knife to do the deed. He knew they were all killed by the same man. He was sure of it. And he should have seen the note as part of this.

'Hello, Brian.'

Darrow turned off the tap and turned to see a plump, rubicund man in his late fifties holding a tattered black medical bag. Darrow recognised him as Derek Miles one of the Police Surgeons.

'That was quick,' said Darrow.

'I was in transit when the call came through,' he explained in Received Pronunciation English. He looked at his watch. 'It took me three minutes to get here.' He took in the bloody scene and sighed. 'Dear me, this is a mess.' He bent down and brushed the hair away from Christine's face. He winced. 'Poor child.'

'She died about five minutes ago,' Darrow informed the Surgeon bitterly as he checked her pulse. Miles smiled but said nothing.

Darrow watched the Surgeon as he scribbled in a notebook and began to feel a little nauseous. Always too late. He quickly crunched down a spearmint. It offered no relief. 'If you'll excuse me...'

Miles shifted his attention from Christine to the Inspector. 'Hmm? Oh, yes, of course.'

*

Price tucked a copy of the *Daily Mirror* into his back pocket, tore the cellophane from a twenty pack of Lambert & Butler and lit one with a match. He removed the cigarette from his lips and regarded it fondly, blowing the thick smoke over the smouldering tip. 'That hits the spot,' he declared and quickly took another drag.

There's no time for this.

'There's always time for a smoke,' he explained, dragging deeply again.

A teenage boy with a centre parting, wearing a thick blue bubble coat, black jeans and white training shoes swaggered past Price's right-hand side. He tipped Price a wink and said, 'Don't allow complacency to deceive you. Speed is of the essence.'

'You must kill the whore and move on,' echoed a thin woman pushing a baby in a buggy. The child turned its finely haired head to Price. 'Kill the whore!' it gurgled with glee.

See?

Price nodded. 'All right, I'm going. But first we have to make a short stop.'

Where?

He tossed away the cigarette and lit another. 'I need to purchase the tools of our trade.'

Splendid.

*

Darrow watched as a paper suited SOCO circled the blood stains on the wall with white chalk. Neither man offered any conversation, the SOCO absorbed in the task at hand, Darrow frantically trying to correlate the Bell murder with the two bodies in the kitchen. Thus far he had only the sliced throats of Bell and MacNeil, and the use of household knives, the notes. But why? As far as he knew none of the women knew each other. Did they have to? Fuck.

'Sir!' called an excited Constable Jay as he ran towards the Inspector.

Darrow's eyes widened expectantly and hurried towards the Constable. This looked like good news.

Jay took a moment to compose himself. 'The neighbour, Mrs. Sharp, saw McNeil's boyfriend, a David Price, call round this morning. She says she heard what could have been screaming about twenty minutes later but couldn't be sure if it wasn't them acting the goat. She also says she didn't see him leave.' He drew a much-needed breath. 'She didn't know his address but did know that he worked for a pay office in Bootle. So, I made a few calls...' Jay beamed triumphantly. 'I've got his address.'

Darrow could have kissed him. 'Good work, Simon. Well done.' He began walking briskly back towards the house, Jay fell in behind. 'I'll get onto the Chief Inspector and let him know what we're doing. With any luck he'll rustle up a few bodies for the trip.' He turned to Jay and fixed him with an icy stare, his lips pressed in a tight snarl. 'Start the car.'

*

It had started to rain by the time Price stepped out from 'Carl's DIY' and onto the pavement. Price tilted his head and allowed the moisture to soak into his skin. Opening his mouth he drank, feeling the fine rain dancing on his tongue. He pulled a displeased face at the people putting up hoods or umbrellas for fear that the sensation of cold rain on their dry skin might snap them out of their slumber. With a snort he tore the price tag off the claw hammer and threw it to the wind. The weight of the hammer was reassuring in his hand, feeling more like a natural extension of his arm than a carpenter's tool.

Now can we go?

'Not quite,' he said, putting the hammer in his pocket. 'One more stop.'

Where?

Price pointed further up the street. 'There.'

A pet shop? What on Earth for?

'Questions, questions, questions. For once I would like you to trust me. Do you think you can do that?'

A sullen silence.

'Good. Then it's agreed.'

Price began to walk.

Chapter thirty-five

I took in the row of terraced houses, sweeping my eyes from left to right. My eyes drawn instinctively to number twenty-one.

Breathless with excitement I stepped up to the front door as memories crowded upon me: my first visit here, Julie on my arm and a throbbing in my loins. And suddenly there she was beside me, her blue eyes glinting with desire, her fingers entwined with mine. Her lips brushed my cheek like a cool breeze and I shivered. This was going to be a day to remember.

I pressed the doorbell and heard a faint chiming from within. Such was the feeling of power as I waited that I felt sure I would faint under the pressure.

The door opened and I promptly lashed out with my foot. There was a thud as the door smashed her head and there followed a second thud as she crumpled to the floor. I pushed the door, but her body blocked it from opening further. Shoving with my shoulder I forced the door wide enough to gain entry and quickly shut it behind me.

And there she was, sprawled on her back. Julie the whore. Julie the adulteress. Julie the condemned.

She moaned, the blow of the door having stunned rather than incapacitated her completely.

'Good morning, Julie,' I chirped throwing the dog choker I bought from the pet shop around her neck. I stepped over her so that I was behind her and gave the choker a hearty yank. Immediately her hands flew to the metal which dug into the plump flesh of her neck and she emitted a deliciously terrified gurgling sound. How I had ached to hear such music, for so long it had been everything, and now, as it filled my ears, I could scarcely believe it. It was just unfortunate that I didn't have more time to cherish it.

I dragged her to the living room like a disobedient puppy, allowing the chain to slacken slightly then suddenly yanking it taut with such vehemence that it hoisted her diseased body from the floor. She gasped and gurgled and kicked her legs but succeeded only in rushing the blood to rock hard penis.

Once in the living room I pulled the choker as tightly as I could, the muscles in my arms jutting like sculptured stone, and explained the situation. 'To begin with I feel I must apologise for the brevity of our session. The reason for this isn't really any of your business so I shan't go into it. Agreed?'

I removed the hammer from my back pocket. 'The first strike is to ensure that you don't make any noise,' I said, and with that I smashed the hammer into her jaw. There was no scream; only a muted, inarticulate howling and I would be lying if I said I was not disappointed. But what is life if not one long learning experience? However, the crunch of impact was deeply satisfying.

She fell limp but retained a dazed consciousness. The fear in her eyes was something special, the recognition, the uncertainty, the pleading, and even, perhaps, a small measure of repentance.

'The second and third strikes are to ensure that you don't leave before the fat lady sings.' Raising the hammer above my head I popped both her knees in quick succession. I say popped because that is the sound the kneecaps made as they cracked. Onomatopoeia I believe it's called. The steady howl from her shattered jaw rose in pitch.

'The fourth and fifth strikes are to prevent you from interfering with my work...' I pulled her arms away from her body, encountering little resistance, and lay them in a rough crucifixion position, intending to mash her hands to a bloody pulp when inspiration took me.

'One moment, Dearest,' I whispered and strolled to the wall and took down that awful reproduction Turner hanging above

the fireplace. Behind it were two hooks held in place with nails. Encouraged by this good fortune I removed the nails from the wall with the claw end of the hammer (such a tool useful tool) and weighed them in my palm. The nails were not as long as I would have liked (approximately an inch and a half) and I cursed myself for not having thought of the idea whilst in the DIY shop.

Undeterred, I pressed the tip of the nail gently into the centre of her palm, piercing the flesh. Then I tapped it further into her hand with the hammer then swiftly dealt the final blow to drive the nail home. Her moaning grew to a new intensity as she tried vainly to retract her arm and, if I'm honest, she was beginning to grate on my nerves a little. However, being the staunch little trooper that I am I moved over to her second hand.

Her pain impaired brain had managed to grasp my intention and was attempting to hide her hand beneath her body.

To avoid all that tedious mucking about trying to force her hand in position I stomped on her stomach with as much force as I could muster. The air whooshed from her provoking a tremendous hawking sound as she desperately tried to suck the air back into her body. This highly satisfactory outcome was made all the more so by the fact that it brought temporary respite to that God-awful howling. And so, whistling the chorus to one of my favourite songs (which I shan't mention because I am weary of the press's inclination to link this particular type of music to crime) I nailed her other palm to the floor.

I stepped back a pace and marvelled at a job well done. She certainly was a work of art; a tired mental image refreshed in actuality, a personal demon stripped bare and conquered.

'How does it feel to have your life turned inside out?' I asked, unable to prevent the hatred from reducing my question to a low snarl. The loathing bloated inside me, constricted my

chest and left a bitter taste in my mouth. 'Answer me!' I screamed, the words forming black clouds before my eyes.

How the pathetic wretch tried to answer, rolling her eyes, trying to coax the words from her shattered jaw, managing only to whine in pain. Had it been anyone else in the world I might have felt sorry for them but not her. The pain she was wrapped in was but a fraction of the agony I had endured. If the circumstances had been different I would have left, leaving her to heal her wounds and wrestle with the nightmares until her end.

'How I love thee, my dying bride,' I said and kissed her forehead. 'And it is love that has brought me here today.'

Slowly, I unbuttoned her jeans and pulled them from her hips. After removing her training shoes and socks, I dragged her jeans from her ruined legs without much care. Tipping her a wink I sniffed the crotch and detected the bitter tang of urine.

'Someone's not house trained,' I declared with a laugh and reprimanded her with a wagging finger. Her white knickers were stained yellow and I wrenched them from her and wrung them out over her head. Urine dripped into her eyes and she blinked it away clumsily.

I switched my attention to her genitals and was touched profoundly at the sight of her coffee-coloured clitoris and labia. 'Hello, old friends. I'm back.' Her vagina smiled up at me, clearly pleased to see me even if the rest of her wasn't. 'Have you missed me?'

With a gurgle of fluid it told me that it had.

'The feeling is mutual. And I intend to take measures to ensure that we shall never be apart again.'

I ventured into the kitchen in search of a knife suitable for the task in hand.

*

Darrow hammered on the door of 57 Winterburn Road and announced his presence through the letter box. He waited for two seconds before nodding to PC Welsh to force an entry. He stepped aside as Welsh smashed the battering ram against the door. There was a resounding crack as the door frame splintered but maintained its hold on the door.

'Again,' barked Darrow unnecessarily.

Welsh pounded the battering ram a second time. The door flew open and the PC toppled inside. Darrow pushed past him and stood in the hallway snapping on his latex gloves, oblivious to the other men brushing past him and darting into the different rooms of the house.

'Sir!' It was PC Grady over in the room to Darrow's right. He opened the door and stepped inside. The walls had been recently stripped and small piles of shaved paper were dotted about the dusty floorboards. The only furniture in the room was a sofa. Opposite this was PC Grady hunched over a large rusty brown stain. He turned to the Inspector, 'I think it's blood, Sir.' Darrow crouched beside the PC and ran his finger through the stain. He brought it up to his nose.

Blood.

'There's a few nails dotted about the floor also, Sir. They look to be pretty recent.'

Darrow appraised them and was inclined to agree.

'Sir!' Darrow turned his head to the direction of his name and hurried from the room. In the kitchen he saw PC Welsh vomiting over the sink and a blanched Sergeant Ball leaning uncertainly over a large fridge freezer. Darrow's eyes darted about the small room searching for the source of their revulsion.

Everything seemed to be in order. Except for one thing: the white refrigerator shelving had been removed and lay scattered about the floor.

'What is it?' he asked, unsure of whether he wanted to know.

Sergeant Ball swallowed. 'In here,' he said and nodded to the fridge but kept his eyes firmly on the Inspector.

Darrow told him to take PC Welsh outside and fumbled in his pockets for a spearmint. Only when the minty taste was fully established in his mouth did he even consider looking inside. Taking a deep breath and holding it, he opened the fridge.

The smell hit him like a blow and he recoiled, covering his mouth and nose with the back of his hand.

Inside the fridge was a body. It was only after glimpsing a torn breast that he was able to determine it was a girl. Her body was stored in such a way that her spine was almost folded in half, the head forced down to the chest, white bone protruding from the back of her neck. The skin was stained with blood and he could just make out a wound to the throat. Her limbs had been smashed and twisted in order to force her in the fridge and they jutted at unnatural angles like branches of a tree. She had been shaven bald, as had her eyebrows, and through the stench of putrefaction he detected a faint odour of bleach. With weary eyes he scanned the body for her genitalia, shifting his head to see through the tangle of limbs. Eventually he located her groin and found only a bloody mess.

'Shit,' he hissed under his breath and crunched on his spearmint. It was as he began searching the kitchen for a second make-shift vase that he heard Jay call him up to the bathroom.

He took the stairs two at a time. Once at the top, pale faces and shaking fingers directed him to the bathroom. Jay stood in the doorway. 'You might want to pop a mint,' he suggested.

Darrow ignored him and peered into the bathroom. A green plastic bathtub with a flowered shower curtain that was still damp, a toilet and sink also in the same unpleasant shade of green. 'What am I looking for?'

'The cabinet to the left of the toilet.'

Darrow dragged his eyes to the cabinet and there it was. Keeping a toothbrush and two disposable razors upright was the missing vagina. 'Shit.'

Jay nodded gravely to himself.

Darrow wiped his lips with the back of his hand. 'It looks like he killed her downstairs. There are nails in the floorboards, could be he kept her there for a while.'

'Should I get on to missing persons?'

'Yes...no, on second thoughts I need you here, get someone else to do it.'

'Like who?'

'I don't know,' he replied irritably. 'Just get on with it, will you.'

Without a word Jay left the bathroom.

Darrow steeled himself and moved closer to the monstrosity on the cabinet. Price had obviously taken his time with this one, he thought. There were no objects employed to hold it in place, the knife work was less clumsy. Darrow's face tightened in sympathy with the protestations from his stomach and he moved away. The image remained in his vision, burned into his retinas like a blinding light. He closed the bathroom door behind him and wandered into Price's bedroom.

The room looked more like a music store than a bedroom and if it hadn't been for the double bed and single wardrobe he would have forgiven anyone for jumping to that conclusion. Every wall, save for the one with the window, was crammed with thousands of CDs, DVDs and even videos.

Upon closer inspection he noticed that the CD's were all placed in alphabetical order and covered the gamut of musical genres: *Abba, Abigor, AC/DC, A-ha, Amazulu, Aphex Twin, Art of Noise, Asian Dub Foundation, Aswad, Autechre.* The videos were much the same mix of styles, although didn't appear to be in any sort of order. He ran his eyes along the length of the shelf: *Carry on Camping, Inception, King Ralph, Bottom, Linda the neighbourhood Slut, Die Hard, Horny Housewives, Rambo III, Shut up and fuck me white boy 3,* a selection of *National Geographic* documentaries, *Brady Bunch: The Movie.* He quickly estimated the total value of the room to be somewhere in the region of twenty thousand pounds.

Dotted about the room were speakers of various sizes connected to the most impressive Hi-fi Darrow had ever seen.

'That must have cost a pretty penny,' he mumbled to himself and gave up trying to guess its value. The television was top of the range, too.

'Looks like this was where he spent most of his time,' said Jay.

'You say he worked in a Pay office?'

Jay nodded. 'He must be a sad and lonely individual.'

'They usually are,' agreed the Inspector.

Darrow caught a muffled 'Sir!' from under the bed. Moments later the head of DC John Ryan emerged, blonde hair ruffled, from under the duvet. 'I've found something,' he said and moved away from the bed, turning it on its side with a grunt.

Darrow moved over to the DC and saw a large metal chest about a metre and a half wide and half a metre deep. It was old and dented but sported a shiny silver padlock. 'Don't bother looking for a key,' he instructed. 'Smash it open.'

DC Ryan walked to the door and called for the battering ram.

'Do you think it's another body, Sir?' asked Jay coolly.

'I won't know that until we get it open, will I?' snapped Darrow. He shook his head. 'I doubt it,' he said quietly. 'It'll more than likely be a stash of weird porn and sex aids...'

Welsh appeared with the battering ram, looked mystified for a moment, until Ryan told him what to do.

The padlock fell apart with the second strike.

DC Ryan opened the chest allowing the lid to drop to the floor behind.

Darrow frowned. The chest contained not aberrant pornography but a selection of modern classics: *The Collected Poems of T.S. Eliot*, *The Portrait of the Artist as a Young Dog*, *Ulysses*, *Finnegan's Wake*, *Mrs. Dalloway*, *The Waves*, *The Bell Jar*, *Coming up for Air*. There were also a few compact discs: Mozart's *'Don Giovani'*, Verdi's *'Aida'*, *'Madame Butterfly'* by Puccini.

'What the bloody hell has he got them locked away for?' asked Darrow to no-one in particular. He turned to Jay, frowning. 'Why would a man with *King Ralph* and *Horny Housewives* blatantly displayed on his shelves feel the need to conceal his collection of literature and opera CD's? If anything, it should have been the reverse.'

Jay shrugged. 'I have no idea, Sir.'

'Anyone?'

DC Ryan and PC Welsh shrugged their shoulders in unison.

Darrow's frown was replaced by a broad grin. 'I'll tell you why. For the purpose of creating a false impression. We come here and see poor comedy films, testosterone drenched action films, pop music, pornography; not a book in sight and we think he's a bit dim. Then we start to underestimate him...'

'But why leave it here for us to find?' interrupted Ryan.

'I don't think he was planning on us finding him so soon.' The Inspector crossed to the shelves containing the CD's beginning with A. 'See the gap between the *A-ha* CD's and the *Amazulu* ones? It's only slight.' He waited as the other men examined the shelf. 'Notice how those discs are at a slight angle, and the others are perfectly vertical? That was where *Aida* was before he moved it. He was planning on leaving and more than likely would have taken the trunk with him.'

'Maybe he'll try and come back for them,' offered Ryan.

Darrow shook his head. 'I doubt it. He's no fool. He's been planning this for a long time. He wants us to think he conforms to the sad loner profile...' he trailed off continuing the discussion privately. The other officers waited patiently. 'If we don't come up with something soon, he'll be long gone.' He addressed the room, 'Look for anything; diaries, address books, anything.' Then Ryan specifically, 'See if there's anything at the bottom of the chest.' Darrow searched the room for his DC. 'Jay?'

Jay stepped into the bedroom.

'Get back to McNeil's. I think there's a photograph of Price on the mantelpiece, check with the neighbour that it's him, then get it circulated.'

Jay turned and left. Darrow called after him, 'And you may as well see if there are any others knocking about, while you're at it.'

'I think I've found something, Sir.'

DC Ryan stood, his arms filled with blue hard backed note-books. Darrow snatched one from the top and opened it at random. As he scanned the page his eyes narrowed. He turned to another page, then another, eyes widening. Tucking the book under his arm he took another from Ryan and opened it. He flicked through it frantically, turning page after page.

The colour drained from his face. 'Oh my God.'

'What is it, Sir?' asked a concerned DC Ryan.

'Come with me,' he barked and bolted out of the room.

*

Unfortunately, Julie was never one for preparing her own meals and the poor selection of kitchen utensils reflected her lack of culinary expertise. Eventually, I decided upon a neglected carving knife that was hidden away in a draw of bits and bobs. It was part of a house warming present from her mother. The blade was dull with disuse and, as I ran it across my thumb, failed to draw blood or even mark my skin. All the better for the purpose I had in mind; the duller the blade the more intense the pain. A bit of extra elbow grease would be required but I was more than capable. Before I returned to my darling, I filled up an empty milk bottle with cold water and carried it into the living room.

To my surprise she was still with us but, not wanting to have wasted my time, I poured the water over her head anyway. She shook her head, spluttering and moaning in her usual fashion. I placed a finger to my lips. She somehow managed to do as she was bid. If only she had been this co-operative when we were together.

She said nothing; for what could she have said? She was all too aware of her guilt and knew any protests and pleas would have fallen on deaf ears. I was most gratified that she saved me the distasteful task of listening to her inarticulate, unintelligible excuses.

With horror I realised I had omitted the bleach scrub. Panic gripped me. Would a slut such as this possess such a cleaning agent? Doubtful. Would I be able to slip out and purchase a bottle without incident?

I paced up and down the room rapping my knuckles against the side of my head, cursing my carelessness.

I noticed my odd behaviour was causing her some distress. Excellent. I shook my fist to the heavens and cursed God and all his angels in theatrically deranged manner.

As anticipated, this increased her distress and I giggled. The more I tried to suppress my glee the harder I laughed; there is, after all, no laughter like forbidden laughter. Tears streamed from my eyes and my ribs started to ache.

'Stop it!' I screamed slapping my thighs as if this would help.

My inner voice warned me to compose myself and I did.

The voice explained the bleach was not necessary on this occasion as no intercourse was to take place.

Reassured of my safety I knelt between Julie's legs and tickled her perineum like the chin of an adorable child. Adopting an equally condescending tone reserved ordinarily for women conversing with their spawn, I said, 'Hello there my little baby. You're a little stinker.' I nodded emphatically; teeth bared in a wide grin. 'Yes, you are. You're a little stinker.'

Julie was beginning to slip away, her eyes closing, head lolling to one side, which simply wasn't cricket. I skipped over to the large wooden desk in the corner of the room and searched the drawers for something to regain her attention.

In contrast to the kitchen I found a wide range of stationary at my disposal, most of which appeared to have been purchased recently. I selected a shiny red stapler.

Julie was unconscious when I returned, so I pressed lightly against her broken jaw with my index finger. With a howl she opened her eyes and fixed me with a look of such despair, such incredulity, that I was overcome with the urge to slash the wretched whore's throat and be done with her. Instead I reached down with the thumb and forefinger of my left hand, took hold of her left eyelid and pulled it with care away from the eye, turning it inside out and stretching it to her eyebrow. I then proceeded to staple the thin flesh to her eyebrow. Yet another low howl of pain crawled its way up from her throat, so I added another staple for good measure. I repeated the process for her right eye.

Now I was assured of her complete attention.

Pleased with my handiwork I attempted to staple her lips together but was unable to manoeuvre the base of the stapler beneath them to do so effectively. I gave it up as an unnecessary whim and opted to staple her nostrils shut instead. That worked a treat.

'You'd suit a nose-stud,' I remarked. The only reply I received for this generous and spontaneous compliment was a *desperate hissing sound as she sucked in precious air through her shattered jaw.*

She was nothing if a survivor, I had to give her that.

I held the knife above her pubic hair and just below the curving smile of her flabby stomach, about four inches below her navel to be precise. I turned the knife horizontally, so the cutting edge was facing her left hip, and raised myself up to a crouch. Gripping the handle with both hands, and hunching my shoulders over the knife, I pressed the tip against her skin.

'Now, this might sting a little,' I warned and pushed the knife deep into her abdomen. For the first time that day she managed to scream (quite competently, I might add) but it soon diminished to that insufferable moaning as I worked the knife across her abdomen. Soon even the moaning faded leaving only, yes, you've guessed it, that damned twitching. I increased my efforts, sawing with renewed vigour to put an end to that twitching. It really is the most distracting thing, ruining the atmosphere I had worked so hard to cultivate.

As I commenced slicing vertically, I noticed with some relief that she was virtually dead and stepped away just in time to avoid being soiled by her excreta.

It was at this time that things took a turn for the worse.

Suddenly there was a loud bang at the front door, and I frowned in its direction. There swiftly followed another bang, accompanied this time by the splintering of wood and the sound of the front door hitting the inside wall. Muffled voices and stomping feet were audible an instant later.

I am rather ashamed to say that I found myself rooted to the spot, sweating profusely, my spine burning hot then chilling me with cold, unsure of what to do next. So, wearing a face that is colloquially referred to as a smacked arse, I stood and waited for the heavy footsteps to reach me.

The living room door burst open and a man filled the frame. He was about six-foot four and heavily built. The first thing I really noticed about him was his eyes; a piercing cadmium-green (the type of ocular colouring one expects to be the exclusive domain of Supermodels and Hollywood actresses) which was accentuated by his close-cropped grey hair. They took in my work and he thundered across the room, his features glaring with contempt, and in that split second I recognised the jacket, coat and unimaginatively grey tie of Detective Inspector Darrow. I raised my chin in what I hope would come across as a defiant gesture and raised the knife to slash at his neck when he came into range. He was far too quick for me and in a blur of movement his strong hands wrapped around my wrist before I knew anything about it. In a rather impressive manoeuvre he bent my arm back behind my shoulder and such was the pain I was forced to relinquish my hold on the knife. He continued to force my arm backwards and I felt my knees buckle and, although I was trying my utmost not to do so, I let out a small yelp of pain.

As I collapsed to the floor in an embarrassingly feminine fashion, he brought his knee up and into my stomach with considerable force. Suddenly deprived of air I gasped and wheezed and retched like so many women had done before me. It's moments of supreme irony such as this that reaffirm my belief in the existence of God. And remind me that He/She/It has a wicked sense of humour.

'Police. You're under arrest,' he said gruffly and quite unnecessarily I thought, although I was in no position to voice this opinion as his heavy size ten boot was crushing my face into Julie's poorly vacuumed carpet.

This was not how I expected it to be.

*

Darrow was well aware that he was pushing his foot down far too hard on Price's face and was surprised to find that he didn't care. For the first time in his career he wanted to tear a perp limb from limb, wanted not only to show him the pain all those women he had mutilated felt, but to destroy a part of Price that witnessing his violations had destroyed in him.

DC Ryan rested a reassuring hand on his superior's shoulder. Darrow gave a start and turned to the DC, eyes clouded as if he had just woken from a dream. He gave a slow nod and removed his foot.

PC Watts secured Price with handcuffs, reading him his rights as he did, and dragged him to his feet.

Price, a large red footprint on his cheek, swayed slightly and winked at the Inspector. 'That was quite an impressive little move, I must say. If I ask you nicely to you think you could teach it to me sometime?' he asked, receiving a scowl from Darrow. 'No?' said Price, disappointed. 'Are you sure you won't reconsider? There are an infinite number of women who need such a manoeuvre performed on their brittle bones...'

'Get him out of here,' snapped Darrow, jerking his thumb towards the door.

Watts gave Price a shove, but he held his ground. 'Oh, go on,' he urged Darrow. 'Don't be a spoil sport.'

'Move!' ordered Watts with a firmer shove.

Price looked at the DC over his shoulder arrogantly. 'My dear chap, all you had to do was ask.' He returned his attention back to Darrow. 'See you at the interview,' he sneered.

Darrow reached for his spearmints.

Chapter Thirty-six

The interview room was pretty much as I expected. This came as no surprise; after all they featured on television screens almost daily and even the most frugal and discerning of viewers would have seen one at some point in their lives. As this is the case I see no reason for me to describe the room or the programmes in which such a location would appear. Suffice is to say they all conform to the same tired formula and I was quite looking forward to seeing how much of it was based on actual practice and how much of it was indolence excused as creative licence; also known as the storyteller's lie.

With this in mind, I compiled a selection of the most memorable constabulary aphorisms and bon mots *in preparation for a game of spot the cliché should I become bored during the interview. I shall confess in advance that if the phrase 'You're going down, son' doesn't reveal itself during the proceedings I shall be heartbroken.*

One of the PC's (number 102) was kind enough to fetch me a cup of tea. I assume that this is one of my rights, but not having brushed up on that area I cannot be certain. Nevertheless, I conveyed my thanks most sincerely, receiving in return a thin smile.

He was a terribly emaciated sort of fellow; tall and gangly and painfully carbuncular. He looked no older than twenty. Not the type of officer one would be relieved to see arrive at the scene of a violent assault, American style baton or no American style baton.

This aside, I was fascinated by this young man as he stood in the corner of the room avoiding my eyes. I was bursting with questions regarding his training and experience. How long had he been in the job? Was I the first murderer he had seen? Was he frightened? Did he find me objectionable? Even repulsive?

For me the whole experience was incredibly exciting. Here I was waiting to be interviewed regarding the murders of five women, wearing a paper suit while my clothes underwent forensic examination...the sense of importance was overwhelming.

Reason told me I should be nervous, even afraid as I was undoubtedly going to prison. However, I countered, by the time I was tried and sentenced my twelve months of life would almost be at an end. Pleading insanity would waste a few weeks of the court's time, too. For this reason, I found myself relaxed, almost amused by my predicament. This state of mind was compounded by the fact that I was unable to dispel the sensation of being on television. At any moment I expected DCI Meadows to storm into the room, beat his meaty fists on the table and declare something intimidating in that broad Yorkshire accent of his.

My voice was sulking (something he was becoming increasingly adept at). All the way to the Police station he griped and moaned at my admittedly pitiful and swift apprehension: I told you not to send those notes, why didn't you run or at least give the impression that you were capable of resisting arrest? *and so on. He was right of course. It was a pretty dismal end to a promising career, even one destined to be a mere twelve months long. But at least this way I can shed light on my motives, communicate my ideology to the media, pontificate from the stand, that sort of thing. The first opportunity that arises I shall ask for a pen and paper and compose a monologue. Although, I expect I would only be permitted to use a crayon. If so I will draw a pretty picture for Detective Inspector Darrow.*

The door opened. Speak of the Devil.

Darrow walked straight to the tape machine without even a glance in my direction and, after placing five large folders on the table, opened the tape decks and unwrapped two audio cassettes.

He was a menacing figure but as I know he is shackled by the law I am only mildly uneasy in his company.

The man who entered behind the DI was less impressive. Another youngster, but one who possessed a visible confidence, a characteristic absent from 102, whom he dismissed. His attire was straight off the rack at Burton's and well worn. The fabric noticeably lighter around the elbows. It looked like it was purchased by his mother for a second cousin's wedding. I caught a faint whiff of stage fright on a cloud of Lynx when he sat opposite me to my right. He studied the Inspector carefully which my arrogance interpreted as an unwillingness to look me in the eyes. When I noticed his fingers trembling I realised I was not mistaken.

Am I worthy of such fear? Were the things I did so abhorrent? In my eyes I did no more than a High-Street butcher does on a daily basis. Then again if that so disgusts Animal Rights activists it is a logical progression that it would equally effect a Human Rights activist which, in its most fundamental sense, is exactly what the Police Force (sorry, Service) consider themselves to be. But how much of that is actually born from genuine compassion or a dread that if they don't reject the likes of me, they too will eventually fall foul of someone like me.

A loud electronic screeching filled the room then stopped when the cassette began recording. Darrow talked to the tape. 'Taped interview between Detective Inspector Darrow and David Price. Other officer present, DC Jay...The time is...

*

'...Two thirty-nine on the thirteenth of October. David Price, I must remind you that you are still under caution and that you have refused a solicitor. I must also remind you that you are free to ask for legal representation at any time. Do you understand?'

'I do.'

Darrow folded his hands neatly on the table before him. 'Do you know a Christine MacNeil?'

Price smiled, gave a nod and said, 'For the benefit of the tape, Mr. Price has just nodded.'

Darrow chose not to comment on this. 'And what is your relationship with Miss MacNeil?'

'Ah, well, that is so difficult to define. There are so many labels attached to this sort of thing today: lover, partner, girlfriend, bird, Judy, tart, lass. They pretty much mean the same thing. What's your preference?'

'I think we'll take girlfriend. If that's all right with you?' added Darrow.

'That's just Dandy.'

'And how long have you known her?'

'Biblically or chronologically?'

'Chronologically.'

'About six months.'

'And how would you describe the relationship?'

'I don't understand the question.'

'Did you get on well together?'

'Naturally, I can only speak for myself...but I had no reason to complain. As for Chrissy? You'll have to ask her yourself.'

'I can't do that.'

Price leaned forward and steepled his fingers. 'And why not, pray?'

'Because she's dead.'

'I agree that it does present you with some difficulty in obtaining a balanced perspective.'

'It does.'

'Then I suppose you will just have to take my word for it, then.'

Jay cleared his throat and asked, 'You don't sound very concerned to hear she's dead.'

For a moment Price regarded Jay as if he had remarked upon something peculiar, before raising his eyebrows in both surprise and amusement. 'My dear chap, we're all dead,' he replied as if humouring a senile resident of a retirement home. 'It just takes some of us longer to decompose than others. Christine was in a great deal of pain, emotionally speaking. Demons I believe they're called. They plagued her every waking moment. Sometimes she was crippled by their taunting. It is for this reason that I view her passing in much the same light one would view the demise of a long-suffering cancer patient who finally found relief in death.' Price quickly made the Sign of the Cross. 'Rest in peace, darling,' he whispered to the interview room ceiling.

'That's very noble of you,' remarked Darrow.

'What is?' asked Price.

'Well, if someone had just murdered my girlfriend, I doubt that I would be as understanding.'

Price crumpled his brow into a frown. 'I'm surprised at you, Inspector, I really am. Am I to be treated with suspicion because I fail to correspond to the traditional definition of grief? I thought you were better than that. Would it be easier for you to grasp if I wailed and wept and threw my arms about the place enraged at the injustice of it all?'

Jay answered for the Inspector. 'You have to admit your behaviour is odd.'

'I don't have to admit anything. I have just displayed a personal reaction to an event. The key word here is personal. How can I react any other way? Wailing and gnashing of teeth and demanding revenge are, granted, more popular reactions. But they are not mine. The average cadaver in the street's head would implode if it attempted to stray from the norm and therefore reacts to stimuli in the expected manner. Should it even consider stretching its sensibilities to a different perspective it would be resented and ultimately ostracised. It...*they* prefer safety, to belong to the indifferent whole even if it does involve the sacrifice of certain freedoms. The television is their preferred method of communication and experience. Every day billions of people travel the world on their backsides, or only achieve through mouse-clicks and joy-pads, their veins hooked up to the net. It is, in their sightless eyes, the most desirable form of contact with others in their condition. No risk of contamination, you see? Also, there's no need for them to compromise themselves further to get what they want.' Price signified the end of his speech with a curt, satisfied smile.

Darrow who had found this opinionated outburst most enlightening and informative regarding Price's mental state, chose not to credit it with any further discussion. 'There was another body at your girlfriend's house-'

Price was baffled. 'Hasn't anything of what I have just said touched you in any way?'

'I can't say that it has,' replied Darrow evenly.

'Really?'

'Yes.'

Price turned to Jay. 'What about you?'

He shrugged. 'Not particularly.'

Price deflated back into his chair, leaned it on to two legs and began rocking it gently back and forth, his fingers locked behind his head. 'I'm disappointed,' he revealed to Darrow. 'I believe I may have misjudged you...I thought you were different.'

'I'm heartbroken.'

The rocking ceased. Then started again. 'It's unwise to mock me.'

'And why's that, David?'

'Because if you don't indulge me in my verbal digressions and participate in the discussions they provoke...I shall say nothing further. And I mean nothing. Is that clear?'

Darrow shook his head. 'You're in no position to dictate to me.'

'Oh, but I am,' said Price returning the chair to all four legs. 'Correct me if I'm incorrect but I was under the impression that the purpose of an interview was to obtain information. I expect achieving this goal would be severely hampered if I suddenly became deaf-mute.'

'An interview is not merely utilised to determine guilt, it is also an opportunity for you to prove your innocence.'

Price waved his hands airily. 'I'm not interested in that. My main concern is ensuring that my motives are understood and documented.'

'Motives to what?'

'All in good time, all in good time. Rest assured, however, that if you permit my circumlocution you shall receive all the information you require. Agreed?'

Darrow paused more for effect than any need to consider the offer. 'Agreed.'

Jay also agreed.

'Excellent,' beamed Price. 'Now what was it you wanted to know?'

'There was another body at your girlfriend's house. Have you any idea who that was?'

'Didn't you check the body for ID?'

'I know who she is, I was asking if you knew?'

'Oh, I see. I assume you're referring to Janine Taylor?'

'I am. Did you know her well?'

'Well enough.'

'Could you elaborate on that?'

'I knew her age, address, that she was voraciously heterosexual and had an excruciatingly nasal voice.'

'Was that why you killed her?'

'Was what why I killed her?'

'Because she was 'voraciously heterosexual'?'

'Did I say I killed her?'

Darrow ignored the question. 'Was her promiscuity offensive to you?'

Price repeated his question to Jay. 'Did I say I killed her?'

Jay gave no indication that he had heard him speak.

Darrow continued. 'Did it get to you? All those men she went with, let them inside her. She'd have anyone, but not you. She thought she was too good for you. But you showed her, didn't you? You tied her up, raped her, then killed her-'

'Excuse me but I really would like to know how you arrived at this conclusion. Did I refer to her as a whore or slag or use any other pejorative term in reference to her? No. So I'm at a loss as to where you conclude that her sexual proclivities were in any way connected to her death. If you must know, it was her irritating voice that prompted my dispatch of her.'

'You did kill her, then?' asked Jay.

Price's expression displayed his disdain for the question. 'I believe I just made that clear.'

Jay was undeterred. 'And Christine?'

'Has he been asleep or something?' he asked Darrow, then turned to Jay and said slowly, 'Are you in any way hearing impaired? Do you need someone to sign my answers to you?' He returned his attention to Darrow. 'Or is he just too dim to grasp the agreement we just made?'

'It's okay, David,' Darrow soothed. 'Tell us about Janine...'

Price pinched his eyebrows and closed his eyes. 'I've lost my train of thought now.' He threw Jay a scowl.

'You were telling us about Janine's irritating voice...'

'So I was...Dear God, you should have heard it! I have no idea whether it's inherited, taught or simply the result of years of practice, but she was able to find the precise point in pitch and volume between a child's howling tantrum and a dentist's drill. Unfortunately, the Good Lord didn't see fit to provide her with an off button, so I was forced to smash her head against the wall a few times. That ceased her whinging.'

'What was she whinging about?'

Price wriggled uncomfortably in his chair. 'Is it terribly important?'

'We think it is.'

Price released a long sigh. 'Very well, but I'll keep it short. Chris had received a threatening letter and was suitably distressed. Janine wanted me to play the protective boyfriend. I told her I was on my way but didn't arrive until the following morning. Janine felt she was justified in chastising me. She was mistaken.'

'Why didn't you go around when she asked you to?'

'I was otherwise engaged.'

'Doing what?'

'We'll get to that later...'

'Okay. Weren't you concerned for Christine's safety?'

He shrugged. 'Not particularly.'

'And why was that?'

'Two reasons really. Firstly, anyone breaking into the house with intent to cause harm to Christine would have encountered Janine and she would have shagged him into submission.'

'And the second reason?'

A smile turned up the corners of his mouth. 'I sent the notes.'

'You sent them? Why?'

'I don't know. For a laugh?'

'I don't follow you. A few minutes ago you said that your relationship with Christine was fine-'

'I'm certain I said I had no reason to complain...but go on...'

'And yet you send her a note saying you're coming to rip out her cunt?'

'Extremely crude phraseology but rather effective, wouldn't you say?'

'But why?'

'I've already answered that question.'

'I'll re-phrase it. What did you hope to achieve by it?'

'I wanted to smell her fear. I wanted to make her tremble.'

'To what end?'

'Who can tell?'

'Did you tell her that you sent the notes?'

'I tried but she was in shock.'

'Why?'

'Because she had discovered Janine's corpse in the kitchen.'

'And how did she react to that?'

'She was stunned. The colour drained from her and she withered...' For a moment he was there again, in the kitchen. 'It was a disturbing sight. The poor girl just couldn't comprehend what had happened. 'I don't understand,' she said. 'I don't understand."' Price buried his head in his hands and slumped over the table.

Darrow leaned forward and spoke softly in his ear. 'Do you regret killing her?'

Price suddenly sat upright, composure restored and declared in a casual tone of voice, 'Not really. It was necessary. I made a decision and I stand by it. Everything comes down to choice in the end. For instance, when I chose the girl you probably have already discovered in my refrigerator there were several aspects of appearance and manner I was looking for; youth to hopefully provoke an outraged reaction, beauty also. But also sexual promiscuity to inform the world that things are not always how they seem.'

'I think people already know that.'

'Do you think so?'

'Of course.'

'I know that isn't true. How can a man in your profession still have faith in human nature, when every moment of every day is spent with cheats and liars? No, no, no, no, I find that very difficult to believe. There's no reason to be ashamed of thinking that the world is filled with the ignorant and stupid. It's no great secret. It's everywhere. Even in the professional circuit.

'Let me give you an example. I used to work in a bank and at the time I believed I would be working with people who were...how shall I say...of reasonable intelligence. One day I went for my tea-break and the Assistant Manager was already in the staff room smoking a cigarette. We struck up a conversation, during which he made the most ridiculous statement I had ever heard. I can no longer remember what it was, which is an indication of how ludicrously misinformed it was, but I think it was something to do with Hitler. Naturally I questioned the validity of his statement and he became quite offended and tried to convince me that it was genuine. But still I would not accept it. So what does he bring to prove his point? *The History of Germany* by AJP Taylor? *The Rise and Fall of the Third Reich* by Walter S Shirer? Or any book promoting historiographical debate. No. He reaches for a copy of *The Sun*, holds it aloft and declares, and I quote: 'It must be true it's in here!''

'Not everybody is like that.'

'Aren't they.'

'I'm not.'

'That's specious reasoning. 'I'm not so therefore there must be others like me.''

'You're not.'

'Ah, but then again...I've seen the light.'

'What light?'

'The dead sun at the top of the Hill of Bones.'

Darrow looked coldly into Price's eyes and was answered with a similar lack of warmth. He saw how women would have been drawn to those dark orbs; they were heavy with a sadness that some women would have wanted to ease.

There was also an indifference which Darrow had picked up on during the course of the interview. His eyes would briefly glaze over and wander aimlessly about as if blind. It was unsettling to watch.

Price's eyes were not the window to a soul, they were simply utilised for sight. Price could not be unfolded so easily.

He'd given up trying to read his eyes a few minutes into the interview, preferring to allow him to ramble. There lay the true David Price.

'Where's that, David?'

'It doesn't matter.'

Darrow decided to move in a different direction. 'Where were you last Wednesday at around midnight?'

Price did not appear to be phased by the shift in questioning. 'At home.'

'Doing what?'

'If I remember correctly I was masturbating to my favourite scene in Horny Housewives. The double penetration of Madeline.'

'Are you sure.'

'Oh yes,' he smiled fondly. 'Came like a rocket I did.'

'Can anybody confirm this?'

'Well, you could try asking Madeline. But as her mother taught her not to talk with her mouth full you might have to wait until she's not so busy. Or at least rewind the tape to the beginning.'

'So, nobody can confirm this.'

'It would appear so. You could check my television screen for deposits of semen, if you like.'

'Does the name Pamela Bell mean anything to you?'

Price didn't even flinch. 'Should it?'

'I think it should.'

'And why is that?'

'It's funny you should ask because it's something that has been playing on my mind. The girl we found in your fridge...What was her name again?'

'Lucy Eliot.'

'Right. Well, her vagina was cut out and used as a holder for your razors and toothbrush.'

Price laughed.

Darrow smiled in return. 'Nice work, if I may say so?'

'You may, and I appreciate the praise.'

'But, and this is the thing that's bothering me, sometime in the early hours of Thursday morning a student nurse by the name of Pamela Bell was murdered and her vagina was also hacked out. Only this time it was used as a vase to hold some dried flowers.'

Price suppressed his laughter long enough to ask, 'And?'

'Don't you think it's odd that two such distinctive acts should occur purely by chance?'

'Not really. I think any man wanting to defile a woman has very little choice but to attack the vagina. After all, that is the source of her power. A woman without her genitalia is of no use to anyone.'

'I can see the logic in that. But both women were shaved bald and scrubbed clean with household bleach...'

'Now that is too much to be dismissed as coincidence...'

'My thoughts exactly.'

'But what can I say? There's very little originality in the world today. The music industry has run out of combinations of notes to play and so churn out the same drivel under a different name. Television dramas are guilty of the same thing. Take the rise in period dramas recently. It's not because people like them, it's because no-one can come up with something new. But what is there to write about that hasn't already been written? How many ways are there to kill that will remain in the minds of those who witness them?'

'I agree. When I saw Pamela Bell's corpse I thought 'Oh no, not another woman with her vagina mutilated. When will there be a crime committed that isn't just one cliché after another?'

Price narrowed his eyes. 'But you were bound to say that. A gynaecologist probably thinks the same when-ever he sees a vagina in Razzle, he no longer feels desire towards something he cannot become sexually involved with, the desire is no longer there, he is immune to its charms. But that doesn't prevent someone who rarely comes into contact with a vagina becoming aroused. Or, to return to your point, being repulsed by the sight of a vaginal vase. The reason behind my action was to extend my own life. It's immortality in other people's minds that I crave. Whoever witnesses the vase will carry the image with them as long as they live and more than likely pass it on to a few souls along their way.'

'What? You want to be the most remembered murderer?' his tone was contemptuous. 'Kill the most women. Set the standard for other budding psychopaths to aspire to?'

Price shook his head sadly. 'Do you sincerely believe that of me?'

'I don't know.'

'It's hardly like that. I was simply trying to bring a little slice of life to their grey, empty existence-' began Price.

'You're pathetic!' shouted Darrow. 'There are no excuses for what you did, there is no ideology that will justify it! Look at you! I can't even call you a serial killer!'

Price looked pained. 'Why not?'

'Because you have to kill five people before you can be classed as a repeater.'

'Oh, in that case. Yes. I killed Pamela Bell.'

Darrow calmed himself. 'Now we're getting somewhere.'

'Aren't we?'

'How long have you known her?'

'I don't know her. I met her for the first time that night.'

'Then how did you get into her house without forcing an entry?'

'Pam was also voraciously heterosexual but where Janine would sleep with anyone who showed an interest, Pam was very selective. Very. She was beautiful and finding sexual partners was not a problem. But finding sexual partners who would be happy with one night of sex and nothing more was. And so, if she liked the look of you she would ask a few direct questions to gauge compatibility and to explain her philosophy. If an understanding was reached, then Bob was your aunt's live-in-lover.'

'Which you did.'

'I'm a very understanding man.'

'I can see that, David. All the same that was a piece of luck. Finding a woman who was so easy to get home.'

Price snorted. 'There all easy. All of them. And anyway it wasn't luck. I was pointed in her direction.'

'By whom?'

'The voice in my head.'

'The voice in your head?'

'For the benefit of the tape Mr. Price has just nodded his head.'

'And it's this voice that tells you to kill people.'

'Oh, nothing so melodramatic. He's more of an independent adviser.'

'And how long have you been hearing this voice, David?'

'A few days, now. He claims to have always been there.' Price's voice dropped to a whisper, 'I let him think he's right. He's a bit of a sulk...'

'And it was this voice that told you all about Pamela Bell, and presumably Lucy Eliot...'

'Yes.'

'Now that is interesting,' Darrow opens the folders before him and removes the contents. He proceeds to lay out five blue A4 notebooks in a line. 'Because according to these journals of yours, you stalked Pamela Bell for six months. These wonderfully comprehensive journals contain details of her daily movements, her sexual partners, a small biography and even a few sketches of her. How do you explain that?'

Price remained silent.

'Nothing to say? I understand. These diaries also show that you stalked Lucy Eliot for an identical length of time, and also Christine for two months before you finally introduced yourself. You also stalked someone by the name of Margaret Henderson for three weeks and three of her friends. According to your diaries you also were keeping Susan Lally under surveillance because she had not accepted your offer of a drink in a nightclub. Am I correct in assuming that it was you who was responsible for assaulting her on Tuesday?'

He said nothing.

'Okay, we'll come back to that one. But you could help me with another matter. Who's Julie?'

Again, Darrow watched as Price's eyes seemed to die. They dulled and darkened. His lips trembled, trying to reply. The words wouldn't come.

'I'm only asking,' said Darrow, 'because the sketches of her on the diary pages which detail her surveillance have all had their faces violently scribbled over.'

'I hate her,' Price said finally.

'Who? Julie?'

'The whore, the perfidious wench! Words are not enough to describe what that thing did to me. Nowhere near enough.'

'But what does she look like?'

Price was amazed. 'What do you mean 'what does she look like'?'

'What I say...'

'You were there, you saw her on the living room carpet...What is your problem?'

'Ah, you see, her name is Elizabeth Murray, not Julie. Elizabeth and her husband have only lived in the Merseyside area a month, previously they were contractors in Dubai. And when we showed a photograph of you to her husband of ten years...he said he had never seen you before in his life.'

Epilogue

It came as something as a shock to be showed evidence of my delusional state of mind. I really had no idea. I must have looked so foolish.

Even worse was to come.

After Darrow's splendidly timed revelation I became complacent, after all, I still had the brain tumour ace up my sleeve; what did I have to be worried about? It was at this point that Darrow, ever intuitive, informed me that he had read in my diaries about the worms and the tumour. He said my descriptions were very detailed and graphic. It was nice of him to say.

He contacted Dr Mason who advised that I was in perfect health and the MRI mentioned in my journals did not show a tumour but had been taken as a precaution. He told the good inspector that I had suffered a severe knock to the head when drunk the previous weekend.

Now that was a blow. I had lost my get out of jail free card as it were and there seemed no other direction to move other than the insanity plea. To this end I began muttering away to myself, holding conversations, that sort of thing. I received no reply from my inner voice. Even now, as I move into my second year at Parkhurst, he has not spoken.

But quite the worst thing was the realisation that there were no worms. It sounds awful to have a clump of worms squirming inside your head, but I have to admit I was attached to the little chaps. Once they had made themselves known to me the world seemed ordered. It was as if every chaotic and painful segment of my hitherto pointless life had been for a purpose. Never before had I felt so valued, so revered.

To suddenly be deprived of that respect and admiration, to be wrenched from their warm bosom of belonging, is a pain I never thought would be mine. Now I can truly know what it is to be heartbroken. I can't say I care for it a great deal.

Perhaps it is for the best; a sentiment shared by Dr Unsworth, my therapist. It is his opinion that his absence lends me the time to reorganise myself and be able to find and return to my place in society that keeps me going. In a strange way I don't even miss him. I mean, what is the point of aching for someone you know for certain will return.

48600317R00193

Printed in Poland
by Amazon Fulfillment
Poland Sp. z o.o., Wrocław